Death in a Budapest Butterfly

JULIA BUCKLEY

BERKLEY PRIME CRIME
New York

BERKLEY PRIME CRIME
Published by Berkley
An imprint of Penguin Random House LLC
1745 Broadway, New York, NY 10019

ISBN: 9781984804822

First Edition: July 2019

Printed in the United States of America
1 3 5 7 9 10 8 6 4 2

Cover art by Sara Mulvanny
Cover design by Vikki Chu
Book design by Laura K. Corless

I moved closer and peered into the cup, which sat next to Ava's shiny red purse. The tea was half-gone, and just above the midpoint of the cup's interior it looked as though Ava had scrawled something—with lipstick? Eyeliner? Something waxy, it seemed, that did not wash away. Almost the color of blood. And upon closer examination, it seemed to be a phrase or a sentence, but in Hungarian. That's when the feeling in my gut returned—the misery—and this time I was aware of it.

"What is this?" I interrupted. I pointed at the Hungarian words, and my mother, alerted by my tone, bent over the cup and looked inside.

Then she stood up. "This is bad," she said, merely affirming what I already knew, what I felt all around us. She reached for the cup and I grabbed her arm.

"Not the cup. Touch only the saucer."

She nodded. We both understood that something was amiss, and that whether Ava or someone else had scrawled those words, they had been written with malice.

My mother's blue eyes were fearful. "Where is the woman?"

"Her name is Mrs. Novák," I said, my lips partly numb with sudden fear.

"We need to find her."

"I'll go," I said, but I had to drag myself across the floor. I turned left into the little hallway where the restrooms were. I didn't even need to enter the ladies' room. Ava Novák was slumped on the floor, staring at the wall in front of her.

I realized then that the tea hall had grown silent. Then I heard my grandmother's voice, loud and horrified. "Vasorrú Bába," she intoned.

"No!" one of the women cried out.

So that's what it had said in the cup. I knew what it meant because my grandmother had told me Hungarian fairy stories since I was a tiny child. Vasorrú Bába translated to "the witch with the iron nose," and had come to mean something along the lines of "horrible old woman."

This is what someone had written on the teacup that they had given specially to Ava Novák, and now Ava Novák was dead.

Berkley Prime Crime titles by Julia Buckley

Hungarian Tea House Mystery

DEATH IN A BUDAPEST BUTTERFLY

Writer's Apprentice Mysteries

A DARK AND STORMY MURDER
DEATH IN DARK BLUE
A DARK AND TWISTING PATH
DEATH WAITS IN THE DARK

Undercover Dish Mysteries

THE BIG CHILI
CHEDDAR OFF DEAD
PUDDING UP WITH MURDER

To my Hungarian grandparents,
Julia Veronika Vig
and
Joseph Rohaly
(who was "too poor for a middle name")
And to my father,
William Edward Rohaly

Acknowledgments

Thank you to my father, William Rohaly, for all of his knowledge of Hungarian language and culture, shared with me over fifty years. Thank you to my aunt Maria, my Mariska *néni*, for her stories of the Old Country and related Chicago traditions. Thanks as well to my uncle Joseph Rohaly for sharing his stories at family gatherings over many years. Finally, I send much gratitude to my dear deceased grandparents, Julia and Joseph, who loosely inspired the tale of Hana's grandparents.

Thanks to Hana Somogyi Steil, a fellow Hungarian girl, for letting me borrow her name for this story; to Katinka Kallay Adams, a dear friend since college and a Hungarian American who answers my questions about Hungary whenever I have them; and to my friend Mary Karen Muehleck Reynolds, another half Hungarian who told me, long ago, that Hungarians stare at people.

I am grateful to my late grandma Julia for all her cooking; I will never forget the smell of her kitchen. She never wrote down her recipes, just said, "A lilly bit of this, a lilly bit of that." My mother tried to duplicate the flavors, but she could never quite do it, although her cooking was delicious, too.

I am grateful to my father again for being a discerning editor and pointing out that, with some Hungarian words, if an accent mark is removed, the meaning might be changed to something utterly unacceptable.

A final thanks to my siblings, four other hybrids of our Hungarian German household. Because of my parents and the traditions of their respective cultures, we five children grew up loving food, music, language, a good story, and a good joke.

Tea is quiet, and our thirst for
tea is never far from our craving
for beauty.

–JAMES NORWOOD PRATT

I admit I have a Hungarian temper.
Why not? I am from Hungary.
We are descendants of Genghis Khan
and Attila the Hun.

–ZSA ZSA GABOR

Chapter 1

The Butterfly

I sat polishing teacups with my mother and her cat. The latter wasn't so much helping to polish as he was regarding me from his chair with a stern expression that he wore only when I had disappointed him. I tried reason.

"Major, I will feed you right after we finish. Isn't this a pretty teacup?" I held up a beautiful specimen of pale green with pink-painted flowers. Major scowled and twitched a whisker at me—a sure sign that he was irritated.

"It's past his lunchtime," my mother said mildly. "You know how he likes to keep to a schedule. Hana, hand me that dish." I did so, still contemplating the cat.

Major licked one of his elegant gray paws. "Yes, I know." I paused my polishing to scratch his head. "He runs this place, and you are just under the illusion that you do."

With a sigh I got up, stretched, and said, "I'll feed him, then, so I can finish up without his judgmental eyes on me."

I went to the counter and got a whiff of my grandmother's cooking; I closed my eyes to fully appreciate the aroma.

There is nothing like the smell of a Hungarian kitchen. The pure sensual experience is one that a visitor cannot forget, any more than she can duplicate it. If these aromas were to be compared to music, then the song would begin with bass notes of sautéed onions and paprika. (There is always paprika on the shelf of a Hungarian cook, and not the kind that you can buy cheaply at your grocery store.) Above these bass notes is the melody—perhaps the deep, satisfying aroma of chicken soup filled with *kis négyzet tészta*, square noodles made of only flour, eggs, and salt—or the mouthwatering fragrance of pork, beef, and Hungarian sausage stuffed into boiled cabbage, called *töltött káposzta*—or perhaps even the soul-filling incense of *gulyásleves*, known here as goulash. Above all of the wonderful scents that work on the soul like melodies floats a sweet descant known as Hungarian dessert. There is the deep-fried wonder of *fánk*, a bismarck-like doughnut stuffed with delicious jam; or the thin Hungarian pancakes known as *palacsinta*, filled with jelly and covered with sugar; or the deep, dark, and delicious plums baked into cakes called *szilvás lepény*. To those who have never experienced this confluence of sights and smells that somehow become a symphony, it is hard to understand why these food memories would follow you wherever you go. I closed my eyes for one second, appreciating the aromas that permeated the house, partly because of my mother's cooking, but mostly because of my grandmother, who cooked whenever she came to her daughter's house to "make sure you got all you need."

I prepared Major's food and set it down for him. He strolled over, still glaring slightly, and began to pick delicately at the meat in the bowl. I laughed and looked back at my mother. "If we're set up by three, that should be plenty of time, right?"

"Yes. I told Mrs. Kalas not to arrive before three forty-five." My mother looked serene, as always, in the domain of her kitchen, the largest and nicest room in her little house. We had set up at the long center island my father had built for this purpose, and the September sun shone on the array of teacups on the shining white surface. Soon we would transport the tea set to Maggie's Tea House, a business my mother and grandmother had established and which I co-ran.

"Mrs. Kalas is kind of a lot to handle," I said. "Although she's not much different from Grandma in that respect."

My grandmother, who had superhuman hearing, floated in on the scent of Odyssey, her favorite Avon perfume. "Vat did you say about Mrs. Kalas?" She picked up a teacup and began to polish it with the edge of her sleeve.

My mother sent me a subtle but urgent glance. I said, "Oh, just that she's getting there about fifteen minutes early and we want to be sure everything is all set. This isn't just a regular event, right? It's high tea for her Magyar Women group. So we want things to be just perfect."

She looked mildly suspicious, but then she nodded, tucking a bit of gray hair behind her ear; the errant strand had escaped from the bun at the nape of her neck. She wore our tea house uniform with a black sweater and some sparkling earrings. Although she'd been in America for almost forty years, my grandmother still clung to some traditions from her youth, and one was her preference for vintage jewelry, including the cruel clip-on earrings that invariably left her in pain after a "fancy" tea event.

"Ya. I will go early, make sure the floors vas done properly."

"*Were* done, Mama," my mother corrected. She, too, was an immigrant, but had been only twelve when they left Hungary, and she had mastered American grammar and intonation with a child's resiliency. She didn't always like her mother's lingering accent or her refusal to adhere, sometimes, to American usage. My mother was convinced that Grandma knew exactly how to say things, but merely refused.

My grandmother shrugged. "Ya, yes. I don't trust that cleaning crew." She turned to me. "Sit up straight, Haniska."

I had thought I was sitting up straight; my parents had always been sticklers about posture. Sometimes Grandma just said things on autopilot because she felt it was her job as matriarch. These comments included her feelings about my posture, my hair, my makeup, or what she considered swearing (these were especially reserved for my brother, Domo).

My mother said, "Are you reading tea leaves today, Mama? The ladies always like that. Why don't you set up your table, and we'll do it after Mrs. Kalas's raffle."

Grandma shrugged. She loved the whole theatrical event that reading tea leaves had become for her, but she always wanted to be coaxed into it. "I suppose," she said. "If they vant. Mama would do it better."

At the mention of her, we turned toward the picture of my great-grandmother on the sideboard. She looked, in the photograph, just as I remembered her from childhood—sweet, smiling, wearing her favorite green sweater and sitting in a lawn chair under the large elm in our backyard. My favorite memory of her, distant and lovely with the fog of time, involved me at five or six, standing next to her knee beneath that same tree while she showed me a monarch that had landed on her veined hand.

I leaned forward. "The ladies love it when you do it. Even the American guests like it when you read the tea leaves. Everyone likes to think they can get a glimpse into the future. And it's free, which they like even better," I said.

She moved closer to me to examine my hair, as she had done throughout my life. I knew that she was secretly fascinated by my hair, but she pretended to be critical of it. When I was a child I had overheard her telling my mother what a remarkable shade of reddish-brown it was, how thick and glossy. "Like the color of autumn," she had enthused. "Prettier even than mine used to be." I had been surprised and pleased at the time, having never thought much about my hair at the age of eight or nine. As I grew up, though, I remembered her words and developed a special pride in my auburn tresses.

"Do I see split ends?" my grandmother asked, pretending to study the lock in her hand.

My mother sniffed. "No, you do not. Why do you obsess over that child's hair?"

I laughed. "This *child* needs to get to work. And I'll remind you both that I'm turning twenty-seven next month so you can probably lay off thinking that I am perpetually twelve."

Both women looked somewhat disappointed. I said, "Hey, Grandma! If you're setting up the leaf-reading teacups on your table, I'll give you a special centerpiece: my Budapest Butterfly!"

"Ooohh," my grandmother said, clapping her hands. "Can I see it?"

"Yes. I just brought it to Mom's this morning." I moved to the counter, where a teacup sat in a box, tucked into tissue paper. This had been a recent find, and a spectacular one. Since I had grown up in and around Maggie's Tea

House, I had of course developed an interest in all things tea, especially teacups, which to me were like jewels, tiny treasures, and individual pieces of art. I had done a great deal of research on teacups, and some of my favorites were from Hungary (I suppose because of my family origins). The great Herend Porcelain company was located in Hungary, the makers of exquisite pieces of china that dated back centuries; I also loved the work of Zsolnay porcelain and Hollóháza porcelain, and I scoured china shops, antiques markets, and eBay for affordable pieces by these makers that I could add to my currently small collection.

The Butterfly, though, was my jewel of jewels, and a recent acquisition. I frequented a little antiques shop called Timeless Treasures, and the proprietor, Falken Trisch, knew of my predilection for European china. He had come across a single piece with the maker's mark of Anna Weatherley, a porcelain artist in Budapest. The cup, normally listed at about five hundred dollars, had a tiny chip in the plate, barely visible, but still an imperfection, making it hard for Falken to sell it for what it was worth. He had called me in to look at it, and we both marveled at its beauty before he gave me the good news: he would sell it to me for seventy-five dollars.

This was an outrageously low price for a piece of art like this, and I had pounced on his offer and borne home my treasure in a collector's euphoria.

Now I took it out and showed it to my grandmother, who looked no less enamored than I felt. Perhaps I had inherited my love of beautiful things from her.

She scrutinized the piece like a scientist with a specimen. The handle of the cup was the butterfly itself, with wings of vibrant blue, purple, and yellow. The white china was edged in gold, and the front was dominated by a large painted orange flower—the butterfly's destination—with bright green leaves flourishing on a trailing vine. Another butterfly, Persian blue and lavender, graced the plate itself, along with two more leaves trailing along a green swirling vine tucked up against the gold trim. Beauty, color, and fragility combined to make a lovely objet d'art.

"Oooh," my grandmother said, lightly touching the butterfly handle.

"Isn't it amazing? We can put it at the center of your tea table, and I'll get down the bag of nylon butterflies and greenery."

This was our strength and our special talent. We three generations of women, who between us had run a tea house for a total of almost three decades, were masters of stored decorations. Every event had a different theme, although our specialty was the European high tea. Occasionally we purchased specialized decorations according to season or customer request, but we saved everything. We were frugal and smart and we took our decorations seriously; we had a library of them sealed in ziplock bags. The butterflies were particularly lovely—they looked close to real, with vibrant, multihued, iridescent wings and legs that could be bent for attaching to vines or trees or stalks of plants.

"Ya. That will be nice," Grandma said, running her finger around the gold rim of the cup. Good porcelain seemed to have the effect of a magic talisman on our family; she literally brightened after contact with the lovely object.

"I'll transport it with the other teacups, and I'll set up the decorations for your table. You have your sign?"

"In the car," she said. "I will go now. Magdi, make sure to mingle, talk to all the Hungarian ladies."

My mother half rolled her eyes as she began packing cups into their travel container. "I always do, Mama."

Grandma marched past me on a fragrant cloud, her earrings flashing with multicolored stones. "I meet you there," she said.

When we arrived at the tea house, beautifully landscaped and maintained once a week by someone my grandmother called "a man Grandpa knows," and whom she paid with mysterious white envelopes handed to him in the shadow of the building, I lifted one of my boxes and carried it toward the entrance, where a brick walkway led to two grand wooden entrance doors. Halfway across the bricks I stopped—or, more precisely, my body stopped—and I couldn't bring myself to go closer.

My mother trundled up behind me. "Come on, Hana, we're running late." She paused, studied my face, and seemed to grow pale in the shady entrance. It was actually a bit warm on that September day, but it felt cold on our threshold. My mother frowned, hesitated, then pushed past me and unlocked the door. My grandmother walked up with her leaf-reading sign; she also took a moment to study my face. She didn't pale, but she did look interested. "Something is wrong?" she asked.

"No, I—it's weird. I feel like I don't want to go in. Am I having an anxiety attack?"

She touched my arm and stared at her own hand for a moment, as though it were an interesting bird that had landed on my sleeve. Then she looked up at me. "No. But we should be watchful. Come, we go in together."

I had no free hand, so she touched the middle of my back, and I felt almost immediately better. "Thanks, Grandma. I don't know what's wrong with me today."

She nodded at me with a wise expression. Wise, and somehow commiserating.

Inside I gradually forgot the strange feeling I had experienced in the doorway because we had a great deal to do; I lost myself in work.

I made Grandma's tea table a visual treat, one that would arrest the attention of anyone walking by. The Budapest Butterfly, my Anna Weatherley treasure, sat on an elevated, velvet-covered platform. Cascading down the white velvet were some artificial-yet-lifelike vines, to which I attached some of the winged art. The butterflies' tiny pipe cleaner legs could easily bend around any intended location. Over the rest of the table I scattered the remaining butterflies, some of them attached to the rims of the alabaster teacups that Grandma used to read leaves.

She had set up her little sign, which said, "Juliana Horvath reads your fate in tea leaves."

A jar of loose Earl Grey leaves sat near the sign along with a tiny scoop. Generally people scooped leaves into their palm; cast the leaves into a chosen cup, and filled the cup with boiling water from a nearby carafe. Grandma presided over a line of people, instructing everyone to drink their tea down to the leaves, then, when they reached her, to pour out any liquid that remained at the bottom, turning the cup a few times to eliminate excess tea, dry the sides of the cup, and allow the leaves to take their fateful shape.

Grandma followed some of the basics of reading tea leaves, but she generally incorporated her own mythology. While the traditional tea-reading symbols included things like an acorn, an owl, a palm tree, birds, and hearts, Grandma gave her readings a Hungarian flair by adding shepherds, wolves, hawks, spirits, and even fairies, a staple of Hungarian folklore. These fairies, depending upon the shape of their wings, could bode either good or ill.

My mother approached the table and said, "Lovely, Hana. But I need your artistry on the actual dining tables, and then we have to check out the tea and coffee. And make sure François is all set."

"Right," I said. I did tend to linger over the aesthetic things; my mother was the necessary taskmaster who kept me moving.

We moved around the little hall that my parents had bought decades earlier with a special-rate business loan for young entrepreneurs. My mother was the entrepreneur, with a business degree and a sharp mind. My father was a history teacher, but he spent a lot of his time helping at the tea house, even if it just meant that he could grade papers and "catch glimpses of my girlfriend."

Today's tablecloths were crisply ironed and standard white; each table had been accented with individual pale blue place mats on which we had set teacups in their saucers and dessert plates for the tea sandwiches and petit fours prepared by François, the French culinary student who worked for us part-time. François had been a real find, because our former pastry chef had retired to have a baby, and we had suddenly found ourselves juggling too many jobs.

François liked to have the kitchen to himself, which was fine with us once we saw what he could do with confections. He was young, handsome, talented, and blessed with a French accent—and he made cakes. He was like something a woman would invent for herself if given magical powers. He was moody, too, but so far that had only added to his glamour for the (mostly) women who showed up for events at the tea house.

My mother consulted her watch, her bearing straight and alert. She looked like an attractive general. "They'll be wandering in soon; let's just make sure the—oh."

A determined-looking Mrs. Kalas, wearing a flowered dress and flat nurses' shoes, was marching through the door. She paused briefly to speak to my grandmother, which involved a spate of Hungarian that I could not understand—I, the first woman in my family to not know the language that was Mom's and Grandma's native tongue. I did understand the words "Mariska" and "*Law & Order*." Both of the ladies enjoyed watching the entire television franchise, specifically the show with Mariska Hargitay in the starring role, because Mariska was partly Hungarian. Now, after comparing notes on whatever episode they had seen, the women scanned the room to see if it was up to Mrs. Kalas's standards. Some more ladies entered, clutching their purses and looking like people from another era.

"This will be interesting," my mother said with a smile. Her strawberry blonde hair was swooped up in an elegant twist today. She wore the same outfit that Grandma and I wore: white blouse, black skirt, and apron embroidered with Hungarian colors—red, green, and white.

"You look nice, Mom."

"Thanks, sweetie." She gave me a quick peck on the cheek. "So do you. I like that eyeliner you put on. It makes those big brown eyes look even prettier, and so dramatic! My sweet baby girl." She swept away and started whisking the newcomers to tables.

I smirked. My mother was under the abiding impression that if I dolled myself up like a movie star I would meet the man of my dreams. The ride toward dreamland had been particularly bumpy so far, with two ultimately unpleasant relationships as all I had to show for the last four years. At this point I was more interested in devoting myself to my career at Maggie's Tea House and my side job of collecting. Someday I thought I might even open my own shop, similar to Falken's, where I could buy and sell beautiful things.

Mrs. Kalas was suddenly next to me, clutching my arm. "Hallo, Haniska! You look so pretty today, so pretty!"

"Thank you, Mrs. Kalas."

"Which is my table? I like to sit with the other officers." Mrs. Kalas was the president of the Magyar Women group at their church. Riverwood had an unusually large population of Hungarians.

"Right over here. We made tiny place cards, see? So you are here, and Mrs. Pinkoczi is here. And Mrs. Guliban is on your other side. Wait until you see the tea cakes François has made today. Delicious!"

"Did your Grandma make *kiflis*?" she asked. Sometimes my grandmother supplemented François's work with some Hungarian staples, but this week we had all been busy and she hadn't made her delicious sweet dough crescents filled with jam.

"No, not this time, but you won't be disappointed."

Mrs. Kalas still had her fingers around my forearm, and they tightened when a woman I didn't recognize walked in. The newcomer wore a tweed coat and carried a large red purse with some sort of fancy red stone decoration on the front. She had dyed blonde hair and wore bright red lipstick—that was my first impression. She also looked young until she got close enough that I could see she was the same age as most of the other women in the room—somewhere between sixty and seventy.

"Who is that?" I asked.

Mrs. Kalas pursed her lips. "She doesn't come to these events much. Her name is Ava Novák."

"She's pretty," I said, mostly for something to say, but it was as though I'd pressed some terrible button.

"Hush!" said Mrs. Kalas, her face flushing with strong emotion. "She is not."

This struck me as funny. I laughed and said, "What do you—?"

She squeezed my arm with a hand that felt like an eagle's talons. "Don't pay any attention to Ava. Pretend she is not there."

I opened my mouth in shock and indignation, but before I could summon words, Mrs. Kalas had let go of me and walked swiftly away.

In retrospect, I realize it was at that very point that I started to feel the misery, not in the form of sadness or depression, but more in a sense of something in my gut, a sensation I'd never experienced. I barely noticed it at the time, that gut feeling. Now I know it was like a symptom, alerting me to a terrible disease, but the disease was not inside me.

It was in the room.

Chapter 2

The Magyar Ladies

Still reeling from Mrs. Kalas's rudeness, I took a deep breath. "All in a day's work," I murmured. I was tempted to go to the back room, where I could text Domo or my friend Katie and tell them how weird Mrs. Kalas was, but I caught my mother's eye and saw that she wanted everyone seated; I helped her to usher the ladies present to their chairs, and we went to the kitchen to get our wheeled carts containing the hot tea. There were eight round tables today, although we could accommodate larger groups. Mrs. Kalas had told us there would be approximately seventy women in attendance, and it looked as though there were almost that many already present.

I took my cart to the first table and began to pour tea; there were sugar and creamer packets at each table, along with traditional porcelain sugar and cream containers that could be passed around. As I poured, the women thanked me politely, some of them predictably commenting on my appearance or asking if I had a boyfriend. Mrs. Toth, a regular attendee, told me that I had "grown into my looks."

"This is the year you will find a man," she told me.

My mother, pouring tea nearby, overheard this and shook her head at me, as if to say, *These old ladies—what will they say next?*

It was true that much of what they said was incredibly inappropriate or even insulting, but they always said it with fondness or what they considered helpfulness, and it was hard to look at their faces and read negative intention there. Except for that strange reaction by Mrs. Kalas . . . "Well, thanks, Mrs. Toth. I don't really need a man, but if I run across a really great one I'll give him a try."

This made all the ladies laugh as they stirred their tea with dainty spoons. François peered out of the kitchen and pointed at his watch. François needed everything to go according to schedule or he got upset; he ran his kitchen with compulsive precision. I waved and nodded, and he pushed out a large cart covered in sandwich trays. The sandwiches, as always, demonstrated the talent of our chef. Cut into various pleasing shapes and adorned with colorful sprigs of parsley or shaved red and orange peppers or paprika blends, the tiny meals looked like little works of art. Between the three of us—François, my mother, and me—we delivered the trays to every table. François disappeared into the kitchen to arrange his pastries on dessert trays.

"Who is that young man?" asked Mrs. Guliban. "He's awfully handsome, Haniska!"

"That's François," I said, moving the sandwich tray closer to an elderly woman with rather short arms. "He is a genius in the kitchen. He also has a lovely girlfriend named Claire."

The ladies tutted about this. "You would make a wonderful

couple, honey," Mrs. Sarka said. She called everyone "honey." She sat up straight in her chair, trying to extend her four-foot-something frame. My mother once joked that she could fit Mrs. Sarka into one of our teacups. "Your babies would be beautiful."

I put my hands on my hips. "What do you ladies talk about besides men? Shouldn't you have a woman-focused agenda today?"

They looked at me for a moment, then burst into laughter and some scattered Hungarian. Shaking my head, I headed back to the kitchen. I heard Mrs. Kalas stand and start her program. She clinked a glass and said, "Welcome to all the Magyar Women from St. Stephen's parish."

A smattering of applause. I caught the eye of the woman named Ava and smiled at her. She smiled back. I gave a little wave and escaped into the kitchen, where François tried not to scowl at me.

"Sorry—I know it's your space—but they're driving me crazy. If one more person asks me why I don't have a boyfriend I'm going to start whipping little sandwiches at them."

This earned a small smile from François. "Even the old women are obsessed with romance. It is the same in my country."

I leaned against the counter, keeping out of his way, and said, "What brought you to America, anyway?"

He shrugged. "At first, it was on a visit, with a host family. I stayed in Chicago, very lovely. I walked in Millennium Park and saw The Bean and Navy Pier—all the sights, you know."

He was repairing the frosting on a tiny petit four, a white-iced cake with a large pink rose on top. "But then I start to examine the Chicago culinary schools. They were good, some of them, and in France there is more competition for these things."

"I can imagine."

"So I get a visa, and I start going to school. My dream would be to live here six months, live in France six months. But I could only do that once I had my own restaurant and have a trusted staff. This is the big dream, yes?"

"It sounds wonderful," I said. And if anyone could do it, François could. "What would you call your restaurant?"

He looked thoughtful as he placed the tiny cake on a large tray with many other tiny cakes. "I would call it after my name."

"François's Patisserie?"

"Yes. Something like that." He smiled at me—two in one day!—and gave me a thumbs-up.

The noise in the hall was escalating, so I waved to him and went back out; Mrs. Kalas had done some sort of icebreaker activity, and the women were all standing again, milling around with their teacups and chatting loudly.

My mother moved swiftly through the groups, waiting for a chance to make them sit back down. She was starting to look nervous, so I waded in, telling the ladies that there would be pastries soon and then a chance to have their tea leaves read.

As I passed Grandma's table, I gasped, my heart thudding in my chest. The butterfly teacup was gone!

I scanned the room. I didn't think that anyone would have stolen the cup; could Grandma have taken it somewhere to show someone? That seemed the most likely answer. My mother, like a teacher with wayward preschoolers, was trying to shoo women back to their chairs with promises of sweets to come.

I did a quick visual survey, scanning for deep blue tones

instead of the pink and green of the tea service we were using today. Finally, at table eight, I spotted it. The new woman, with the red lipstick and the red purse—what was her name?—Ava. A woman in a blue dress, not someone I knew, had leaned down to chat with her, and she laughed at something the woman said. The woman patted her shoulder and moved away, leaving Ava alone at her back table, like the person at the wedding who doesn't want to dance. In fact, many of the women had drifted out of their seats again and were talking in clusters on our tiny dance floor, or what my mother called "the networking area." Ava seemed untroubled by her aloneness; she took a sip of her tea, and sure enough, she was drinking out of my Budapest Butterfly, my five-hundred-dollar-when-brand-new Anna Weatherley treasure.

How had she gotten the cup? Why would she drink tea from there and not from the one that was set at her place? Had Mrs. Kalas warned me against her because she was some sort of thief?

I pursed my lips. The moment I could think of an excuse, I would be reclaiming what was mine. With a sigh I did a quick sweep of the room with my cart, picking up stray napkins, empty teacups, dropped silverware. I passed a little cardboard box lying on the floor. I pictured one of the women pulling out her boutonniere or her club award or whatever she had received in it and then just casting the box aside. The rudeness irritated me; we were hostesses, not maids, not janitors. Still, I picked it up and set it on my cart. I looked at the cardboard box for a moment, and in that brief time something happened inside my mind—what felt like the flipping of a switch, as though I were a camera and someone had put on my telephoto lens. I saw the pores of the cardboard, the crease in a bent corner of one flap. I shook my head and pushed my cart into the back room, where I tossed the box away, then came back out to scan the assembled guests, milling here and there, and to consider what might be needed.

François appeared with his tall frame and dark curls, brandishing his dessert cart, and an "Ahhh!" went up among the crowd. I wasn't sure what they found more delicious—the frosted treats or François.

This provided a nice distraction, and the ladies returned to their seats in order to eat cake. Just when I thought they had all settled in, the loner called Ava, my teacup thief, rose from her chair and began to walk toward the front door, or perhaps toward the restrooms, which were near the entrance. She seemed distressed; she held one hand to her abdomen as though she felt sick. Concerned, I watched her for a moment as she reached the back hallways where the bathrooms were. She tripped once; was she drunk? Is that why the other women avoided her? I considered going after her, but if she were sick to her stomach, she probably wouldn't relish having a witness. I'd give her a minute or two, I decided. Then I wondered, perhaps inappropriately, if she had finished her tea, and if I might be able to reclaim my cup. But then I saw Grandma take her place at her table, looking grand and mysterious with her black sweater and flashing earrings.

Mrs. Kalas stood and made an announcement about tea leaves, and a line of women formed, each member casting her leaves into cups and pouring in the hot water. They stood in line, drinking their tea so that when they reached the front they could display their leaves. Grandma sat like a queen, clearly enjoying the drama.

I darted to the back to see if François had any cakes left, which he did. "Can I take this last tray, François?" I asked.

He was in a corner of the kitchen, texting. I sighed. We loved everything about François except his addiction to his phone. I loved my cell as much as the next person, but François, at the tender age of twenty-three, seemed to view it as a part of his body. His girlfriend, Claire, a pretty blonde classmate at the culinary institute, often appeared in our doorway with a slightly haunted expression, as though she couldn't live without a glimpse of her French lover.

A part of me envied her: longing for a man that much, French or otherwise. It had never happened to me. "How's Claire?" I asked, my voice dry.

He looked up, his eyes wide. "This is my mother, in France. My father is ill."

"Oh, François! What can we do? Will you have to go back?"

He shook his head. "I don't know. He is in hospital; something with his heart. She will contact me later today." He looked vulnerable for the first time since I had known him.

I crossed the room quickly and gave him a hug, which he accepted gratefully, judging by the strength of his return embrace. "Go home. Talk to your mom or just relax until you hear from them. Let me know if you need anything."

"Okay. Thank you, Hana."

He took off his apron and hurried out of the kitchen. I looked around, noting with approval that he had already done most of the cleaning up.

I put away a few remaining dishes and wiped down the counters, then went outside to monitor the group. My grandmother had started her readings. A small woman with white hair sat in front of her, and Grandma was giving her a pretty standard reading. "Good fortune," she said, staring into the cup. "And marriage. Any marriages happening soon?"

The woman brightened. "Yes! My granddaughter."

Grandma leaned closer and pointed in the cup. "This. See? The letter *M*. Could be bad luck, the shape of a serpent, but it is next to the birds flying toward it, which means you will have contact with someone whose name begins with *M*. Who is this?"

The woman clapped her hands. "My brother Miklos is flying in for the wedding."

My grandmother swept the line of fascinated women with her triumphant gaze. "You see? The wedding will be a success. Good fortune for you and your visiting family."

The woman moved away, pleased, and Mrs. Kalas moved forward with her cup. She swirled her tea leaves in the cup three times, as instructed by my grandmother, then inverted the cup so that the liquid drained away and the leaves were left behind. My grandmother stared into the cup and stiffened. "Oh," she said.

"What is it?" asked Mrs. Kalas, alarmed.

Grandma pointed at a shape on the side of the cup. "You have the woman here, see? But are these wings, or is this her flowing long hair?"

Mrs. Kalas gasped. For Hungarians who bought into legends, one interpretation would make the woman a standard fairy, a potentially good omen, but another would link her to the mythical Fair Lady, or Szépasszony, who was dangerous and vengeful. Neither of those, however, was as menacing as a witch, a common character in Hungarian folklore and one my grandma enjoyed employing for the sake of theatricality.

Grandma studied the cup some more, but this time there was no humor or even drama in her eyes. For a moment she almost looked worried. "You should not trust things on their face. Question things and people. Do not assume they are what they seem. Be careful in this way, for many weeks to come. There is something bad—not for you, maybe, but for a friend, a family, something near."

Mrs. Kalas, now pale, nodded and walked away from the table.

Grandma normally didn't leave people without some positive spin, so this was strange. I would have to speak to her—or perhaps my mother would—about keeping things upbeat at the reading table.

I noted again the empty velvet platform on the table and headed toward my butterfly cup, sitting on the place mat in front of the seat where Ava had been. I hesitated near the table, wondering if she had finished her tea, and if I needed to check on her in the washroom. I moved closer and peered into the cup, which sat next to Ava's shiny red purse. Why had she left her purse behind? Something was different about her purse, but the teacup distracted me. The tea was half-gone, and just above the midpoint of the cup's interior it looked as though Ava had scrawled something—with lipstick? Eyeliner? Something waxy, it seemed, that did not wash away. Almost the color of blood. And upon closer examination, it seemed to be a phrase or a sentence, but in Hungarian. That's when the feeling in my gut returned—the misery—and this time I was aware of it.

My mother appeared next to me. "Hana, what are you doing? We need to—?"

"What is this?" I interrupted. I pointed at the Hungarian words, and my mother, alerted by my tone, bent over the cup and looked inside.

Then she stood up. "This is bad," she said, merely affirming what I already knew, what I felt all around us. "I have to show this to Mama." She reached for the cup and I grabbed her arm.

"Not the cup. Touch only the saucer."

She nodded. We both understood that something was amiss, and that whether Ava or someone else had scrawled those words, they had been written with malice.

My mother's blue eyes were fearful. "Where is the woman?"

"Her name is Mrs. Novák," I said, my lips partly numb with sudden fear.

"We need to find her."

"I'll go," I said, but I had to drag myself across the floor, heading toward the entrance and feeling tempted to walk out into the sunshine and never return. Instead, I turned left into the little hallway where the restrooms were. I didn't even need to enter the ladies' room. Ava Novák was slumped on the floor, staring at the wall in front of her. I knew the truth before I reached her, before I made myself touch her cool wrist and realized there was no pulse at all. I fumbled for the phone in the pocket of my skirt, dialed 911 with one hand even as I made a vague blessing over Ava Novák with the other.

I told the operator that a woman had collapsed; I told her our address.

"Is the patient breathing?"

"No," I said.

"Does the patient have a pulse?" the operator asked.

"No," I said. My eyes felt wet. Ava's eyes, staring at nothing, were still beautiful.

I realized then that the tea hall had grown silent. Then I heard my grandmother's voice, loud and horrified. "Vasorrú Bába," she intoned.

"No!" one of the women cried out.

So that's what it had said in the cup. I knew what it meant because my grandmother had told me Hungarian fairy stories since I was a tiny child. Vasorrú Bába translated to "the witch with the iron nose," and had come to mean something along the lines of "horrible old woman."

This is what someone had written on the teacup that they had given specially to Ava Novák, and now Ava Novák was dead.

Chapter 3

A Wolf in the Henhouse

The emergency crew confirmed Ava's condition and said that they would not move her until the police could come, given the strange circumstances of her death. One of the EMTs made a call and the other stood guard at the hallway; I moved back into the room, where the women now stood in troubled clusters, speaking in low tones and assuring one another that they knew nothing about what had happened, although several had seen Ava move rapidly toward the bathroom, as though she had been in distress.

The police arrived soon after the ambulance, and then more police arrived, and then some people who were clearly police of higher rank, who wore not uniforms but suits and grave expressions.

One of these people, a large red-haired man with a mustache, announced that no one should leave until one of the police officers had gotten their contact information and a basic statement. Another man, in a gray suit that seemed slightly short for his tall frame, appeared next to my mother and me while we talked with my grandmother, who was still recovering from seeing the dangerous vision in the tea leaves and then the reality of death in the tea house.

"Are you the owners?" the man asked.

"Yes," my mother said. "This is my mother, Juliana Horvath, and I am Maggie Keller. This is my daughter, Hana Keller. We run this place."

He held out a card. "I'm Detective Wolf with the Riverwood Police."

My grandmother moaned and said something in Hungarian. He looked at me. "Is she all right?"

My face grew hot. "Oh yes. Uh—she finds your name rather—predatory."

He smiled. "What?"

"My grandmother is superstitious. She was reading people's tea leaves today—"

"Okay," he said, clearly out of his element.

"And she saw a bad omen in the leaves. Then moments later I found Mrs. Novák—" I gestured back toward the hallway. "And then, as my grandma sees it, a wolf entered the room."

"Okay," he said again. He was scanning the hall over my head, probably looking for better people to interview. "So your grandma is . . ."

"Hungarian," I offered.

He made eye contact with me and grinned. "Is there somewhere we can sit down? Maybe out of this room?"

We led him to François's workspace, where we would have access to a wooden table and some folding chairs. We all sat down and Detective Wolf took out a small notebook that he flipped open like an old-timey reporter at a press conference. "Did any of you know Mrs. Novák?"

I shrugged and shook my head, as did my mother. My grandmother said, "I met Ava once or twice, years ago. I know Mrs. Kalas. She goes to a different church from me. She said Mrs. Novák was a parishioner at that church, St. Stephen's. Mrs. Kalas did not like her. Many of her friends did not like her, either."

He jotted down some notes. He had rather thick blond hair; I had never known a man with blond hair before. I wondered if he were Nordic. Wolf sounded like a Nordic name . . .

"Miss Keller?" he said.

"What? I'm sorry, I was spacing out."

"Why didn't she like Mrs. Novák?"

"I have no idea. Grandma?" I asked.

My grandmother shrugged.

He tried again. "Did any of you speak with Mrs. Novák today?"

I recalled her solitary seat at the back of the room, her isolation and probable loneliness. This made me remorseful, especially when I recalled my suspicions and Mrs. Kalas's fierce warning, and that no one had really been sitting with her before she ran out of the room. "I don't think she spoke to many people, aside from that dark-haired lady in the blue dress. She seemed pretty friendly, though," I said. "I wish I had talked to her. Mom and I were moving around, pouring tea, and then I was back here with François."

He lifted his head and looked at me with interesting green eyes. "And who is François?"

"Oh—he's our pastry chef. He makes the tea sandwiches and the desserts. You can see them there."

My mother had gathered up some untouched trays and brought them to the back room; now she got up and set one before Detective Wolf. "Help yourself," she said.

Detective Wolf glanced at the tray and raised his eyebrows. "Did any other women show signs of distress after eating these? Or drinking the tea?"

My mother gasped. "You think our food was *poisoned*? I can assure you that François has been with us for several months and has done an amazing job."

"We're not certain what caused Mrs. Novák's death. But we had reports from the first officers on the scene that she was threatened, so murder has not been ruled out."

"Murder," my grandmother gasped. Her skin looked gray.

"Do you mean the words written on the teacup?" I asked. "Is that the threat they reported?"

"What words?" Wolf asked, his eyes wide.

"There was a teacup on my grandma's reading table. It was a decoration, not part of today's service. I saw at one point that Mrs. Novák was drinking out of it. When all the women were milling around, I went over there to take it back. It's a very valuable cup—anyway, I saw that someone had written something on the inside, probably before they poured her tea. It translated to mean 'horrible woman.'"

He jotted this in his notebook. "Where is the cup?"

I pointed to the counter, where my mother had put the cup and its saucer for safekeeping. He got up and bent over it. "You touched this?" he said, looking disappointed. "You carried it back here?"

"Well, yes, but only the saucer, I think. I told my mother not to touch it. She put it back here because, as I said, it's a very valuable cup, and I didn't want—"

He darted away and leaned out of the kitchen door. "Wallace! Bring me an evidence bag."

Moments later a uniformed officer appeared with something resembling the ziplock bags we used for our decorations. Wolf was back at the counter, reading the message on the cup. He jotted some more things in his notebook, then pointed with his pen. "Bag this," he said.

"No!" I yelled.

Both men looked at me. "It's—very valuable, and fragile. You can't just throw it in a bag, it will break. The handle will come right off. Plus it will collide with the saucer and cause damage. And also—it's mine. It's one of my personal treasures."

Wolf became indulgent. "We have special padding to keep it from breaking. Once it's cleared and processed, I'll be able to give it back to you."

I looked helplessly at my mother, who put an arm around me. "See that she does get it back, Detective Wolf."

Wolf nodded. The officer went in search of packing material, and Wolf came back to us. "Why would someone write that in the cup? What does it mean?"

My mother said, "It's vengeful. It's an insult in any language, but the Hungarians are superstitious, at least the old-time Hungarians are. Witches are a part of their folklore, and witches are always bad. Evil, treacherous."

Wolf chewed on the inside of his mouth for a moment, thinking. "And none of you knew this Ava Novák? Or ever saw her before?"

We all shook our heads. "We have several tea events per week, Detective," my mother said. "This was just another group, although they have been here before. Just not Mrs. Novák. She was new to us."

He put his notebook in the pocket of his shrunken suit. "Thank you, ladies. If you could all leave your contact information with Detective Benton before you leave, I would appreciate it."

My mother and my grandmother agreed and walked out

to talk to their guests. I stayed to watch the bagging of my lovely teacup. I couldn't complain, of course. I was losing a teacup, but poor Mrs. Novák had lost her life. Had she really been murdered?

"Bag these, too," Wolf was saying to the tech, who wore gloves and was carefully wrapping the saucer in bubble wrap.

"Bag what?" I said. Then I realized he meant the sandwiches and desserts on the tray. "So you do think we poisoned our food," I said, mortified. What would happen if this ended up in the newspapers? We would never get customers again.

He moved back toward me. "I'm just doing my job, Haniska."

The Hungarian nickname, spoken by this dry policeman, sounded ridiculous, and I laughed.

He tilted his head, confused. I said, "Who told you that was my name?"

"One of the ladies out there," he said, looking at his shoes.

"It's Hana," I said. "Haniska is just what my grandma calls me. A diminutive similar to hers. She's Juliana, but her mother called her Juliska."

"Ah."

"When will you know what happened to poor Mrs. Novák?"

"I'm not sure. But I'll be sure to notify you when we know. In the meantime, we'll need you to postpone any other events."

"What? Oh—yes, I see. We don't have one planned for tomorrow, but Saturday we have a bridal shower . . ." Assuming we were even allowed to be open for that, what would happen if François had to go home? Suddenly everything was going wrong. Hadn't I sensed this, somehow, that morning when my body refused to move forward into the hall?

"Do you happen to have any security cameras here?"

I ran a hand through my hair, a gesture of helplessness. "Oh. No, I'm sorry. It's not something that ever dawned on us. There's not a lot of crime at tea parties, as a rule."

He smiled, and it altered his face. "I guess not."

"But someone must have seen who brought that cup over. If it wasn't Ava Novák herself, then it was—the person who wrote that message. And they prepared a cup of tea just for her, and said, 'Here, Ava, a special treat,' and gave it to her and watched her drink it and die." I gulped, suddenly on the verge of tears. That poor woman. And who, among those sweet ladies with their big purses and their lavender-scented bosoms and their flowery scarves—who was angry enough to kill?

"Don't upset yourself, Hana. We don't know what happened yet. We will interview everyone, and we'll piece everything together and find out the truth."

"Good," I said, and sighed. "I'll let you go back to your interviews."

"Don't worry," he said. My eyes were back on the teacup, which was now so sealed in plastic that I could barely see its vibrant colors. The tech had moved on to bagging the food. "I'll contact you personally when we know something conclusive. Here, you can write your information by your name."

He handed me his notebook, where he had written the names of my family as Horvath, Juliana; Keller, Maggie; Keller, Honnishka. I crossed the last word out and wrote "Haniska/Hana" instead. Then I jotted my phone number and address. I gave the notebook back to him, and he tucked it into the pocket of his ill-fitting suit.

He nodded and went into the hall—the wolf going out to agitate the chickens.

With one final glance at my mummified butterfly, I left the room, thinking that the Fair Lady, Szépasszony, had truly been set loose among us. In the lore of fairies, she could appear in different guises, as an animal, or a beautiful woman, even as someone's lover.

But she could also make herself invisible, so that people never saw her coming.

And that made her dangerous.

Chapter 4

The Missing Jewel

That night I went back to my little sanctuary of an apartment, where I apologized to my own cats for my lateness. Antony and Cleopatra were siblings, one black and one gray, that I had found at a local shelter. They had won my heart immediately because they were sitting together in their cage with their little arms around each other, their fuzzy heads together. They still liked to sit this way, although right now they were stropping around my legs and chiding me for being gone so long.

"I know, my babies. Let me get your food." I poured kibble in both of their bowls and set the dishes on the floor, where the felines got busy crunching and occasionally looking at each other while they chewed. "You guys are hilarious! Even food can't distract you from each other, can it? You remind me of François and Claire."

I recalled then that I hadn't heard back from François, so I called him. "Hello?" he said.

"François! This is Hana. How is your dad?"

There was a smile in his voice. "He is much better! He had what they call an anomaly. I don't know what this means, but it was not a heart attack. He will be fine with medication."

"Oh, I'm so glad! Really, that is wonderful." I paused, reluctant to bring any negativity into his happy and relieved state of mind. "Listen, there's something you need to know."

"What is it?" He was alert now.

"The thing is—after you left today, a woman died in the hall."

"What?" He fired a bunch of questions at me before he realized he was speaking French. "I mean, what happened? Was this also a heart ailment?"

"No. We called an ambulance, and then they called the police. It's possible she was poisoned."

"Not by my food, no!" I pictured his face, a mixture of surprise and defensive fury.

"No, I don't think so, and I don't think they are leaning that way, either. It might have been one cup of tea. Just the one."

There was silence for a moment. "So—murder?" he asked in a hushed tone.

"It might be. The police are investigating. I don't even know if we'll be allowed to have our Saturday event. Mom and Grandma made it clear to the police that it would be very problematic if we had to cancel on a customer."

"I am sorry to hear this," François said. "I will say a prayer. Let me know."

"I will, thanks. I'm glad about your father."

"Me, too," he said.

I said good-bye and ended the call, then wandered into my little living room with its built-in shelves full of books and treasures. I was just about to plop down, and my two cats had followed me, ready to jump into my lap, when the doorbell buzzed.

I went to the intercom and pressed the button. "Yes?"

"It's Domo," said my brother.

I buzzed him up and left my door open. Then, carrying a bottle of water and a jar of peanut butter, I went back to my chair. I felt too tired to make myself any dinner.

Domo wandered in, looking at home in my small place. His own apartment was bigger and more expensive; Domo worked in computers and was always flush with cash. "How's it going, sis?"

He plopped into the chair opposite mine and smiled at me.

I had the peanut butter open and was digging a spoon inside. "Not the best. Someone died at the tea house today."

"*Again?*" he joked, scanning the books on one of my shelves.

"They think she was poisoned."

He sat up straight, his smile gone. "What? I thought you were just being sarcastic, like someone was so bored she died. I don't know. What the heck happened?"

I told him, and his eyes grew wider as the details emerged. "That's crazy!"

"I know!"

"And how weird must it have looked to the cops that Grandma was sitting there with her tea leaves and her mysterious expressions."

"I know!"

"I hope they don't think she's a suspect."

"I don't know. He was pretty inscrutable."

"He? He who?"

"This one cop, the detective. Or one of the detectives.

He was asking us tons of questions about Mrs. Novák and the words on the cup and the tea leaves and stuff. Oh, and his name was Wolf."

"I'll bet Grandma loved that."

"She did *not*."

He shook his head in disbelief. "Are you okay?"

"I think so. It was hard because—I'm the one who found her."

He leapt out of his chair and put an arm around me. "Oh no. Did you know, right away, that—?"

I nodded. Domo gave me a hug and went back to his seat. "Okay, do you want me to distract you?"

I nodded again. This was what my brother did best.

He leaned back in his chair and sighed. "First of all, you smell like peanut butter."

"I'm eating peanut butter. Do you want some?"

"No. I'm not always an elegant diner, but I don't generally have to eat dinner out of a jar."

"Special circumstances," I said.

"Second, your cats look like executioners." Antony and Cleopatra had in fact taken up stations on either side of Domo's chair and were sort of glaring up at him. This was because they wanted to be petted, but a paranoid visitor could assume that they had darker intentions.

"They just want love," I said mildly.

He ignored this. "Third, your eventful Thursday beats mine. I just sat at a desk, mostly, and longer than I wanted to. Which is partly why I'm here."

"What? I assume you need a favor."

"Yes."

"And that favor is you need a gift for Margie."

"Yes, God. Somehow I missed another one of the many anniversaries she keeps track of. It's not the anniversary of the day we met, or the day I asked her out, or the first time we had dinner, or of our 'making it official.' It's some other obscure thing."

"Domo, make her tone it down with the anniversaries."

"I know, but in all other respects she is a really mellow girlfriend." My brother's handsome face was earnest, and he was right. Margie was a really nice person who didn't insist on a lot of relationship drama—but she did love her anniversaries.

"Well, I've got you covered. Just go to the Margie basket."

Domo knew I loved shopping, and when I ran across a likely gift for anyone in my family, I would buy it and keep it handy for the next occasion when a gift might be needed. This worked far better for me than trying to think of a random gift with very little time to plan. With my prepurchased gift baskets, I was always ready. This had helped Domo out of many a dilemma with Margie.

He got up and retrieved the wicker basket from the top of my shelf. In it were a necklace I had found at Falken's antiques shop—a lovely faux ruby on a silver chain—and a book about Audrey Hepburn. Under those was a bottle of Éclat d'Arpège, which I knew was one of her favorites. Domo rooted through these and decided on the necklace. "This is really nice; thanks, Hana."

"I have some little gift bags in the drawer by my fridge. Tissue paper, too."

He jogged into the kitchen, and Antony chased him. Domo scooped the cat up and gave him a big kiss on his sleek black head, then put him down again.

Cleopatra had relocated to my lap, where she had started making dough on my legs.

Domo came back, bearing a silver gift bag with a red heart appliqué; he had inserted red tissue paper. It was a good choice for a romantic gift. "Margie will love this. Thanks again."

"Sure. Are you going to take her out to dinner or something?"

"Something," he said with a grin.

I glared at him. "Women don't always want sex as a present, Domo. And when are you going to ask her to marry you?"

He shrugged. "Someday soon."

"Men," I said to Cleopatra.

"Anyway, gotta run. You're not going to OD on that peanut butter, are you?"

"No. Just a few more spoons, and then I'll devote myself to Cleo. She's been neglected, as you can see." Cleopatra was already purring and tucking into the chair against my hip, ready for a long nap.

"Thanks again; you're a lifesaver." Domo kissed me on the cheek, then went to my little kitchen. "I'm leaving some cash on your counter here. It should cover the necklace and the bag and paper." I was sure it would more than cover it—my brother was generous that way. "Keep me apprised about that other stuff. Maybe it will turn out to be a natural-causes kind of thing."

"Hopefully." I waved to him and he departed, closing my door behind him. I heard him checking the knob in the hallway, making sure the door had locked.

Antony jumped into my lap and tucked on the side opposite Cleo. Suddenly my chair felt much smaller.

"You guys aren't as little as you used to be," I said fondly, scratching their soft heads.

They purred loudly, competing for my attention.

I laughed and leaned my head back on the chair. I didn't have the concentration for reading or for watching television.

I closed my eyes and saw again the crowded hall, the milling women, the bright teacups, Mrs. Kalas's face when she looked at Ava Novák with her red lipstick, Ava's red purse lying on the table. The red purse with its bright red stone decoration . . . except that, when I saw the purse sitting next to the teacup with its terrible message, something about the purse had been different. Had the stone been missing?

I sat up—surely it had been missing, because when I glanced at the purse, just before I became distracted by the teacup, I had noticed a tiny strip of white—something like Velcro or glue, perhaps. Something that may have held the stone on her purse. And later, when the police had bagged the purse as evidence, I had glanced at it and seen both sides.

Somehow the gemstone decoration had disappeared.

Chapter 5

Mrs. Kalas's Story

We arrived just before eight on Friday morning. My mother had brought a huge portable urn so that she could make coffee for the police officers; she had also brought some prepackaged pastries from a European market in Chicago. "So they don't think we're poisoning them," she murmured. My mother was not pleased about the potential loss of face for her establishment, and she wanted to help the police expedite matters and finish their work in one day.

She set up the coffee, and soon the aroma lured policemen out of the various corners of the hall and encouraged them to suspend their investigations for the few moments it took to seek a cup of bracing java. Detective Wolf, wearing a different and better-fitting suit (though still a bit wrinkled), met us in the back room, François's space, with a large McDonald's soft drink in his hand. I raised my brows and he held it up. "My caffeine addiction takes a different form. Diet Coke."

"They sell that at eight in the morning?" I asked.

He nodded. "It's a crime I should investigate." He took a sip of his drink, then got down to business. "Mrs. Keller, Mrs. Horvath, we're going to be sitting at that table there." He pointed through the doorway at one of our round tables, now stripped of its white cloth, which had been carted off as evidence, along with just about everything that could be lifted. "If you two ladies would sit nearby and listen, and just hold up a finger if there's an issue—something you know to be untrue, or a discrepancy from what the witness might have mentioned to you at some other time. Anything like that. Since you both speak some Hungarian, I might occasionally ask for your translation help."

My mother nodded, as did my grandmother. The latter wore an expression that indicated her conflicted feelings. She wanted to dislike and mistrust Detective Wolf on principle, but she was clearly pleased to have an important role in the investigation. In addition, Detective Benton intrigued her because he had told her the day before that he had spent a summer in Budapest, and my grandmother had once lived there, as well. This made her feel generally favorable toward Benton, despite his mustache.

As the two women moved toward their station, Wolf pointed his Diet Coke at me. "Hana, I have a different task for you, if you'll be willing. After the ladies make their statements, Detective Benton will print them out. I'd like you to go over the printed statement and jot down any notes you have about what was said. I'll want to keep both of them in the file."

I studied Wolf. His blond hair was still damp, and his

collar needed smoothing down on the left side. "I get it. You want layers."

"I do, yes. It gives me a way to find the little discrepancies, the little crevices in the stories that can be broken into giant holes. Will you do it?"

"Yes, whatever I can do to help. Do they know anything yet about—you know—how it happened?"

"I'm still waiting for final confirmation."

I continued to stare at him, trying to read his expression. "She was most likely poisoned, though."

His mouth became a grim line. "Yes."

"And the sandwiches?"

He shook his head. "Not the source."

My sigh of relief must have been louder than I thought, because he patted me on the shoulder. "I'm sorry you had to worry. We hope to give you your space back soon."

He turned to go, but I touched his arm. "There's one thing."

He raised his blond brows.

"Yesterday, I noticed that Mrs. Novák had this interesting stone on the outside of her purse. You know, a decoration. But when she left the table and I saw the purse by her teacup—I think the jewel was gone."

"What?" he said. It was a rhetorical question, because he already had his phone out. "Wilson," he barked, "look at the Novák evidence and see if the purse had a jewel attached to the outside. A stone." He turned to me. "Color?"

"Red. Red and gray."

"A red jewel. Yes. Okay."

He hung up. "Thanks for that. We'll check."

"Thank you." I looked over at the round table, where Benton, with admirable politeness, was seating Mrs. Kalas, while my mother offered her a cup of coffee.

"It looks like you're on," I said.

"Yes. I'll be back soon." He strode to the table, set down his drink, and seemed to be introducing himself to Mrs. Kalas. He opened up a notebook while Benton opened a computer. I saw a printer set up near one of the pillars, all of which bore electrical outlets. Wolf's face was solemn, focused, and Mrs. Kalas, normally so intimidating and larger-than-life with her loud voice, her flowered dresses, and her bosom as large as the prow of a ship, now seemed shrunken and old in her folding chair.

I sighed and sat down in the back room. I texted François. Interviews going on today. Enjoy your free time. I'll get back to you tonight about the wedding shower.

Restless, I called Domo at work. He sounded cheery. "Hey, Han Solo."

"Hey."

"What's happening?" He was typing something; I could hear the keys clacking, but apparently he was willing to chat while working.

"They're doing interviews of the ladies all day. They want us Hungarian hostesses to serve as witnesses. Verifying statements and such."

"How do they know one of *you* didn't do it? Who's going to verify your statements?"

"First of all, as our *family member*, you know that we are free of guilt. Secondly, maybe he will have someone check our statements. Playing us all against each other, I mean. I wouldn't put it past him—he seems tricky, somehow."

"Interesting."

"They've got poor Mrs. Kalas out there, looking all deflated and nervous. Can you really picture one of these old ladies committing murder?"

"Of course I can. They're a scary batch of Old Country women, full of superstition and paprika-scented resentment."

"Don't be ridiculous. Hey, how did Margie like the necklace?"

"She loved it. A *crazy* amount. Apparently I am the best boyfriend in the world." His voice was smug; in the background I heard phones ringing.

"No, *I* am the best boyfriend in the world. If only Margie knew."

My brother remained unfazed. "She wouldn't leave me for you. I provide things you cannot. She probably already knows that you're the mastermind behind the presents; when we first started dating I gave her a *Star Wars* T-shirt as a birthday gift. She knows I'm not good at that sort of thing. The fact that my gifts suddenly became elegant and thoughtful? I think she's savvy enough to know the source. By the way, it's time for another Hana and Margie adventure."

"Oh—yeah. I'm not sure how long these cops will want us, but I'll let you know."

"She really likes them. I need you to do this, Han."

"Yes, I know." Domo's Margie was painfully shy. Her full name was Marguerite LaSalle. She was an introvert to the fifth power, and she was dating the gregarious Domo only because she had happened once to call him to her house to solve a computer problem (Domo moonlighted as a home tech), and Domo immediately saw the blonde, pretty Margie as a social challenge. He could barely get two words out of her, but he spent the whole evening working on her computer and practicing his patter, until he had her laughing and talking more naturally. Because he needed to order a special part, he was able to return to her apartment two days later, and this time he lured her out even more. In the process he found that he hadn't just succeeded in entertaining a shy woman—he had become attracted to her.

For their first few dates, Domo came to her house,

bearing pizza or a sub sandwich or whatever else they decided to dine on at her little kitchen table. Margie worked for an architectural firm; she drew up blueprints and e-mailed them to clients for a fee. She barely ever had to leave her cozy little space to do this, so she barely ever did. She had a wolfhound named Boris, who kept her company and guarded her home, and she didn't even have to walk him because one of her neighbors walked Boris along with his own dog, Wookie, in exchange for Margie making enough dinner for two and sharing it across the hall.

Domo found all this diverting yet sad, and he wanted to lure her out into the world for different adventures. He had done this himself on several occasions, but he also wanted Margie to have more women friends. He solicited me to take her to the zoo one day; God knows how he convinced her to meet me there, but I'd spent the previous evening listing topics of conversation. Initially it had been challenging; I found myself asking her about her favorite books and whether or not she'd had pets as a child. Once, in desperation, I had actually asked her if she would ever eat her dog's food if someone paid her to do it. Gradually I'd realized that Margie, beneath her silent exterior, was a fascinating person, and eventually my questions became more personal, more natural, and we ended up having an interesting dialogue as we strolled past the lions, tigers, and bears.

Domo's voice was loud in my ear. "She really liked that last outing you had; the one where you saw the play."

"Ick. The play was horrible!"

"That's why she liked it. She said you were cracking hilarious jokes about it all the way home."

"That's me. Hilarious Hana."

"Anyway. I was thinking this time you could take her to the mall."

I sat up straight. "Are you nuts? There are zillions of people there. And weird escalators and staircases. She might get vertigo, or have an episode, or something."

"She's not insane, Hana. She's just shy. And she's getting a lot more sociable with the Keller Treatment."

"The Keller Treatment! Sounds like a movie."

"My boss is coming. Gotta go!" my brother said, and I got a dial tone.

I hung up with a sigh. Feeling restless, I stood up and peered through the doorway. Mrs. Kalas sat up straight in her chair, her mouth moving in an almost robotic way. She looked as if she were reciting the Pledge of Allegiance. My mother and grandmother occasionally patted her hands or touched her shoulders. Detective Wolf looked at ease in his chair, but his eyes, even from this distance, seemed to have a laser focus that would have been disconcerting to the person he studied. He jotted the occasional note, but Detective Benton typed away, looking so absorbed in his work that one would think he wasn't listening to Mrs. Kalas at all.

Suddenly Wolf unfolded himself from his chair and reached out to Mrs. Kalas; she shook his hand automatically. I heard him say "thank you" and then murmur something else more quietly. Detective Benton smiled and bowed from his seat, and then Mrs. Kalas was walking toward the exit, looking exhausted.

"Mrs. Pinkoczi?" Wolf called.

Lili Pinkoczi, dressed in a pink nubby suit, walked toward the table, her head held high. She exchanged a glance with Mrs. Kalas as they passed in the doorway, but the women did not speak. I almost laughed; one would have thought they were being interrogated by the Grand Inquisitor.

"Shall I sit here?" she asked daintily, and Wolf lunged toward a chair to pull it out for her.

"I'll be right back," he said, and moved toward the front hall, perhaps to make a phone call or use the restroom.

Benton said something; it sounded as if he wanted Lili to spell her name.

An officer in uniform appeared at a side table. He spoke to my grandmother, who joined him and jotted something on a paper; a moment later I realized the officer was coming toward me. He handed me a copy of Mrs. Kalas's testimony and said, "Detective Wolf asks that you verify the contents of this report."

"Oh, okay," I said. I laughed with a sudden nervous impulse, and the officer gave me a surprised look before moving toward the entrance, where the other women would show up for their various appointments.

I took the sheet of paper to my table and found a pencil in my purse. Then I read.

Testimony of Luca Kalas

Luca Kalas, born 23 September 1949 in Chicago. Parents born in Szeged, Hungary, and emigrated in 1948.

Mrs. Kalas describes herself as a good leader and a good friend to members of her church group, called the Magyar Women. Ladies in this group are generally Hungarian but are not required to be; anyone with an interest in Hungary can apply for membership. The group takes monthly tours of sites of interest to Hungarian Americans. They occasionally sponsor cook-offs such as last year's Goulash Games. Mrs. Kalas's goulash earned third place.

Mrs. Kalas did not know Ava Novák well, although they had been acquainted for four years. Ava had been a member of the Magyar Women for less than one year, at the invitation of Mrs. Pinkoczi, and generally did not mingle with many others at meetings. This did not mean that the women were not friendly to her.

I paused in my reading, and, after hesitating, wrote a note beside this.

"I don't think this is true. Mrs. Kalas implied that Ava was not liked in the group. When I said that Ava was pretty, it made Mrs. Kalas angry, and she told me not to acknowledge Ava. I found it jarring at the time."

I had written too soon, however, because Benton's notes soon turned into more of a deposition-like dialogue, with Wolf as interrogator. I read some of it and whistled. "He *is* the Grand Inquisitor," I murmured. Then, like someone addicted to a soap opera, I devoured the story.

Mrs. Kalas admitted she was disturbed by the death of Ava Novák, not only that the woman had died, but that she had done it at Mrs. Kalas's event. She called this "very upsetting."

WOLF: *Was it upsetting to you because you had been unfriendly to Mrs. Novák?*

KALAS: *Who told you?—I wasn't unfriendly.*

WOLF: *We have been told you did not like her.*

KALAS: *I did not—? How dare you!! (indignant) I'll have you know it was I who took that woman around four years ago when she showed up in this town, I who introduced her to other Hungarian ladies, people she could speak to in her own language. How was I to know—*

WOLF: *What did you not know, Mrs. Kalas?*

Kalas: *You must understand, we are supportive of each other. Mrs. Pinkoczi was going through troubles, she needed the women around her. She needed people who understood.*

Wolf: *I'm sorry? Are we talking about Mrs. Pinkoczi or Mrs. Novák?*

Kalas: *Lili—Mrs. Pinkoczi—was having marital troubles. Her husband (something Hungarian muttered here) had moved out and was living in a small apartment.*

In the margin, my grandmother had written, in her perfect script, "*Egy férfi kanos kutya*." Then she had helpfully translated: "She is calling him a horny dog."

Wolf: *How does this relate to Mrs. Novák?*

Kalas: *It relates because that woman sniffed out Mr. Pinkoczi where he was staying, and the two began dating. Shameful.*

Wolf: *Were the Pinkoczis legally separated?*

Kalas: *That does not matter. He is her husband. Her man. Ava was the intruder. The thief.*

Wolf: *Did this make you angry, Mrs. Kalas?*

Kalas: *Of course! It made us all angry. And I was guilty. Felt guilty, I mean. I had introduced them, just casual, and then she stole him away. He was infatuated with her because she was different, pretty, mysterious. And then—*

Wolf: *So she did not "sniff him out." You introduced them.*

Kalas: *Well, yes, but she obviously kept seeing him.*

WOLF: *What then?*

KALAS: *She left that poor fool Pinkoczi. She had moved on to Joe Novák.*

WOLF: *The man she eventually married.*

KALAS: *(grim) Yes.*

WOLF: *Why does it upset you that she married Joe Novák? Was he also separated from his wife?*

KALAS: *No. He was a bachelor. He is the vice president at Adler Bank, and a Hungarian on both sides.*

WOLF: *So this was good for your friend Mrs. Novák, right? To find an eligible bachelor and to fall in love with him?*

KALAS: *No. Not good. Other women had been waiting a long time for Joe to settle down. Women who put in their time. The amount of* paprikás *that man consumed—and yet he chose Ava, who made him nothing.*

WOLF: *Mrs. Kalas, you are a widow?*

KALAS: *Yes. My husband died in 2011.*

WOLF: *And were you one of the women who made* paprikás *for Joe Novák?*

KALAS: *Of course. We all did.*

WOLF: *So after Mrs. Novák married Mr. Novák, none of the women wanted anything to do with her. Is that right?*

KALAS: *(reluctant) We were civil to her.*

WOLF: *Did some women dislike her?*

KALAS: *I suppose.*

WOLF: *Hate her?*

KALAS: *I—don't know. Some women were kind to her. Lili was good to her, despite Ava's betrayal.*

WOLF: *What you saw as a betrayal.*

KALAS: *Yes. I guess Lili didn't see it that way. They were friends. Lili has a generous heart. She went on outings with Ava, that sort of thing. They were not seated together yesterday because Lili sat at the officers' table, but normally they would have been together.*

WOLF: *Did you hate Ava, Mrs. Kalas?*

KALAS: *No! I don't hate. I am a good woman. I—was kind to her when she came to town, as I told you. I gave her gifts. I gave her a plate, a beautiful plate with a picture of the Danube. And I—*

WOLF: *Were you surprised when you heard she was dead?*

KALAS: *Yes. Well, not entirely. I knew something bad would happen.*

WOLF: *How did you know that, Mrs. Kalas?*

KALAS: *Because of the tea leaves. Juliana Horvath saw something disturbing in them. I could see in her eyes she wasn't even telling me the whole truth.*

WOLF: *Do you really put any credence in the reading of tea leaves?*

KALAS: *Of course. Have Juliana read yours. You'll understand. Her family all have the gift, did you know?*

WOLF: *What interactions did you have with Mrs. Novák yesterday?*

KALAS: *None. I—did not speak to her. I was upset to see her, to be honest.*

WOLF: *Didn't you expect to see her? She is a member of your group.*

KALAS: *She had never come to one of our teas before.*

WOLF: *Because she was not invited?*

KALAS: *All members are invited.*

WOLF: *Was Mrs. Novák persecuted by your group?*

KALAS: *No! We do not persecute. We might hold grudges. That is not the same.*

WOLF: *Do you think it might have felt the same to her?*

KALAS: *I—I can't know how she felt.*

WOLF: *Did you at any point remove a large jewel from the purse of Ava Novák?*

KALAS: *(surprised) What? A jewel? I do not look in people's purses.*

WOLF: *Will you be attending Mrs. Novák's funeral, Mrs. Kalas?*

KALAS: *(hesitating) I had not considered—yes, I'm sure I will. I'm sure our whole women's group will attend.*

WOLF: *Thank you for your information, Mrs. Kalas.*

KALAS: *Yes, of course.*

WOLF: *We'll contact you if we have any further questions.*

KALAS: *Yes, thank you.*

I pushed the paper away, full of admiration for Wolf and his questioning style. Mrs. Kalas had always struck me as one tough cookie, and he had made her feel defensive and confused for much of the interview.

He looked innocuous in his rumpled suits, with his big soda pop, but I found myself hoping that he would not be questioning me.

I peered out the door. He was back at the table and introducing himself to Mrs. Pinkoczi. I saw that there were some coffee cups lying around the room, so I grabbed a tray and began collecting them, moving closer and closer to the interview table. In this way I hoped to be able to hear the actual interview. This one was going to be a doozy; Wolf and Benton had no idea what they were facing.

Mrs. Pinkoczi, as one of the Hungarian ladies had once put it, "could talk the hind legs off a donkey."

I wanted to hear how these professional interrogators dealt with a woman who had no conversational cutoff valve. I busied myself with the tray as Wolf took a sip of his cola and then leaned forward.

Chapter 6

Mrs. Pinkoczi's Story

Lili Pinkoczi was already talking by the time Detective Wolf had reopened his notebook. She leaned toward Benton, smiling. "That is a lovely tie, Detective. My boyfriend has one just like. Silk?"

Benton cleared his throat. "It's polyester," he said. "Please direct your conversation to Detective Wolf. I need to focus on my notes." He smiled at her briefly and began typing something. Her gaze swiveled over to Wolf, who said, "Mrs. Pinkoczi, can you state your name, age, and place of birth?"

Lili smiled. "Oh, ladies don't like to say the age. But I am born Liliana Bas, in Keszthely, near Balaton."

"Balaton?"

"Hungarian Sea."

Wolf stared at her, tapping his pen on his pad. "Hungary is landlocked."

My mother took pity on him. "It's a lake. The largest

lake in Hungary. The locals are very proud. They call it the Hungarian Sea."

"Right," Wolf said. "Mrs. Pinkoczi, when were you divorced from your husband?"

Lili's smile paled slightly, as did her skin under her rouged cheeks. "We are in the process. We have been legal separated for three years."

"Did you know, three years ago, that Mrs. Novák was dating your husband?"

She sighed. "Oh, I can barely talk about this. My poor Ava. Poor lady. I can't believe she is dead."

"Did you know she was dating your husband, back when it happened?"

She shrugged. "Sure. Armin and I had been fighting, long time. We were much happier apart. So I think—good for him. Ava was nice, pretty. She would have made a good wife for him."

Wolf waited until she met his eyes. "But you were his wife. You still are."

She didn't take his bait. She said, "How old are you, Detective? Young still, yes? And too thin. You are still here tomorrow, I will bring some *hurka*. Have you tasted? So good, and will put meat on your bones, and on this one." She gestured to Benton, whose face grew slightly red.

My mother shook her head, and my grandmother pursed her lips in disapproval. They knew how hard it was to keep Lili on track, as did I; she had cornered me more than once in an effort to "solve your man problem."

Wolf was undeterred. "Mrs. Pinkoczi, how long had you known Ava?"

Lili's eyes grew sad. "She came here, oh, about four years ago. She had been in Austria many years, then come to the States, I think. She was always sad, but I could distract her. We did things together. Went to the museums and the senior citizen bus trips. Went to dances, things like that. I think I was like a sister to her, and she reminded me of a friend from my childhood, a sweet girl. We would always play in the fields with her dog, Farkas."

My grandmother moaned and shifted in her chair.

Wolf looked surprised and turned to my mother. "Means 'wolf' in Hungarian," she murmured.

"Ah," Wolf said. I could have sworn he was smiling slightly as he looked back at his notes, but then he said, "And when she started dating your husband? Did that change your friendship with her?"

Lili pursed her lips. "Enough about this. I *told* her she should date my husband. She was lonely. I was already looking at men on the line."

"Online," my mother said.

"Where did you seek out men, Mrs. Pinkoczi?"

She shrugged. "Mrs. Kiraly showed me a site for Hungarian Americans. You can shop on there, find someone to go out with you."

"And did you find someone?"

"Yes, many. I had dates—dancing, dinner."

"So your separation was not acrimonious?"

"Not what?" She laughed a little, but I could tell she was uncomfortable.

"There was no anger, fighting?"

She brushed at some pilled fabric on her nubby sleeve. "No, not much. A little, maybe. We been together forty years."

"Is that why you're not divorced, Mrs. Pinkoczi?"

She raised her penciled brows. "We have children. You have to think of them."

"How old are your children?"

We tried to stop Wolf midway through his question, all of us sort of diving toward him as though bullets were flying at his head. He looked at my mother and grandmother, then at me, surprised, and in that time Lili had already gone for her purse and was now laying out family photographs like a deck of cards.

Wolf was the one to turn pale now as Lili launched into her family spiel. "This is Lizabeth; she's forty. Then Michael—he's thirty-eight. And their little brother, my baby, is thirty-five. Lazslo is his name." She went on to tell Wolf a fuller account of each one: Lizabeth's career as a nurse, Michael's work in the research lab, Lazslo's impressive credentials as an educator.

She looked brightly at Wolf, prepared with what was clearly her proudest accomplishment: "They are all married, one to a Hungarian. I have eight grandchildren so far. I think there will be more, many more. I can put the pictures in order here by age. This is William. I don't have a portrait, so here he is on the potty. Isn't he a little devil? Look at his expression. So mischievous. Then is little Johanna—same name day as our Hana there."

She pointed at me.

"Name day?" Wolf said. "Same birthday, you mean?"

"No, no." Lili held up a hand to stop him. "Name day is very special. The name you share with your saint, see? Who you are named for. So Hana's saint is St. Johanna, whose name day is March twenty-eighth. I know all the children's name days and all the birthdays. Nagymama has a mind like a trap." She pointed at her head.

Wolf glanced at me for verification, and I nodded. I was conscious for the first time of the activity around us; police officers moving here and there, quietly, all over the room, in François's back room area, in the front lobby. Some of the investigators seemed to be taking pictures, some examining a table or a wall or a piece of flooring and taking notes or even samples. It felt suddenly surreal. This was a strange dream in which Lili Pinkoczi was telling one of her long stories and showing family pictures while policemen loomed in the foreground and we all seemed to ignore the fact that a woman had died here. A woman had expired quietly and politely at a tea party as though it would have been the height of rudeness for her to explain she had been poisoned, that someone had called her a witch, that the last thing she probably saw before she felt ill was a beautiful blue butterfly . . .

Wolf was back on task. "Mrs. Pinkoczi, those are very cute grandchildren, but I am more curious about Ava Novák. Did she suggest to you that anyone bore her any grudge?"

Mrs. Pinkoczi hesitated, clutching a picture of a boy in a graduation gown. "Well—some of the women were upset, you know. About her and Armin. They had some dates. She cooked for him. This upset the women, as you can imagine. But I told them all it was fine. Better to have someone cooking for him than for him to get skinny. I tell Ava to ignore the women."

"Ignore what? Did they threaten her?"

She shook her head. "No. Cat comments only."

Wolf looked to my mother, who said, "Catty comments. Snarky."

Wolf nodded. "How many languages do you speak, Mrs. Pinkoczi?"

This surprised all of us. He had not asked this of Mrs. Kalas. "I speak three," she said. "Hungarian, English, French."

"And what about Ava Novák?"

"I think she speak the same—maybe some German as well."

"Did you and she ever speak to each other in another language?"

She paused; she seemed to be trying to read Wolf's intentions in his face, and she was still holding the boy's picture, as though hoping for a way to work him back into the conversation. "Just Hungarian," she said. "We mostly spoke in Hungarian—some English."

"I see. And did you speak to Mrs. Novák on the day she died?"

To my surprise, Lili Pinkoczi's eyes filled with tears. "Only once. I was at the officer table, and Mrs. Kalas kept talking in my ear. Then while some of the ladies were having tea leaves read, Mrs. Toth came to complain about an outing we plan. She wants the aquarium, but the ladies all vote on the planetarium. We talked for quite some time. I once did stop by Ava's table and say hello to her. She was drinking out of a lovely teacup, with butterflies on. I said, 'Ava, that cup is as pretty as you are.' She laughed a little but said she didn't really like the tea and perhaps her taste buds were off."

Wolf stiffened, but said nothing.

Lili wiped at her eyes. "She had a pretty purse with a reddish stone on it. I said it was perfect for her, because her lipstick was red. I said, 'You are the lady in red today.'"

Benton paused to sneeze and we all looked at him.

Wolf's eyes were on his notebook when he said, "Did you admire that stone? Did you take that stone from her purse, Mrs. Pinkoczi?"

She looked at him, then at me, her watery eyes confused. "Why would I take? I have my own stone." She held up her purse, a black square thing with a garish rhinestone on the outside. She opened it to retrieve an embroidered handkerchief, the stitching of which she showed to both detectives before she dabbed her eyes and blew her nose.

Then, while her purse was open, she dove inside it to retrieve a photo album that said "Baby's First Year" on the front. "Did I tell you that my daughter had a baby last fall?" she said, her voice still tearful.

"Mrs. Pinkoczi," said Wolf sternly.

Lili opened the album and displayed a picture of a fat baby with little hands that barely reached above his head. "This is Edward," she said. "Thirteen pounds at birth. What were you, Detective Wolf? A big boy, I bet. You still have a big appetite, yes? When I bring the *hurka*, I'll also bring some *paprikás*. And some good homemade *nokedli*. Dumplings."

"That won't be necessary," Wolf said. I thought Benton looked disappointed.

Mrs. Pinkoczi dabbed at her eyes again and said, "Everyone should eat Hungarian food, Detective. It is healthy."

Wolf looked to my mother, who subtly shook her head. "But it is delicious," my mother said.

Wolf took a moment to study his notebook, still tapping it with his pen. He took a sip of his Diet Coke and said, "What was your husband's response to Ava's death?"

Lili tucked her handkerchief back into her purse and closed the flap with a snapping sound. Then she sighed. "I don't know. I haven't talked to him since before our tea event. I haven't had the courage. He will be sad, of course. Perhaps he has heard by now."

Frowning, Wolf said, "Is there anything you think I should know about Ava Novák?"

Lili thought about this; for the first time she was silent

for more than ten seconds. I exchanged a glance with my mother, who was obviously noting the same thing. I couldn't catch my grandmother's eye; she had seemed out of sorts all day.

Finally Mrs. Pinkoczi lifted her chin and looked at Detective Wolf. "You should know she was my friend," she said.

Chapter 7

Mrs. Guliban's Story

When Mrs. Pinkoczi finally left the room, still promising to bring Hungarian food to the detectives, Wolf looked at his list and called Mrs. Guliban. He pronounced it *Gulliban*, and my mother and grandmother giggled. He looked at them, brows raised. "That's not how you say it?"

My grandmother pushed out her lips. "*GOO-lee-bonn.* Accent on first syllable. In Hungarian, always accent on the first syllable."

Wolf bent his blond head and made a note of this in his book. My mother said, "Detective Wolf, may we stretch our legs for a moment?"

He sat up straighter. "Of course. I'll tell Mrs. Guliban she can get a cup of coffee." This time he pronounced it correctly; Wolf was a quick study.

I followed my family to the coffeepot, and then to our back room, where we could talk in private. "When can we leave?" I complained. "I have things to do at home."

My mother frowned. "And when will we know if we can host the shower tomorrow? Mrs. Anderson will be murderous if we drop out on such short notice. Hana, you ask him."

"Why me?"

The two of them exchanged a glance. "He likes you best," my grandmother said.

My face grew warm. "That's ridiculous. We haven't exchanged more than a few words. Stop it! Don't look at me that way."

"Fine," my mother said. "Meanwhile, do you think we have to stay through all the testimony? I saw twenty names on that list."

This made us all broody. A police technician came into the room and seemed to be studying the refrigerator, both inside and out. My mother lowered her voice. "Maybe ask him now, Hana. About the shower, and about today. How long we're needed." She and my grandmother looked at me expectantly, and I snorted.

"Fine. Cowards. We have every right to ask those questions, and any one of us could ask them, but I'll do it." I marched out of the room and saw that Wolf, too, was stretching his legs. He stood near the lobby, looking out of the glass door. We had a lovely view of an open field beyond the entrance to Maggie's Tea House. Riverwood was a very green town—lots of forested areas, flowered fields, swaying grasses at the roadside.

"Uh—Detective?"

He turned. "Yes?"

"We were wondering—my family and I—when we would know about the event we have scheduled tomorrow. It's very short notice to leave them in the lurch, and we have the reputation of our business to consider . . ."

Wolf nodded. "Of course; I'm sorry. Let me talk to that

technician over there. Hang on." He moved swiftly on his long legs to one of the people wearing gloves. I heard him say "estimate" and "completion." Then they were talking quietly, their heads close together. He nodded once, then walked back to me. "We'll be finished by five o'clock today. Will that give you enough time to prepare?"

Relief washed through me. "Oh yes! Thank you. They will be so glad to hear this."

"Good." He started to move away.

"Uh—one more thing."

He turned back. Normally I wasn't intimidated by authority figures, but something about Wolf's bearing, about the badge that poked out of his pocket, about the gun I could sometimes glimpse when he moved his arm, had me feeling like a child talking to a stern teacher. "Do we—do you need us here for every testimony? It's just that you seem to have quite a long list there. And we have—other jobs."

Wolf nodded. "Number one, I really appreciate your help. This is a group of women brought together by a shared culture, and you three also share that culture, that heritage. So your input will be invaluable to me." He started walking back toward the interview table and gestured that I should come along. "Number two, no, you don't *have* to stay for any of them, but I would ask that you consider hanging around for at least the first five or six. From what we gleaned, those women had the strongest connections to Ava and perhaps the most interactions with her on the day she died. The ones at the bottom of the list claimed to not know her at all. So if you could stay—perhaps another hour? That would help immeasurably." We had reached the table, and he picked up a piece of paper. "And if you could take a look at this."

It was Mrs. Pinkoczi's printed interview. "Homework," I joked.

"Just give it a once-over, see if you note any discrepancies." He cleared his throat, then coughed a little. I realized he'd been doing a lot of throat-clearing during his interviews. Perhaps he was getting a cold. He paused a moment, then said, "Hana."

I looked up at him; his green eyes were gentle, but serious. "I know that you all feel bad about this woman dying in your establishment. I saw your face yesterday when she was taken away on the stretcher."

That had indeed been terrible. A rush of guilt had overcome me; why had I not spoken to her, chatted with her, made her feel at home? Instead I had begrudged her my teacup. "Yes," I said softly.

"And I figured you would want this opportunity to help her, or at least honor her memory."

I think my eyes must have grown huge. In my astonishment, it seemed that they were dominating my face. "You're guilt-tripping me!" I said, pointing at him.

Wolf expressed no surprise at all. "Is it working?"

I snatched the paper out of his hand with what my mother would call "ill grace." I looked at my shoes and then at him. "Yes, it's working. Thank you for the information. I'll go over this at my table in the back."

I walked away, not sure if I was right to feel indignant, but feeling that way nonetheless. I returned to my mother and grandmother and gave them Wolf's time estimates. They clapped and said, "Good job, Hana."

"Now you go out and listen to Mrs. Guliban while I fact-check the Pinkoczi notes."

"What are we, detectives? Are we Charlie's Angels?" My grandmother asked. She liked watching old TV shows on cable.

"They need our help," I said. "Just one more hour. So

let's do a good job, and we can say we did our part for poor Ava."

They agreed and went back out to Wolf; I sat down to study Lili's comments. After a moment, I jotted in my notebook. "Mrs. Kalas was defensive; Mrs. Pinkoczi is evasive."

This made me curious; did every witness have a pattern of behavior under interrogation? I stood up and peeked out at the Guliban interview. Mrs. Guliban was saying in a loud voice, "How dare you suggest that I had anything to do with this?"

Wolf's quiet response, unintelligible. Then a cough.

Her volume lessened slightly, but she remained on the offense. "I just don't think you police are handling this well, at all . . ."

I went back to my notebook and added, "And Mrs. Guliban is confrontational."

How would I act, I wondered, if Wolf fired a million questions at me? Considering how upset I had just gotten with him over something rather trivial, I did not think I would fare well. It was difficult to sit in that seat, to be interrogated. Wolf, on the other hand, did his job well, and he retained his composure no matter what people did.

I wondered what it must be like for a detective to have to face people's various defense mechanisms. People yelling, crying, lying, accusing, demanding. It was not a job I envied.

Jotting a few notes on the interview before me, I stood up and went into the main room. I walked to the table behind Benton and set my paper on top of the Mrs. Kalas notes. Then I moved to the coffeepot, eavesdropping on the current interview.

Mrs. Guliban, short and squat in her dark suit, was muttering something in Hungarian.

Wolf, unfazed, said, "English please, Mrs. Guliban."

She huffed. "You think I am some enemy to Ava, but we were friends. We went to church together, sometimes. She had this special quality that all the ladies liked, at first."

"What special quality?" Wolf said, beaming in on her with his green eyes.

"A quality like—she draws people to herself. They like her personality, and how pretty she is."

"Charisma?" Wolf asked.

"Yes, yes. That is Ava. So we all liked her."

"You said 'at first,' before," Wolf reminded her.

"Yes, at first, because then she started dating around. Some of us thought she seemed too eager, too forward. And then she was dating Mr. Pinkoczi. She told me once she wanted to find her soul's mate."

"Her soul mate?" Wolf asked, clearing his throat.

"Yes. With another woman's husband. But she didn't end up liking him, anyway. She liked Joe Novák." Mrs. Guliban's face softened, and she pushed her slightly smudged glasses up on her nose. "Everyone like Joe. He is a good man, handsome man."

"And were the Nováks happy together?"

Her face grew sad. "Yes. Very happy, I think. Joe is with Father Istvan today. Praying and crying."

Wolf nodded. "Did you personally resent Ava Novák, Mrs. Guliban?"

She shrugged. "Like I say, at first we were friends. Then she spend more time with Joe, and we start to think she was stuck-up."

"I thought you said she was too forward."

Stubborn, Mrs. Guliban thrust out her chin. "But also stuck-up. Joe always went on about how beautiful, how talented she was. He said she would be famous."

Wolf tensed. He seemed to practically shimmer when he was on the verge of new information. "Famous for what?"

"She sing and dance, and play instruments. Joe said her soul was all music. Melodies made her the happiest." She looked briefly sorry. "Now he has to pick songs for her funeral."

Wolf held up a hand. "Let's go back. Did she use her musical talent in some sort of profession? Did she teach piano, or music?"

Mrs. Guliban shrugged. "I don't know."

"No one wanted to hear Joe speak of his wife's talent?"

She looked a bit guilty. "We already knew. She sang in the church choir."

"What is the name of the choir director?" Wolf asked, his pen ready.

"Mr. Carmichael. Not Hungarian, but very talented." She sat with her hands folded, nodding like a sage as Wolf jotted down the name.

Benton paused in his typing and flexed his fingers. Wolf rubbed his eyes, studied his notes, and then said, "All right, thank you for coming in, Mrs. Guliban."

She nodded at him, then at my mother and grandmother, and made her way out of the room, resembling a beetle with her square black suit and scuttling black shoes.

I leaned toward Wolf and pointed after her. "That's not a Hungarian trait, you know—to be mean and judgmental like those ladies. That's just this group. Their jealousy, or peer pressure, or whatever it was. Encouraged by their, their *girls' club*."

Wolf nodded. "I understand." He covered his mouth and sneezed three times.

My mother said, "You must see all sorts of bad behavior

from people. All of their ugliness exposed to you through an investigation."

"You bet we do," Benton said at the same time that Wolf said, "You have no idea."

~

We stayed for the testimony of Mrs. Balogh, Mrs. Veres, Mrs. Cseh, and Mrs. Samsa. Benton was starting to look cross-eyed as he processed all of the stories, rumors, complaints, resentments, and, in rarer cases, praise.

Wolf fired off his questions, treating every woman to his laser beam eyes and his unforgiving follow-up queries. Generally, the women, even the tough ones, walked away looking slightly intimidated.

My mother and grandmother stood up to stretch their legs and get some coffee, and I left the table I was leaning on to join them. Wolf consulted his list, then stood up and walked over to us. "Ladies, I think that I am no longer in need of your aid, which has been invaluable. On behalf of the Riverwood Police Department, I thank you."

My mother was utterly charmed by this little speech; my grandmother looked a bit more skeptical, although she did offer her hand when he reached out to shake it; then she turned abruptly and walked toward the back room. I handed Wolf the last of my notes. "Just so you know, Mrs. Guliban and Mrs. Cseh are sisters. I don't think they mentioned that in the interview."

Wolf's eyes widened. "I think that is a notable detail; thank you, Hana." He took out his notebook and jotted something, sniffling slightly.

By the time he finished writing my grandmother was back, holding a bottle. "So—the place will be empty of your people by five o'clock?" she asked in an imperious tone.

"We promise," Wolf said. Benton appeared in the doorway; he had gone to buy lunch for the police on the site; he beckoned to Wolf.

"Are you ladies hungry? Would you like—?" he began.

"Oh, no thank you," I said. "We'll eat at home."

My grandmother stepped closer to Wolf and put the bottle in his hand. "This is Pálinka," she said. "Good for your cold. Make it go away."

"Oh—is that so?" he asked, his eyes darting to me.

"Grandma thinks Pálinka cures all ills," I said. "It's fruit brandy. You can Google it."

"Well, thank you. Thanks." Wolf did a half bow in our direction and loped across the floor to claim his lunch.

As we walked to our car in the lot, my mother sighed. "Well, that was a very sad two days; I hope we can put it all behind us. We'll need to get started on this Anderson shower tonight, I think, so we aren't rushing around tomorrow. Then we can just worry about finishing touches in the morning."

"They want the standard European tea, so we'll use the traditional set, right? And then weren't we just going with our vines and flowers around the pastry table? And of course I'll put the Dvořák or the Brahms on my iPad. Mrs. Andersen said she wanted the photo booth, so we'll have to remind Dad to set up his little photo corner with the Danube background. His pictures are always so popular. This will be nice, Mom. We can pull this off without them ever knowing there was a chance of cancellation. Right, Gram?"

My grandmother looked distracted, as she had for most of the day. "Mama should be here. She would have known."

We were climbing into my mother's car; I got into the

backseat and studied the part of her face that I could see in the front seat. "What do you mean, she would have known?"

My mother waved the comment away. "I wish your mother were still here, too. She was such a sweet soul. And such a wonderful cook. Oh my gosh, the food that woman made!"

My grandmother peered around her seat and winked at me. "Your mother doesn't like to talk about my mama's gift."

"What gift?"

"Enough, Ma." My mother looked sternly at her own mother, and the latter sighed and looked out the window. Then my mother looked at me over her right shoulder as she started the engine. "Hana, have you told François?"

"Oh gosh, no! I'll call him when we get home. I told him to be on standby. The event has been on his calendar for ages, so he should be prepared."

As we drove, though, I worried over several things. Would François have made other plans? We had no replacement for him. Did the police have some other reason for wanting the three of us at the tea house for half the day?

And why, why had I not talked to Ava Novák, if only to say hello?

Chapter 8

FRANÇOIS AND THE CIGARETTE

I ate a quick lunch with my mother and grandmother, then hopped in my own car and drove back to my apartment. I unlocked the door and found Iris Gonzalez lurking in the hallway. Iris was five, with short brown hair and big brown eyes; her mother joked that she looked more like my child than like hers. Iris's mom and dad were both accountants, and one of them was usually able to work from home so that Iris always had a parent with her. She liked to pretend that the first-floor hallway was a part of her castle, and she enacted some impressively elaborate make-believe sessions on its carpeted floor.

"Hey, Iris," I said.

"Hi, Hana!" She held up a little finger, as though an idea had just occurred to her. "We should make cookies sometime!" We had done this once, at Christmas, when her mother and I decided to do a cookie exchange. Iris had benefited greatly in the form of dough and oven-warm treats, and she still got glassy-eyed with the memory of it.

"That sounds sweet," I said. "Get it? Sweet?"

Iris rolled her eyes and grabbed her stomach, as though my joke had given her indigestion. "That's a bad one," she said.

"You tell me a better joke, then." I folded my arms.

She skipped toward me. She wore tiny jeans and blue socks and a little sweatshirt with a picture of a grumpy cat on it. "Okay, I got one!"

"Sock it to me."

"What? Sock it?" She laughed theatrically, the way only children can. "You're weird," she said in her little voice.

"Let's hear that joke, Iris. Quit stalling."

She put her hands on her hips and thrust out her chin, making a silly face. "Okay. What did the big flower say to the little flower?"

"Hmm. Big flower to little flower. Did it say, '*Leave* me alone'?"

Iris looked disgusted. "No, it did not."

"What did it say?"

She grinned at me. "It said, 'Hi, bud.'"

I laughed. "You know what? That is a good joke. Slap me five, Iris."

She did, hitting me as hard as she possibly could. "Ouch. That was way too hard. What, are you trying out for the Marines, or something? Stop trying to kill me."

"Sorry," she said, still smiling with all her little teeth.

"Give me a hug, then."

She did, very sweetly, and I gave her a kiss on the head. "Who's home, your mom or your dad?"

"My dad," she said, skipping around.

"Does he know you're out here?"

"Yahh!" Iris said, running in circles around me.

"Did you have, like, a whole bowl of candy?"

"No. Is there one?" She was giggling now.

Her father, Paul, peeked out of his apartment. "I hear lots of hilarity out here," he said, smiling at me.

"Iris just told an awesome joke."

"She's got a bunch of them," he said.

"I'm going to go write that one down, Iris."

"Okay," she said.

Her dad waved her back toward the apartment. "Come on in," he said. "Time for a bath."

"Aaaggh!" she yelled, acting now for my benefit. "The undersea world of Iris!"

Paul rolled his eyes at me. "Ready for Broadway," he said.

I laughed, waved at them both, and climbed the stairs to the second floor.

I fed the cats, who had given me a one-minute sermon, in tandem, about how hungry they were; then I escaped to my little bedroom, my haven and comfort, where I flopped on the bed. My room, like anyone's room, was filled with things personal to me, the objects I wanted to see around me as I drifted off to sleep, or woke up in the morning. My bed sat centered under a large window with a view of the grassy hill behind my apartment. The window had a large white sill that functioned as a shelf. On this, in a blue and white china pot, sat my Norfolk pine, Isabella (we named our plants in the Keller family), and a stack of books I planned to read soon, along with one of my treasures—my Zsolnay woman. This was an artful porcelain figure of a nude woman kneeling on a rock and lifting her long hair with both hands. The finish was an alluring blue-green, what the Zsolnay literature called "a vivid green iridescent glaze with peacock blue overtones." This was a distinctive feature of the glazing at Zsolnay porcelain in Hungary. The woman, I had decided when I received her from my parents on my twenty-first birthday, was too mysterious to be named. She was like one of the good fairies in the stories my grandmother had told me as a child, so from the start I had called her Fairy.

I had taped Fairy down so that Antony and Cleopatra would not bat her around my room. In this way, they were able to share the windowsill harmoniously. Generally, the cats even left Isabella alone, although they sometimes swatted her fronds when they were feeling particularly frisky.

My bedspread was a quilt that had been lovingly pieced together by my mother, a fine seamstress, truly an artisan. Someday, when I had my own shop, I intended to sell her quilts. She had matched the peacock tones in my beloved Fairy and created a bedspread with the colors of sparkling green seas and cool blue lakes. I felt restful, calm, whenever I gazed upon it, not to mention when I reclined on its surface. I lay there now, looking at the rest of my room, which included a small white desk that tucked into the bottom of a built-in white bookcase, a giant treelike thing with many compartments; my father, grandfather, and grandmother had combined their talents and made it to order so that I could display books in some shelves and teacups and porcelain figurines in others.

A blue and white rag rug lay across the light wood floorboards. Antony strolled in and sat on this, staring up at me. The whole room had a whimsical feel, a happy aura. I had some flameless candles beside my bed—flameless so that my cats would refrain from setting my apartment on fire. I switched one on now and set it between Fairy and Isabella;

it flickered gently and soothed me with its artificial glow while I dialed François.

"Yes, François here," he said into my ear.

"Hi, François. It's Hana. We're on for tomorrow. The event is at three, so get there by what—noon? One? Just leave yourself enough time to get everything ready. You still have her menu?"

"Yes, yes, it will be fine. These little love pastries are my specialty. She will weep for joy."

Normally I would mock François for his egotism, but I had seen women become emotional at the sight of his creations before. "Great. And save one for me. I love your little heart cakes."

"Of course. And I will use the multitiered tray—it always looks quite grand on the table. But then you must scatter flowers or something, make it look full, since many of the cakes will be on the tiers."

"Got it. We can put out strawberries, too. They'll match your chocolate frosting and red accents."

"I will make a few white-frosted cakes to scatter with the strawberries. A nice visual, but also delicious."

"Okay." I adjusted a pillow under my head and said, "Hey, François."

"Yes?" He sounded distracted now, just as Domo had when I called him at work. Men and their attention spans.

"Yesterday, I know there was so much going on, but—did you see or hear anything odd? I don't know if you saw Ava—she was the lady with red lipstick and a red purse. She was blonde, pretty . . ."

"Hmm. I don't think so. I didn't really go out among the ladies, except when I pushed out my cart. And then I was scanning the cakes, making sure they look just so."

"That makes sense. I just thought I'd—"

"Although . . ." François said, extending the word as he thought it over. "I did hear two ladies fighting. Or one at least, yelling and being—what do you say? Witchy?"

"Sure. Did you tell the police this?"

"They have not contacted me. And to be honest, when I heard it I didn't really pay attention. I had gone out to have a cigarette—just a quick one—before I cleaned up. I like to close my eyes and think, take myself to faraway places. I was leaning on the wall, under a window. I suppose it was the window in the ladies' room."

"What were they fighting about?"

"Oh—I am trying to remember. The angry one was going back and forth—Hungarian, English. Alternating."

"Okay. What did she say in English?"

"Ahh. She was saying—'I can't believe it.' She couldn't believe, she was indignant, that the other had worn something. A hat or something. No, wait! She said stone. She wore a stone. A necklace, perhaps?"

"What did she say about the stone?"

A pause. "I'm trying to remember. It didn't seem like much, just two ladies bickering. I remember I thought—what was so special about this place, our tea house, because the first one said, 'How dare you bring that stone to this place? How dare you flaunt it so—barzenel'?"

"Brazen? Brazenly?"

"Yes, I think. And the other answered in Hungarian, saying something, probably saying *Calm down, you wacko.*" François chuckled a little. "The first one was insistent, though. Oh yes! She said, 'After all these years, all these years I thought it was lost!' and then the other said, 'You knew, everyone knew.' It was hard to follow. I sat and smoked. I did not realize how much I would recall!"

A stone. Could she have meant the jewel on Ava's purse?

Is that why it had disappeared? Had the angry lady taken it away? "François, did you hear any names?"

"No. I heard, but did not listen, you see? I did get the impression they were sisters."

"Why?"

"One said, 'Even at home, you were like this. Always trying to take from others—take attention, take love, take affection.' The other one said that was not true, that this angry one always overreacted."

"And is that all they said?"

"I think, except one of them got the parting blow. Parting—what is it?"

"Parting shot."

"Yes, the parting shot, the final word. She attacked the prettiness of the other. She said, 'People think you are so pretty and good, like a good fairy, but you are the opposite.' Made me think of *Wizard of Oz*, you know? The good and bad witch."

"François, this is important. Did she say 'bad witch'?"

"I don't know—something like that. She said she was the opposite of the good fairy, and then I think she slipped into some Hungarian."

"Did she say 'Vasorrú Bába'?"

He gasped. "She did! You know what? Because for a minute I think they are speaking French. We have this word, too, can mean a dessert, like I make, but can also mean, like, 'I am so surprised, you have shocked me, my mouth is hanging open.' That meaning of 'baba.' So I was half laughing, you see."

He was laughing a little even now because he had no idea what it meant in Hungarian, what it had meant to Ava Novák. "François, I have to run. Thanks for this information—I think the police will want to ask you about it, so remember those details. I'll see you tomorrow."

"Yes, okay, Hana. Au revoir."

I ended the call, then got up and retrieved my purse from my kitchen counter. I dug out the card Detective Wolf had given me. For the first time I noticed that it said, "Riverwood Police Department. Homicide." Then, in the center, it said "Erik Wolf, Detective."

I pondered this for a moment. Erik with a *k*. Did that mean he was Norwegian? The name certainly suggested it. If so, what an interesting mix we'd had in our European tea house—our French pastry chef, our Hungarian guests, and our Norwegian investigator. I dialed the number Wolf had scrawled on the card with the word "cell."

It rang once, and then he answered. "Detective Wolf."

"Uh—Detective—it's Hana Keller." I moved back toward my bedroom and sat back down on my bed.

"Yes, Hana? Is something wrong?"

"Well—sort of. I mean, I got some new information."

I could hear voices in the background; Wolf himself seemed to be moving quickly while he talked. "New information? What sort of information?"

"I was talking with François, our chef. I asked if he had seen anything strange; he said no, but he heard something, when he was smoking a cigarette outside." I told him François's story, and I could almost hear Wolf's energy bristling over the phone.

"Hana, I'm sure I have this François's information somewhere in my notes, but could you save me the time and give me his phone number?"

"Sure," I said. I knew François's number by heart, and I recited it for Wolf.

"Thank you. I will contact him now. I appreciate the information, Hana."

"Sure," I said again. What a brilliant conversationalist I was. I glared at Antony, who still sat on the carpet like a little black statue.

"Please contact me anytime if you think of something important or relevant. Any hour of the day, it's fine. All right?"

"Yes, okay. Have a good evening," I said.

"Good-bye," Wolf said, and I turned off my phone.

Cleopatra wandered in and sat down next to Antony. Her brother turned and began to nuzzle her ear. They were the most affectionate siblings I had ever encountered. "Okay," I told them. "No more police, no more unhappy thoughts, no more interrogations. I need a break. Do you guys want to watch a movie? Nothing scary, nothing intense. Something light and happy. Right? Who's with me?"

The cats looked at me through slitted eyes. They seemed pleased at the prospect. "Okay, good. I'll make popcorn for me, and I'll find some sort of snack for you. Meanwhile, I'm thinking romantic comedy. Grandma and Mom made me a list."

I got up, ready to move to the living room and my flat-screen TV. I paused at my bookshelf; one of the white compartments held framed family photos: Domo and me at six and three, holding hands at the seashore; my parents on their wedding day, smiling from ear to ear; my grandmother with my grandfather, back in Hungary, in a garden behind their house. She was smiling and looking down with a wise expression, and he was looking at her, clearly in love and devoted, his hand linked with hers; and my great-grandmother, Natalia, in a black dress with a red scarf, posing at someone's graduation. She wore that same serene smile that I remembered, despite having lived through several tragedies. There was no picture of her husband, my great-grandfather. He had died in the Hungarian Revolution—one of the brave in Budapest who had risen up against the Russian invasion. Natalia, whom he had sent to stay with relatives in a distant town, was destined to raise her baby daughter alone. Ever after the war, it had been the two of them, Natalia and her little Juliana. Great-grandma Nat had never remarried. When Juliana married my grandfather and they eventually decided to come to America with their children, her mother came with them.

I thought again of my brave young great-grandfather, determined to protect his wife, his daughter, and his country. "Talk about romantic," I murmured.

I left my room and bustled around for a few minutes, making a bowl of popcorn, finding treats for my little friends, and glancing over the list of movies my mother and grandmother said I should watch.

"*Gone with the Wind*, *Indiana Jones*, *Romancing the Stone* . . ." I paused at the third one. Once again I was pondering the word "stone" and thinking of the one on Ava's purse. It hadn't looked like a ruby, but it had been pretty, smooth, elegant. On a whim I grabbed my phone and Googled "stone, red and gray flecks."

An image popped up immediately, looking very similar to the stone I'd seen on Ava's purse. I clicked on the Wikipedia link. "'Heliotrope, also known as bloodstone,'" I read to the cats. "'The red inclusions of hematite are supposed to look like flecks of blood.'" Hence the name.

"Bloodstone," I said out loud. And then, to Cleopatra, whose little face was near mine, "Why does that give me a bad feeling?"

She didn't seem to know.

I selected *Romancing the Stone* and began to watch the tale of Kathleen Turner's character, Joan Wilder, who was an introvert bestselling romance novelist. "Sort of like Margie, at least with the shy part," I mused aloud.

Soon enough, poor, shy Joan Wilder was embroiled in a terrible situation; her sister was a hostage in Cartagena, Colombia, and Joan had to rescue her. Apparently Joan possessed a treasure map, and the people who had her sister wanted it very badly. More and more, as the movie went on (and as the handsome Michael Douglas entered the picture), it became clear that there was a stone at the heart of the mystery.

I felt that there was probably a stone at the heart of Ava's mysterious death, as well. A smooth, reddish stone with gray flecks. A stone that had angered someone so much that she had called Ava a witch. A stone that may have, "after all these years," gotten Ava Novák killed.

A bloodstone.

I sighed and then lost myself in the rest of the movie. Soon I would have to return to the tea house and set up for the next day's adventure, and a fictional drama was preferable to the real-life one that awaited us at Maggie's.

Chapter 9

The Mysterious Mrs. Novák

The sun was setting when we got back to Maggie's Tea House. As we walked in, I appreciated the aesthetics of our building: the pretty brick walkway with the two giant urns flanking the doorway; the sign above the door, large enough to be read from the road, with black lettering surrounded by green fleur-de-lis; the tiny white lights lining the front windows with an alluring glow.

"The weather is nice this evening," my grandmother said. It was true; a cool, gentle breeze wrapped around us as we brought our packages in from the car. This time my father was with us, and he was doing a lot of the heavy lifting.

"Where do you want the photo corner?" he asked.

My mother thought about this as she unlocked the door. "Last time it was a bit too close to the food table. How about over next to the stage?"

For the events, we had a tiny elevated platform on one

side of the tea house. It was perfect for live music—usually someone playing acoustic guitar or classical violin. Once or twice we had even provided chamber music. "Sounds good," said my father, and went inside with my mother.

I moved forward, but my grandmother held me back. "We have a visitor," she said.

A moment later a car pulled into our lot; I sent my grandmother a quizzical look, then moved closer to the parking lot to see who it was. I was ready to approach the driver and tell him we were closed until he emerged from his car and I realized it was Detective Wolf. He was no longer in his professional suit; he wore a pair of blue jeans and a hooded sweatshirt that said "RPD."

"I have to go inside," my grandmother said in my ear, and then she was gone.

"Traitor," I murmured. I was suddenly conscious of my clothes: a pair of faded jeans and a brown T-shirt. I moved toward Wolf, my hands in my pockets. "Can I help you? I thought you were all finished?"

"Yes. I just had a couple of questions, if you have a minute."

"Sure." I sat down on the brick edging of the raised garden that led to our front entrance. My father had set up an elaborate model train in the mulch, in a vaguely European setting with mountains, chalets, and a working ski lift; the train cars weren't running just now, but were hidden inside a tunnel in the Alps, which sat, blue-white and majestic, along the wall of the building. Safe inside the plastic mountains, my father's beloved Euro Express remained protected from the weather and any potential train enthusiasts with thieving tendencies.

Wolf sat next to me. "I spoke with François."

"Oh yes. I've been thinking about that . . ."

"I'll need you to show me the area where he was standing."

"Of course. But I should tell you this. François said that the women were arguing about a stone. I assume this means the stone from Ava's purse."

"It could be, yes. We can't assume anything, though." Wolf's face was hard to read in the waning light.

"Anyway, I looked up the stone online. I think it was heliotrope—also known as bloodstone. It's not particularly expensive."

"That's interesting," he said.

"It seems to me that the stone is at the root of everything. I would want to know why it was on her purse in the first place. Especially if she knew it was going to make someone angry. And why it *did* make someone angry, maybe angry enough to kill her and take the stone. And how—I guess how a person could get so angry that they could actually take the life of another human being." I had tacked the last question on the end spontaneously, and it made me sad.

"Yes." He nodded, looking regretful.

"Another thing, though, was that François said the women sounded like sisters fighting. As I mentioned, there was one set of sisters at the event, but that would mean one of the women wasn't Ava, and that wouldn't make sense."

"No. I think one of the women was Ava."

"But it doesn't quite fit, does it? Why would they fight in the bathroom and then pretend to be friends outside of it? And why was François the only witness?"

Wolf looked at his shoes. "Those are all good questions."

"But there's a more important one."

His mouth seemed to twitch, but I couldn't tell in the twilight. "Yes?"

"I assume you've already asked it. But why would one of those ladies be traveling around with just enough poison to put into a teacup and kill someone? It seems highly unlikely, doesn't it?"

"I can't comment on that." Wolf stood up. "If you could show me the window?"

"Yes, sure. Come this way." We walked around the side of the building and almost to the back, where a large square window was surrounded by brick. There was a small bench in the garden beneath, and this was where François had been sitting with his cigarette.

Wolf walked carefully around the area; he took out a measuring tape, for reasons unknown, and produced the dimensions of the window. He made notes in his notebook and occasionally murmured to himself.

I hesitated, not sure if I was expected to stay. "I should get inside," I said. "They need my help."

"Sure. I just need to come in and look at the ladies' room. I'm sure the techs were there already, but I want to revisit it, given this new context."

"Okay. Come on in."

We went back around the building and through the front door. My father was already busy in his corner setting up a backdrop for the photos he would take and print as souvenirs of the event, and my mother and grandmother had already started on the center refreshment table, smoothing on a starched white cloth and beginning to lay out the green vines that would accentuate the food display.

"You all know Detective Wolf," I said, half joking. My family waved, but kept working.

I turned to Wolf. "You know where the bathroom is, right?"

"I do. Thanks, Hana." He disappeared in the direction

of the ladies' room, I could only assume to measure and take notes and mumble things anew.

I marched to our basket of tablecloths and began putting them on the round tables. My parents looked at me, their faces questioning. I shrugged by way of answer, and they resumed their jobs.

"I think I might need to do some touch-ups with the iron," I said.

"Go ahead," my mother called. "I'm working on the teacups, and Grandma will finish the vines."

I examined the first cloth for wrinkles and began pressing it with our portable steam iron. My mother had opened a window, and the September breeze wafted in, cooling and calming me as I worked.

My grandmother called out, "Let me know if you see Mrs. Kiraly. I asked her to drop off the doilies."

I nodded. Every Hungarian had a house full of doilies, but Mrs. Kiraly was an Old World artisan who made elaborate works of art that were crocheted, knitted, tatted—Mrs. Kiraly could do it all with her magical artist's hands. Grandma had asked her to make some special ones for our wedding events, requesting that she weave tiny red hearts in with the linen thread. Tomorrow we would be debuting her handiwork.

I finished the first tablecloth and flipped another into the air over an unadorned table. Then I centered the cloth and began steaming out the residual wrinkles. Mrs. Kiraly appeared at the front window, peering in like a kindly beggar woman in a fairy tale. I waved and beckoned her in.

She came through the door, holding a little embroidered tote bag, and smiled at me. I was amazed by the lightness of her step and the general energy of her bearing, because Mrs. Kiraly was eighty-five years old.

"Hallo, Anna," my grandmother called. "Thank you for coming!"

Mrs. Kiraly nodded. I pulled out a chair for her, and she sat down to rummage in her bag.

"I can't wait to see," I told her, setting my iron on its resting pad and pulling up a chair beside her. My mother and grandmother wandered over, too, their faces expectant.

Mrs. Kiraly beamed, clearly glad of her audience. "You told me larger, yes? For big display."

"Yes, that will be perfect," Grandma said.

She pulled out a delicate, intricate doily, about three feet long and made of fine linen yarn. Sparkling throughout were little red sequins and flashes of silver-red thread interspersed with the white. It was magnificent, like something spun by Ariadne.

"Oooooh," we all said.

"You like?" asked Mrs. Kiraly.

"It's spectacular," my mother said.

"Just lovely," I told her.

My grandmother went to get her wallet.

Mrs. Kiraly pulled out another long doily, just like the first, and handed it to my mother. "Will make a pretty table," she said.

"It even looks good from here," my father called, still laboring over his backdrop.

Mrs. Kiraly laughed.

Suddenly a shadow loomed over us. It was Wolf, tucking away his notebook and smothering a yawn. "Thank you, Hana, for the tour, and thank you, everyone, for your patience. I think I have everything I need now." He nodded to my mother. "Mrs. Keller. Mrs. Horvath."

I said, "Detective Wolf, this is Mrs. Kiraly. She knew Ava Novák, didn't you, Anna?"

Mrs. Kiraly grew sad and made the sign of the cross. "Oh, poor Ava. My poor child."

Wolf sat down on one of the chairs and pulled out his notebook. "How did you know Ava, Mrs. Kiraly?"

The old woman sighed, resting her hands on the bag in her lap. "She lived two doors away from me. She and Joe. And Joe I know from a child."

Wolf nodded, eager. "And so you've known Ava since she came to the U.S.?"

"Yes, yes. Sweet girl, so excited to come here, to start life."

"Meaning what?" Wolf asked.

Mrs. Kiraly's face was wrinkled, but her eyes were brown and intense. She gave Wolf a shrewd look. "She have a very sad time in Hungary, is all I know. Joe told me she suffered there. So finally, sixty-two years old, she come here, four years ago. And she is happy to start, with new town, new friends, new husband."

"Was she married before?" Wolf asked.

Mrs. Kiraly shrugged. "She never say. I don't like to ask her about the Old Country because it made her sad. We talked mainly about yarn, knitting, cooking. We sing together, sometimes, while we peeled potatoes. We would make double batches of *krumplisaláta* or *paprikás krumpli*."

My grandmother asked her something in Hungarian, and they spoke in that language for a time. Wolf leaned forward, trying to follow it.

"You guys, speak in English," I told them. To Wolf I said, "They made Hungarian potato salad together, or *paprikás* potatoes. At least that's why they peeled potatoes together."

Mrs. Kiraly held up a wrinkled hand. "Sorry, sorry."

Wolf said, "Ava seemed happy to you?"

Anna Kiraly hesitated. "She did, yes. For a long time. But also there was always a sadness." She dismissed Wolf with a look. "You might have to be Hungarian to understand."

Wolf looked at me for explanation.

"We have a gift for sadness," I said. "Or at least that's the stereotype of Hungarian people. But my grandmother says it's in our blood."

"So—supposedly you are all more—melancholic than other people?"

"Exactly," said my mother.

Mrs. Kiraly nodded, wise as an old prophet. "Ya, and Ava had the sadness, like a cloud over her. I always sense it."

My grandmother made sounds of agreement. I pointed at her. "Did you read Ava's leaves that day?"

"No. She never come to the table. I wanted her to. But then I saw she had the butterfly cup, and I vas distracted, telling fortunes." Her accent was becoming more pronounced, which was usually a sign that she was tired and making less of an effort to speak properly for my mother's sake.

"How could someone have done it in front of all those people, with no one witnessing who brought her the cup? How could they have poisoned her without someone being aware of it?" I said, thinking aloud.

Mrs. Kiraly made a regretful sound and got to her feet. Her bones snapped loudly, and she laughed. "The old woman's symphony," she said. "I click and clack and moan."

Wolf stood up, too. "Shall I walk you to your car? It's dark now."

"Such a gentleman," said Mrs. Kiraly. Then, in a non sequitur that brought a flush to my cheeks: "Do you know that Hana was first in her high school class?"

"Really? Valedictorian?" Wolf asked me.

I shrugged. "Not exactly. I was tied with a boy; they asked him to be the speaker at graduation. I was listed in the program, but only he got to make a speech."

Wolf blinked. "That's unfair!"

"Water under the bridge," I said.

"Still, a smart girl and a pretty one. So impressive," said Mrs. Kiraly, moving her creaky bones toward the door.

Wolf smiled at the floor and said, "Good night, everyone. Thank you." He followed our old friend, and they disappeared into the night.

I picked up my iron again and resumed my steaming task. I thought about what Mrs. Kiraly had said and about the idea of the cloud over Ava Novák. I remembered, suddenly, the way my grandmother had gasped when my mother had showed her the teacup and the scrawled message within it. "Grandma," I said. "*Why* did you want to read Ava's leaves?"

My grandmother looked solemn. "Because I knew they would mean trouble. I wanted to warn her," Grandma said.

Chapter 10

What Grandmother Knew

We finished an hour later, and my father ordered a pizza, which we shared at one of the undecorated tables. "Looks good, ladies," my dad said, scanning the room. Then he reached out to pat my mother's blonde hair. My father, after thirty years of marriage, still couldn't resist my mother's charms. He was always hugging her, kissing her cheek, bringing her gifts. Domo said it was disgusting, but I thought it was beautiful. They had met when she was a senior at Purdue University. She had come home for Christmas and gone out shopping in downtown Riverwood. My mother still told the story with shining eyes: It had been snowing, and the shops all glowed with Christmas lights. The street looked ethereal, like something out of a fairy story set at the holidays. She had been rushing along with bags in her hands, and she hit a patch of ice on the sidewalk and went sprawling. She sat there for a second, embarrassed, and a handsome young man bent to pick up her bags and return them to her. "Are you hurt?" he asked.

She looked up; he seemed to have a halo of light around him, a topaz-colored light, my mother always said. She assured him she was all right, and he asked if he could treat her to some hot chocolate. She agreed. He told her, over a cozy table at the local coffee shop, that he had gotten a managerial job at Borden's Department Store, and he enjoyed it, but he was hoping to get into graduate school to study history with the goal of teaching it one day.

He had earned points from my mother with his ambitious nature, and even more points from her family when, two weeks later, he met a roomful of Hungarians and asked them endless questions about their heritage, showing genuine interest.

I smiled at him now as he answered a text message on his phone. His colleagues were always texting him; my mother didn't like it. She said he deserved his private time.

"Dad, that backdrop looks great. I love those pictures where people look like they're in a boat on the Danube."

"Should be popular," he agreed.

My gaze shifted to my grandmother. "Grandma. Tell Mom and Dad what you told me, about how you knew Ava was in trouble."

My mother stiffened. "Mom, really—"

"What? I merely say I knew there would be bad. The leaves said so. Trouble for Mrs. Kalas, or someone connected to her, but also for poor Ava. The fairy was—what is the word for 'unclear, goes either way'—?"

"Ambiguous," I said.

"Yes. Ambiguous. But it seems more like bad fairy. Like Szépasszony when she is angry."

And we came back to the legends, I reflected grimly. My grandmother had grown up listening to old Hungarian tales that her mother loved to tell. These stories were often about a witch, a fairy, or the "Fair Lady" called Szépasszony, as we had told Detective Wolf when he and Benton came to the tea house. What made these three groups fascinating was that they were different except when they weren't—sometimes they had remarkably similar traits. They could all fly, for example, and fairies, while good, could do bad things, just as evil witches could morph into good fairies. Fair ladies could be both wonderful and treacherous. Grandma had absorbed the dualities of these tales as a child, and she wove them into her theatrical readings. "The leaves could suggest something either way?" I asked, humoring her.

"It seem so. But then I look at the leaves, and at Mrs. Kalas, and I know: bad. And I get a very bad feeling."

My mother rustled in her seat, then sighed. "Mama. I know that you've always had—*instincts*. But we're talking about a woman's death here."

My grandmother sat up straight. I didn't think I'd ever seen her look so offended. "My *instincts*, I inherit from my mama, and she is—she was—a woman with gifts."

My father touched her arm. "Of course! We all know that Natalia was a special person. For one thing, she always helped me find lost things. She just seemed to know where they were," he said, and it brought back a memory: my grandmother at our kitchen table, and my father coming in, flustered and late for work, saying "Natalia, help! Where are my car keys?"

The memory surprised me because it was so intact. "That's right! She did help you find things! And I think she found my missing doll once, too!"

My grandmother nodded, pleased with me. My mother

shrugged. "I'm just saying, your reading of the tea leaves is *entertainment*. It's not supposed to be a serious thing."

I realized that I hadn't asked my grandmother an important question. "Grandma—did you know Ava Novák? Before the event, I mean?"

She looked slightly ashamed. "I meet her once or twice, at parties. I hear the rumors, you know, from Mrs. Kalas and the others. I believe them, I guess. Especially because I saw her, talking to men. She was—what is that word?—when you flirt."

"Flirtatious? Coquettish?" I asked.

She shrugged. "Yes, something. But not in a terrible way. She was good at it, you know? She was sparkly. But it got the ladies mad, so I didn't spend time, much. I hear—*heard* that she was so unhappy in Hungary. That she came here to escape memories."

"It's so depressing. Not just what happened to Ava, but the idea that she thought life would be better here, and then she was ostracized and—" I sighed, unwilling to say the final word.

My father clapped his hands. "Enough of this sad talk. You all need to get home, relax, so you can be fresh for your event tomorrow." He got up and started gathering up our paper plates. My mother found a sponge and wiped down the table. They both went briefly to the kitchen at the back of the hall.

I kissed my grandma's cheek and whispered, "I'm with you. There was a bad feeling in that room, even before Ava died." I recalled, with a sudden shock, the way I had felt when I couldn't bring myself to enter the tea house. Could it be that I, too, had sensed something was amiss?

Grandma smiled, grateful, and said, "We all go home and get some rest."

"Yeah. Sounds good." I squeezed her hand and went to retrieve my purse and the light jacket I had brought. By the time I returned, everyone was at the front entrance, ready to leave.

We stepped outside, and my father locked the door; the only lights were the tiny white lights that lined our windows; my father had these on a timer that went off at midnight. "Good night, moon. Good night, tea house," my mother said playfully.

She and my father wandered to their car, my grandmother close behind. They had driven in together, and they would be taking her home. I waved and opened my car door, realizing with a pang that I had forgotten to lock it again. I was going to get a security lecture from my dad. I sat behind the steering wheel, checking texts for a moment, and my family drove off. With a sigh, I put my phone aside and felt for my keys.

My keys! "Oh, don't tell me I left them in the building," I muttered. But no, I was sure I hadn't. They had been clutched in my hand when I walked out with my family. With a mighty sigh I opened my door, prepared to retrace my steps from the entrance. I stalked across the parking lot, scanning here and there, when a sound caught my attention.

A whirring, clacking sound that I recognized, but could not put in context. It sounded like my father's Alpine train, the one he turned on before tea events to please visitors. The one that could be turned on only with a hidden switch tucked behind a gutter pipe.

It was fully dark now, and when I turned to my left to look at the lovely landscaped garden, the train chugged determinedly out of a tuft of wheatgrass, glowing with red, green, and white lights. A ghost train, powered by nobody. But that was impossible.

I cleared my throat. "Hello? Is somebody there?"

My phone was in my right hand. I grabbed it, swiped it on, searched my contacts. I felt somehow rooted to the concrete. I pressed a name, newly added. "Hello?" said Wolf's voice.

"Detective Wolf? This is Hana. I'm sorry to—"

"What is it?"

"I—I'm the last one leaving, and it's dark, and I had to go back for my keys. My dad's train is running."

"I'm sorry?"

"The train wasn't on when I left. It has a hidden switch. But it's running now. I can't explain it. I don't even know why I called you, except I find it very odd, and—no!"

A figure hurtled out of the darkness, a dark-clad figure with a hood and no face. It pushed past me, bumping me hard, and I staggered backward and fell, dropping my phone.

Chapter 11

An Alpine Ghost

I could hear Wolf's voice yelling my name. Shocked, shaking, I crawled forward, my eyes scanning for the mystery figure. Once I had the phone again, I said, "Someone ran out of nowhere. I couldn't see his face. He knocked me down!"

"Is he still there?"

"I don't know."

"Hana. Did you ever find your keys?"

"Uh, no." To my surprise and humiliation, I was on the verge of tears.

"Do you see anyone now?"

I looked around, fearful, feeling exposed. "No—I think he ran away."

"Go find your keys, but stay vigilant. I'll wait. Tell me when you have them."

I didn't have to look for long. They were lying on the

cement walkway just outside the entrance. I picked them up with a shaking hand and said, "I found them."

"Go sit in your car and lock it. I'll be right there. All right?"

"Yes, all right."

"If anyone comes back, you have my permission to run them over."

I laughed a little, as he had wanted me to do. "Okay, thank you."

"Hana? I have to hang up, but I'm already at my car. Give me ten minutes."

"Okay," I said. I ended the call and scanned the parking lot. No sign of the figure. What or who had it been? Why was it here, in our parking lot? Why was the train on?

I looked back at the train, normally such a cheery little vehicle, but tonight it had a ghostly air, a frightening and jarring sight as it loomed up, then receded, again and again, lights twinkling and disappearing in a slight evening fog. And that face that had appeared—so blank and shadowy in the darkness—had there been a face at all? I moved swiftly to my car, climbed in, and locked the doors. I told myself to calm down. Clearly I had listened to far too many fairy legends. My car felt besieged by ghosts and witches.

I started the car and turned on my heater in an attempt to dispel the slight chill outside and the larger cold inside me. When a car turned into the lot moments later, I stiffened, then relaxed when I recognized it as Wolf's.

He pulled up next to my vehicle. I turned off my motor and climbed out. He was just a shadow in the parking lot, but a comforting one. "I'm so sorry to bother you. I'll bet you had just put your feet up for the night."

"It's not a problem. Show me the train."

I led him to the entrance and pointed at the little train. It seemed happier again, now that Wolf was here. "My dad made it—we only turn it on when we're having an event. Customers love it. They take pictures of it, pose with it. At Christmas my dad makes it into a little St. Nicholas train."

"Okay."

"The point is, we never turn it on, certainly not at night. And the switch is very hard to find."

"Show me."

I led him to the side of the building and into a flower bed that extended the length of the south wall. "Here by the gutter pipe. You have to bend down, and there's that little outlet down there? There's a switch just above it." I started to reach toward it, but Wolf put a hand on my arm.

"Let me see if I can get a print."

I stared at his shadowy form. "You think this is related to the whole Ava thing?"

He shrugged. "It doesn't seem to be, and yet the timing is problematic. A woman dies here. A stranger appears in the parking lot not long afterward and knocks you down. Seemingly, the stranger also turned on your train."

"I guess it could be a kid playing tricks?"

"A kid who knew just where to find this switch? You're right, it's well hidden."

"Yes. This is a puzzle."

Wolf was busy doing something with what seemed to be a tiny brush. He lifted his phone, shone a light on the switch, and grunted. "We'll see if we get anything from that. It's only a partial print."

"And it might be my dad's. If the visitor was a witch or a ghost."

His head turned swiftly. "What?"

"Sorry. That was just how it felt. First the train, like a

specter in the dark. And then the figure, which didn't seem to have a face. It freaked me out."

"What do you mean, no face?" He stood up, tucking his materials into a little bag.

"I couldn't see one. Maybe because of a hat or a hood or something."

"Likely. It got kind of cold tonight."

"Yes." I shivered.

Wolf pointed. "Go to the front and tell me when the train is out of the tunnel. I'll switch it off and take a look at it."

I walked to the front of the building and studied the Euro Express. My heightened imagination made me see the little train as exhausted, glad to be heading for the tunnel, where it could sleep for the rest of the night. "Sorry, buddy," I said. It went into the tunnel, emerged again a moment later, and I said, "Now!"

An instant later the train stopped and its lights went dark. Wolf crunched back over some landscaping rocks and squatted in front of the train. I could swear he was making little "hmm" sounds as he investigated, but I wasn't sure.

"This one opens," he said, pointing at the coal car just behind the engine. A little figure of an engineer's assistant stood on a side panel, holding a shovel.

"Yes. When I was little, my dad used to hide presents in there for my brother and me. On birthdays and stuff."

He was still staring at the car and holding the roof in his hand. "Hmm," he said.

"What do you mean? Is that important?"

"I don't know." He stood up and looked left, then across the street, then right. "Any private residences around here?"

I pointed across, where a little log cabin of a house sat back from the road and blended nicely into the vista of swaying grasses. "That's a couple called Dave and Melly. They've lived there about five years; once in a while they come to the tea events that are open to the general public. Sometimes Dave helps my dad plow the lot. He has this big truck—"

"Great, you know them." He looked at his watch. "Let's pay them a quick visit."

"What?"

"It's not that late. Only nine."

"Uh—okay."

Wolf was already walking with long strides across the lot; I jogged to keep up with him. "What exactly do we want to tell them?"

We had reached a streetlight at the roadside, and for the first time I could see the green of his eyes. "We're going to deputize them," he said.

~

Dave appeared at the door, looking sleepy and holding a beer. At first he was scowling, but he smiled when he saw me. "Oh, hey, Hana! What's up?"

"Hi, Dave. I'm sorry to bother you at this time of night. I had a little . . . weird incident over there"—I waved vaguely back at the tea house—"and I called the police. This is Detective Wolf."

Dave's eyebrows went up. He wiped his hand on his jeans and then extended it to Wolf. "Detective, huh? Is this related to all the police cars being there yesterday?"

"We're not sure," Wolf said. "May we come in for a moment?"

"Sure!" Dave backed into the room, where from the sound of things he had been watching a cop show on TV; currently the people on-screen seemed to be involved in a gunfight. "Melly's at a book club meeting, otherwise she would be in on this, too," he said, looking pleased. "Have a seat here in the dining room."

We sat at Dave's dining room table, empty except for a large bowl, in which I spied a Siamese cat, curled into a sleeping ball. "Hi, Serena," I said to the cat.

Wolf said, "Dave, are you familiar with the train that Mr. Keller has set up in the front garden of the tea house?"

Dave took a sip of beer and nodded. "Sure! It's awesome. Serena there can spot it when it's moving. I think she thinks it's some distant mouse."

Wolf nodded; not even the trace of a smile. God, this guy's concentration was amazing. "Have you ever seen it run at night?"

"With the lights? Just at Christmastime. That looks pretty awesome."

"But you could see it from here? If the lights were on?"

"Yeah. It looks all tiny and twinkly, but we can see it." He turned to me. "Hana, you're bleeding."

Wolf and I both looked down at my arm; a trickle of blood ran down from a large scrape. Up until now I hadn't felt anything, but now pain seemed to flow into my arm, and I said, "Oh, wow. That hurts."

Before I knew it, Wolf had whipped a handkerchief out of his pocket and pulled my arm toward him, where he wrapped it up into a weirdly effective bandage. "Wash the wound when you get home," he said.

Dave pointed at him with his beer. "I'll bet you were in Scouts."

Wolf smiled for the first time. "I was. Lots of woodland survival courses."

I smiled, too, trying to picture Wolf as a Boy Scout, traipsing through the woods as a gangly adolescent. I couldn't really envision him as anything but what I saw now—a tall man with broad shoulders and thick, blond hair . . .

Wolf caught me studying him, and I quickly switched my gaze to my watch, whereupon Wolf went back into cop mode. "Dave, I wonder if I can ask you and your wife to keep an eye on the tea house at night—just glance out whenever you pass the window. If you ever see the train running, let me know."

"That's it? Sure, I can do that. Why? What's going on with the train?"

"We don't know. But there was an intruder tonight, and I'd love to catch him if he comes back."

Dave nodded, leaning forward to scratch the ears of the sleeping cat. "This is pretty cool, man. Helping out the cops." He grinned at me; his longish brown hair was uncombed, yet attractive.

"Thanks a lot, Dave," I said. Wolf stood up, and I did, too. "Tell Melly I said hi."

"Sure thing," Dave said, taking the card that Wolf held out to him. "We'll let you know if we see anything suspicious."

Serena the cat lay like a creature unconscious, but when Wolf and I descended the stairs and walked down the driveway, I looked back and saw her little silhouette in the living room window, watching us with glowing eyes.

I thanked Wolf profusely for coming out, and he waited until I tucked into my car and started the motor. I waved to him and drove out of the lot, but went slowly until I saw that his car, too, had safely departed the tea house grounds.

Fifteen minutes later I was back in my apartment, where Antony and Cleopatra were already sacked out for the night, lying close together on my living room couch.

I went to my sink and unwound Wolf's makeshift bandage, then bathed my wound, dried it, and treated it with Neosporin. I soaked Wolf's handkerchief in detergent so that it wouldn't be permanently stained, and I set it on my hamper. Wolf's cold had seemed better, I realized with a start. I wondered if the Pálinka had worked its magic. I also wondered, for no reason, if Wolf had a wife.

I grabbed my phone and sent some text messages. First to Domo: What's up with you guys? Then to Margie: Tell Domo to read his texts. Then to my friend Katie: I need an outing with people under thirty who are not Hungarian. I added a smiley face.

I brushed my teeth, changed into pajamas, and went to my lovely sprawling bookshelf, where I found a book called *Hungarian Tales and Legends*, which I'd received for a long-ago birthday

I opened it up to a tale called "The Wily Shepherd," which was about a young shepherd who had to guard against evil spirits at night—witches who wanted to sneak into his barn and take the milk from his sheep. He sat in the doorway with his pitchfork, vigilant, but saw only a beautiful woman in a white dress; she had long, silvery hair, and she danced around the field, transfixing him with her beauty. It was Szépasszony, the Fair Lady. He ran out and danced along with her; she came closer and kissed him, and he was filled with joy. But a moment later the arms she had draped around him became sharp as talons, and he screamed, realizing too late that this was not the Fair Lady, but Vadleány, the evil spirit who seduced men and then stole their essence. The young man begged her to free him, but she only laughed. His last sight was the bright full moon shining down on his field.

"Ooh, grim," I said. It dawned on me that if my grandmother had grown up hearing tales like this then of course she would have a deeper sense of the duality of human nature, the potential evil beneath a smiling face.

And given what had happened to poor Ava Novák at something as innocuous as a tea party, I couldn't see much wrong with my grandmother's point of view.

Chapter 12

Timeless Treasures

The wedding shower was a success. The women loved everything: they oohed and aahed over the tea service, admired our serving outfits, stood in line for pictures of themselves boating on the Danube, wolfed down dozens of tiny chocolate-raspberry cakes. Several people noticed Mrs. Kiraly's amazing doilies where they sat in splendor on the dessert table, and two people asked where they could buy them. My favorite moment happened when a gaggle of high school girls fell in love with François during one of his rare appearances. This caused him to scowl and mutter under his breath, which was apparently an added allure to the smitten young women. "He's just so *French*," I heard one of them saying in the bathroom. "I heard his name is François. That is just so *European*."

By the time the young bride-to-be finished opening her presents, my mother and I had already done some subtle cleanup, carting teacups and plates to the back. When the group finally left, all we had to do was sweep the last things off the tables, wash a last load of dishes, whisk the cloths into a laundry hamper, and push the large broom across the floor.

Since it was Saturday, and we had the luxury of my father's help, we were done in a jiff. My grandmother found me as I was putting on my jacket. "I make noodles tomorrow after Mass. You want to help?"

"Do I get to keep some noodles?"

"Of course." She shrugged, and I grinned. I always got noodles, and I always wanted to make them with my grandmother—it was a ritual, a tradition, and a joy.

I hugged her, waved at my parents, and was heading home by six o'clock. I had told them about our visitor the night before and about Wolf's deputizing of Dave and Melly. They had agreed with the wisdom of this and expressed dismay over my trauma. My father said that henceforth he would be the last to leave the parking lot. Now, after pulling out first under my parents' watchful gaze, I decided on a whim to stop at Timeless Treasures, Falken's shop, which I knew was open until seven on Saturdays.

Falken's store was visible from the main highway and, with its decor and sense of whimsy, had lured many collectors off the road and into its lot. The sign, "Timeless Treasures," sported green letters burned into a traditional wood shingle attached to the image of an old-fashioned clock. The windows of the brick facade were enhanced with flower boxes, filled now with lovely marigolds and coleus that added a burst of green and orange to the wood-sided building. His covered front porch area held a scattering of larger pieces, from large carved Buddhas to suits of armor. In order to keep things from looking too random or "junky," as he put it, he often created little vignettes, like a staged room with a Victorian bed, table, and chair, with an era-appropriate doll sitting on the bed, or a conversational grouping in which the aforementioned knight chatted with the Buddha while they both held cups of tea.

Inside the main store things were more orderly and enticing: walls of china were arranged in some cases by color and in some cases by time period. If the sets weren't valuable, then he went for color groupings, which made the china wall lovely and irresistible.

In another corner he staged knickknacks and figurines, while across from the china was the shining glassware. Another room held antique furniture; still another held books, old sheet music, and vintage postcards. Timeless Treasures, like any good antiques shop, felt like a delightful labyrinth that drew one back into the past.

When I entered, Falken was ringing up a customer who had bought two antique dolls. "They're so sweet," she said. "They remind me of dolls I had as a child. I still so much prefer shopping in person to going on eBay," she enthused as Falken wrapped the dolls in delicate tissue paper.

He peered at her over his glasses and said, "And I prefer you shopping that way, as well." He punctuated the comment with his gentle smile. He tucked her wares into a bag, and she left, clearly overjoyed with her purchase.

Something brushed against my leg and made me jump; I looked down and saw that it was merely Inspektor, the store cat. Inspektor was ten years old and regal as a king. He was a gray-striped creature with a large noble head, and he was a friend to everyone who came in the store. I bent to scratch his ears, and he purred for me.

"My dear Hana," Falken said. "What can I do for you this evening?"

Falken, despite his foreign name, was American born

and had even been accused of having "a Chicago accent," although he and I agreed that it would be hard to pin down just one accent from Chicago. It all depended on what part of the city you came from. To me, Falken just sounded midwestern.

"Nothing. I just thought I'd browse your beautiful wares." I stood up, and Inspektor, pleased, wandered away.

Falken came from behind his counter to point at some plates. "I got some new blue glass dishes. Lovely stuff."

"Oh, they are."

"And, just for you, I have a Hungarian piece. Hang on, I'll get it." He disappeared into another room and I drifted over to the teacups; he had some new ones, one of which was a beautiful blend of green, pink, and white flowers. I picked it up to see the maker: Wedgwood. Very nice.

"Here we are," Falken said, coming back in. "Cheap, but cute."

He held two little wine stoppers with figures on top, one male and one female, both in traditional Hungarian peasant dress. "Made in Hungary, but not by anyone notable," he said. "Still, as a conversation piece . . ."

"I love them. How much?"

"Ten dollars," said Falken.

"Sold." I loved his store partly because even though he had rare pieces that cost thousands of dollars, he also carried little trinkets that someone like me could afford. "Wrap them up. I think I'll take this teacup next time. It's beautiful."

"Yes! And how are you enjoying your butterfly?" Falken asked, heading back toward the counter. He turned and saw my face. "Oh—what's wrong? Did it break?"

"No." I looked around; as far as I could see, no one else was in the store. "It's the most unlikely thing, Falken. The police have my cup."

"What?" Normally I could not shock him out of his mild-mannered expression, no matter what purposely shocking piece of gossip I used, but this jarred him into an openmouthed stare.

"A woman died at our event. She was drinking out of the Butterfly—long story—and the police think someone poisoned her. In the teacup."

Falken thought about this for about thirty seconds; then he said, "That is *so* unlikely."

"Exactly! I still can't believe it happened. She wasn't even supposed to have the cup. I was using it as a decoration on our butterfly table."

"This could never happen." He shook his head. "I read mysteries all the time. This has too many variables. No one could have known she would take the cup—it was only this cup of tea that was poisoned?"

"Yes, I think so."

"So whoever did it would have had to know that she would take it—"

"They think this person gave it to her. Perhaps as a special treat. Which is so evil . . ." I paused. If Ava had been arguing with someone in the bathroom, and then that person offered her tea out of the Butterfly, why would she accept it? Wouldn't it have seemed unusual for someone angry with her to bring her a gift? Were there *two* people involved? Or perhaps the original person pretended to apologize, to give a peace offering?

Falken must have seen my distress, because he said, "Here—I'm throwing a little treat into the bag. A teacup magnet. Something for your fridge."

"Thanks, Falken. That's sweet."

"Do the police seem to have a handle on this? Something to pursue?"

I shrugged. "They're not telling us much. They're asking a lot of questions, though. Being really thorough. So I guess that's good."

The chimes over his door rang as a group of women entered; I recognized the love of shopping in their eyes. "You've got customers. I'll get going now; talk to you soon, Falken!"

He waved, and I took my little bag to the parking lot.

I sat in my car for a moment, watching the wind blow some early-fall leaves across the concrete. I was briefly tempted to call Detective Wolf again and tell him my epiphany about the teacup, but I thought better of it. I had bothered him enough lately—calling him about François, summoning him to the tea house last night. The last thing he needed was some amateur detective contacting him all the time with wacky (and probably erroneous) ideas. It was his job to find Ava's killer, not mine.

I thought about the fairies, both good and bad. No matter what their form, they were alluring, distracting to the humans who crossed paths with them. Had the beautiful teacup been fairylike in its charm? Falken and I had both been drawn to it, as had my mother and grandmother. Had this piece of art, this mere object, become a talisman of evil?

I shook my head, started the engine, and flipped on the car radio. The DJ was saying, "This is Rumer, with her version of an old classic." And then a smooth, sweet voice began to sing "What the World Needs Now Is Love."

Chapter 13

A Hungarian Connection

We were making *kis négyzet tészta*—small, square noodles—which my grandmother used in her chicken soup, but which worked well in a variety of recipes. Before the day was out, we would make the fine-as-hair *finommetélt*, or thread noodles, as well as *csiga tészta*, which were spiral noodles, and the hand-grated *tarhonya*, which my grandmother assured me went back to the days of Magyars on horseback, who kept the dried noodles in their packs and then cooked them over their campfires.

My grandmother and I usually reserved a whole Saturday to prepare noodles, but today we were making do with half of Sunday. Hungarians are noodle experts; just as Italians have a large variety of pastas, so do Hungarians have a variety of noodles, and I had learned to make no fewer than thirteen kinds. The tools change depending upon the type of noodles; we might cut them, grate them, roll them, drop them, or, in my grandma's case, slice them with a giant sword of a knife that my grandfather had created for her from an old oven door.

Our noodle-making sessions were special to us, and they had become a monthly event. Grandma was usually up first and already rolling out dough when I entered the kitchen. With short, deft strokes of her rolling pin, she managed to spread a chunk of dough over half of the kitchen table. I had suggested that we just use a pizza cutter to cut the *kis négyzet tészta* to precise, small squares, but Grandma scoffed at me and wielded her murder weapon of a knife, which allowed her to slice twenty rows—lengthwise and crosswise—in about a minute.

When we had four hundred little noodles, perfect and square, we put them on the counter to dry. Later we would seal them in airtight containers; I would take a third of them for my home recipes, another third would be reserved for my parents, and Grandma would keep the rest for her home cooking.

We moved on to our next project, and while Grandma took out a new ball of dough, we listened to the little radio she had on the counter. The announcer was saying something about an investigation into potential corruption.

My grandmother shook her head and clucked, saying, "Government always keep secrets."

I nodded. "Maybe some music. I need to bring you my iPad, Grandma."

She shook her head. "I love my radio."

Her front door banged open and my brother appeared (she always left the door open when she knew he was coming). "Hi, Grandma. Hey, Hana. Domo needs his Hungarian food fix."

I stared at him. "Then make some. We've been slaving over noodles for hours . . ."

He pulled my grandmother into a big hug, and she smiled, pleased. She said, "I have your food in Tupperware. In the fridge. Let me go." Domo released her and she went to her refrigerator and began packing things into a paper bag, like a woman at a take-out restaurant. Soon enough Domo had containers filled with chicken *paprikás* and gravy, dumplings, *káposztas tészta tejföllel* (a cabbage, noodle, and sour cream dish), and *sör kenyér*, which was a Hungarian beer bread. It all smelled divine, even through the plastic.

I put my hands on my hips. "I don't suppose you have any of that for Hana, your fellow cook?"

My grandmother tutted. "Of course. I pack you some. I just have to leave some for Grandpa."

At the sound of his name, my grandfather shuffled into the room in his soft slippers. He had long ago retired from his job at the Chicago Railroad, and now he divided his time between reading spy novels, making beautiful wood furniture that he sold on eBay, and sparring good-naturedly with my grandmother (and eating her food).

"Hana, you leave all the noodles for me," he joked with a wink of one blue eye, admiring our handiwork around the room.

I lightly punched him on the arm, which was still solid muscle, after a life of labor on the railroad tracks. "No way. Grandma's leaving you some, and Mom and Dad some, and me some. Domo gets nothing because he's lazy, and he's just going to come and eat food at all of our houses, anyway."

"True," my brother admitted, not bothering to be insulted. While my grandmother packed food and noodles for me, Domo pulled me aside. His handsome face was earnest. His dark hair was uncombed, but somehow he looked better when he was disheveled. Life wasn't fair.

"Hey, Mom said you don't have to work at the tea house tomorrow. That sounds like a great day for you to take Margie to the mall."

I rolled my eyes. "Why the *mall*? I'll just have her over to my place."

Domo grasped my arms and looked into my face. "The idea is to lure her *out* of her introversion, not to introduce her to yours."

"Fine. But only because I like Margie. I'll call her tonight."

"Awesome. And while you're at the mall tomorrow, buy me one of those crazy cinnamon rolls."

I gestured to what seemed like the month's worth of food my grandmother was putting in his bag. "You don't have enough to eat?"

"That's just Hungarian food. I like other food, too." He ruffled my hair, an act he knew I despised, but which, as my brother, he felt was his duty to perform. "Thanks for doing this, Han."

"I love Margie, but you still owe me for being at your beck and call. And that owing will take the form of fixing my computer, which has been acting weird. And a gift certificate to Falken's store. Since I get so many Margie gifts there, it's only right."

"Done and done. No problem. Just remember—I want her to talk to at least three people who aren't you."

~

The Riverwood Mall was fairly large, with two stories of shops, a first-floor fountain, and a second-floor train display (it was this latter phenomenon which had inspired my father to set up his "European Line" outside of the tea house). I walked in with Margie, who looked casually cute in blue jeans, a white T-shirt, and a light blue cardigan sweater. She wore a long beaded necklace with blue, silver, and green stones. She had pulled her blonde hair up into a ponytail, and she looked like the older sister in some 1950s teen movie.

"Your boyfriend wants you to engage other people in discussion," I said to her. "I can help you engineer those interactions, if you wish."

"I wish," said Margie in her quiet voice. "Meanwhile I want to visit the bookstore, the music store, and that clothing store that I see up there on the other side of the fountain." I followed her pointing finger and saw a glass display case with some fun-looking outfits inside.

"Sounds good. I will also need to find some sort of chocolatier. And gross Domo wants one of those twenty-thousand-calorie cinnamon rolls."

"How does he stay thin?" Margie mused.

"It must be from all the making out," I said.

She laughed—a delicate sound, like a little bell. Everything Margie did was quiet, as though she were a doll who was just learning to speak and hadn't quite figured out the notion of volume. The more outrageous I was, the more she tended to laugh, so nowadays I just said whatever I was thinking.

Domo theorized that Margie was quiet because both of her parents, despite their French name, were experts in Russian literature and taught it at Riverwood College. Margie, as an only child, had spent peaceful days poring over books while her professor parents had been immersed in manuscripts, making notations, and softly mumbling to themselves. She recalled her childhood only with pleasure—her parents doted on her in their quiet, academic way, taking her to museums and reading her entire novels over the course of several bedtimes. When she had shown an aptitude for art, they bought her reams of paper, a draftsman's table, and everything from pencils to chalks to paints so that she could find her medium. Despite her cultured and elegant upbringing, Domo said, she had adapted to something unusual—an extremely quiet living space.

"How's Boris?" I asked.

"He's wonderful."

"He is one giant dog. I walked him with Domo once, remember? And he almost took my arm out of the socket when he saw a squirrel."

"That's Boris," she said affectionately.

"Hey. There's someone taking a survey. See the guy with the clipboard? Except he'll want you to come into some back room and talk for at least half an hour, maybe even sell you something. So for your first encounter, all you have to do is say, 'No thanks, not today.'"

"Right! That's easy." She tossed her little ponytail.

I led her past throngs of people and then purposely walked into the path of the clipboard guy that most people were trying to avoid. He beamed a smile at us and I said, "Here we go" under my breath.

"Good morning, ladies!" he said, still grinning. "Can I ask you a few questions about your long-distance plans?"

Margie stared at him in silence. I jabbed her with my elbow, and she blurted, "No thanks. Not TODAY." Somehow the last word came out very loud, while the others had all been quiet. Margie was still working on that volume issue, apparently. Her face turned bright red and she looked at her feet.

The survey guy looked offended. "Okay, no need to yell," he said, and moved off.

Margie looked relieved, but also guilty. "That didn't go well," she said.

I moved closer and looked into her eyes. "Of course it did. He talked to you, you responded, and he did as you asked. Which was basically to get lost."

She nodded. "I got nervous and I sounded too loud."

"Everyone wishes they could yell at the clipboard people. You did us all a favor. Now are you, or are you not, interested in eating one of those little chocolate petit fours that I see in the window of Susie's Bakery?"

"I am interested," she said. She slid her hand into mine, and I led her forward as though she were my little sister. In some ways this was not displeasing to me; I'd had only Domo all my life, and I had always distantly dreamed of a smaller sibling to whom I could dispense advice and on whom I could lavish affection. Margie was only a year younger than I, but she generally fit the bill.

"I'm going to have you order for us," I said. "That will be two interactions already. I'll bet we can accomplish way more than the goal Domo set for you."

"Let's not get crazy," Margie said softly.

By the time we were finished with all our store visits, we were full, we had several packages, and Margie had talked to five people. We were feeling good, and we sat on a bench in front of the train, watching it with the inexplicable fascination that all people have for little models of real environments.

The train had eight cars, including an engine and a caboose, and it traveled through a pretty little town surrounded by a forest (complete with deer), then circled a lake that sported miniature ducks and swans.

"I love the train," Margie said. "I hope they never take it down."

"Has Domo ever brought you by the tea house? We have a train. I'm going to invite you to the next event that we have for young people. You can experience all the fun and escape to the back room when you get overwhelmed."

"Okay," she said. She may or may not have been interested; Margie tended to agree to things in person and then back out of them later on.

"Do you want to go out for lunch? Or are you too full?"

"I'll probably wait to eat," Margie said. "And I should feed Boris."

"Okay, fair enough." I stood up and started to grab my bags when a voice said, "Hana?"

I turned to see Mrs. Sarka, one of the Magyar ladies, rushing toward me on her black ballet flats. She looked even smaller in this setting than she had looked at the tea party where Ava had died. This was the same Mrs. Sarka, four foot ten and smiling, who called all young people "honey," and was more benevolently grandmotherly than my own perfectly fine grandmother.

She reached me and hugged me around my middle. "Hallo, hon-eee!" she said. "You look so pretty, so pretty! Who is this pretty friend?"

"Hi, Mrs. Sarka. Thank you. This is Domo's girlfriend, Marguerite."

"Hallo, hon-eeee!" she said, enthusiastically shaking Margie's hand between both of hers.

Margie looked dumbfounded, but she managed a hello in response. (That made six people.)

"What brings you to the mall, Mrs. Sarka?" I asked the tiny woman. She was dressed up for the visit in a flowered dress and sparkly earrings of the kind my grandmother favored.

"I get a toy for my grandson. His birthday is tomorrow!

Fifteen." She gave me a little push, as though this pressure on my arm, in conjunction with the shocking knowledge of her grandson's advanced age, might knock me down.

I said, "You probably won't want the toy store, then. I'd go there." I pointed to the GameStop three doors away. "If you don't know what to get, you can buy a gift card."

"You think?"

"Does he play video games? The kind on the computer or the TV, with a joystick?" I mimicked the movements of a person playing a video game.

"Yes, yes, always!" she said. "You are right, hon-eee!"

"That's the place, then."

"Tank you. Tanks to you both." She smiled and seemed ready to move away.

On a whim, I said, "Mrs. Sarka, remember the day of the tea—what happened to Ava Novák?"

Her smile disappeared. "Oh yes. How sad, sad, sad." She clapped her hands together and held them against her heart. "Poor Ava—so pretty! So nice."

"Were you—you didn't hate her, then?"

"No! She was such nice lady. For a time, she date my brother Istvan. Steve, you say." She seemed pleased to be able to provide the American version of "Istvan."

"She dated Steve?" My father and Steve Sarka occasionally had drinks together at the sports bar in town.

"Ya. He like her, she like him. But then she meet Joe, of course."

"Oh yes." How many men had Ava Novák dated? It seemed that she had been in America just a short period of time before she had met the man she married, yet her supposed romantic alliances were adding up. Unless they hadn't really been romantic? Had the men assumed relationships when they had really just been friendships?

"Mrs. Sarka, I think your brother should talk about their relationship to the police. Everything he knows about Ava, everything he learned about her when they were dating."

Mrs. Sarka's smile dimmed, and she seemed to shrink slightly. "Oh no, honey. He only date her couple of times. He don't know anything." She looked at her watch and thanked us again, then hurried toward GameStop, where she hesitated in the doorway like a person stepping out of a time machine and landing in the future. Eventually a guy in a polo shirt walked up to her and mumbled something. Even from a few hundred feet away I could hear her call him "Hon-eee!"

Now he was the one who looked disoriented, but Mrs. Sarka had him by the arm. They disappeared into the store.

I looked at Margie, who was starting to grow pale. A true introvert, she needed to recharge in her own space for a while, probably in blissful silence.

"Okay, let's go," I said. She sent me a relieved smile.

As we walked toward the exit, I felt a burst of compassion for the voiceless: not just for introverts like shy Margie, but for people like Ava, who, silent in death, had no control over the things people said about her, regardless of whether those things were true.

Chapter 14

Return of the Stone

We spent the first half of Tuesday preparing for Wednesday's event, a monthly endeavor called The Books and Tea Gathering. This had been the brainchild of an English professor at Riverwood College, a way of reaching out to the Riverwood community to share a love of literature and culture; it had grown in popularity until at least a hundred people came to every event. We provided our standard tea, sandwiches, and pastries, but we also set up a projection screen so that Dr. Caldwell could show some slides with preliminary questions and ideas about the book of the month. Then people could come to the microphone on our stage to ask questions or share ideas. I always found it fascinating, and a couple of times I'd made a point of reading the book so that I could follow the conversation.

Wednesday's book was *The Strange Case of Dr. Jekyll and Mr. Hyde*, the Robert Louis Stevenson classic. I had read this one in college, so I was excited to listen to the conversation. For the literary event, we used dark blue tablecloths and a more generic tea service of white china with gold rims. I printed out tiny book covers, mounted them on poster board, and then put each one in a place-card holder and set it on the plate. We had designed a sign two years earlier which said "Books and Tea: Sponsored by Riverwood College and Maggie's Tea House."

My grandmother, who had an affinity for all things electronic, set up the microphone and the projector. My mother wrapped the base of the stage in what looked like a large navy blue dust ruffle; the effect was surprisingly elegant. When we finished, we stood back and admired our work. "It looks terrific," my mother said. "I think even better than usual."

We had put a basket of alternative teas in the center of each table in case people didn't like the standard black that we generally used for our events. We had large urns on a side table filled with hot water and coffee. We also put out a few cold bottled waters for those who didn't like any of the three other options. "And that," my mother said firmly, "is all we need to offer. This is a tea house."

"Do you guys want to go out for lunch?" I asked. "Or do you have plans?"

My mom put an arm around me. "Grandma has a doctor's appointment. Just a checkup," she assured me when she saw my face. "And I promised your father I would observe his students' project presentations today. They are about heritage; he said they'll be quite good."

"Okay. Then I'm going to warm up Hungarian food. Thanks to Grandma, I have a fridge full of noodles and ready-made meals."

"Yes. And you can sleep in tomorrow; I think we're fine if we meet here at about eleven. The luncheon is set for twelve thirty, and we don't have much more to do."

"Nice." I kissed her cheek. "See you later, then."

I was halfway to the door. "Hana," she called. "I heard that you took Margie out again. Thanks for doing that."

"It's fine. We're friends," I said.

My grandmother marched up to me at the door, holding an extension cord. "Maybe call the detective."

"What? Wolf?"

She winced slightly at his name. "Yes, yes. Call him, Haniska."

"About what? He already has all our statements."

"Just to call, you know. Invite to lunch. It's a nice day—you can have a picnic. I pack you some food."

I stared at her, my mouth open. "Why in the world would you think I would ask Erik Wolf out on a date?"

Her eyes grew wide and she smiled a huge smile; she looked suddenly lit from within. "You know his first name?"

"It was on his card. Stop it, Grandma! For the love of—your endless matchmaking is out of control. As is the interfering of all your love-obsessed friends at these tea events. I am perfectly happy on my own, and I am certainly not going to be desperate enough to call a man investigating a *murder* to see if he wants to have lunch with me!"

"So passionate," my grandmother murmured, still smiling.

I sighed noisily. "I'll tell you what. I'm going to ask out the other police officer. Benton, with the mustache. I'm going to *make out* with him, Grandma."

This did not ruffle even one feather. "No, no. He is not the right one."

"You hate wolves. Even the name 'Wolf' upsets you. Why would you encourage me to talk to this guy? Who shows not the least interest in me, by the way?"

"So, you are blind?" she asked.

"Enough of this," I said. "I have a date with two cats, some refrigerated *paprikás*, and a Netflix movie."

I glared at her, kissed her cheek, glared at her some more, and left the building. Her pleased smile remained, and I saw it when I closed my eyes, as though she were a Cheshire cat in my car.

Ten minutes later my cell phone rang. "Hello?" I said, my eyes on the sunny road and the entrance to my apartment building.

"Hana, it's Detective Wolf."

"Oh, hello."

"I have a couple more questions for you; I wonder if I could stop by the tea house and chat with you for a moment?"

I felt a lingering suspicion. "Did my grandmother just call you? Did she say something to you?"

"What? No, why—has something happened?"

I shook my head, disgusted with myself. Of course a detective in the middle of a murder investigation wasn't going to call some random woman on the phone because her *grandmother* asked him to! I was getting paranoid. "No—uh. It's nothing. Just—she—ugh. Sorry. My grandmother has been driving me nuts."

"Ah." He was not a talkative person, this Detective Wolf.

I pulled into my parking lot and tucked into space number eight. "Well, I'm not at the tea house, as it happens. I just got home. If you want to come here, that's fine. I'll just be making lunch for the gang."

There was a pause. "All right, I'll be there in about ten minutes."

"Do you need my address?"

"I have it here. Thank you, Hana." His voice sounded brusque, and he ended the call without saying good-bye.

I stared at my phone for a minute. "Geez. Everyone is weird today."

With a mighty sigh, I got out of the car and headed to the main entrance of my apartment building, a gray rectangle of a structure on a grassy hill. It reminded me of a piece of driftwood, and I had always found it appealing, especially since my landlords, Ray and Tina, had put flower boxes outside the first-floor windows; they looked pretty and inviting, dripping with leafy trailing plants and purple and red flowers.

There was no sign of my little friend Iris in the first-floor hallway. When I reached my unit, the two cats sang to me, and I fed them. Then I took out Grandma's chicken and dumplings and put them in a pot. Unlike most food, chicken *paprikás* tastes even better as a leftover, and as the gravy heated and my apartment started to smell good, my mood lightened. "Ah, Hungarian food," I said to no one.

My buzzer rang, and I pressed it. "Yes?"

"Hana? It's Erik Wolf."

Erik.

"Okay, you can come up. Second floor, number five." I pressed the unlock button and walked to my door. I opened it and left it slightly ajar. I wasn't sure what to do with myself suddenly; my limbs felt thick and in my way. I walked to the stove and began stirring the contents of the pot.

Out of the corner of my eye I saw Wolf's tall frame enter; I heard him shut the door. "Hello," he said.

It felt strange to see him in a space that wasn't the tea house. This felt less official, and he wasn't wearing one of his ill-fitting suits, but jeans again, with a dark blue button-down shirt. "Hi. I'll be right with you," I said.

"I hope I'm not interrupting?" His eyes were flicking around the room, taking in details.

"Interrupting what?"

"You mentioned feeding the gang."

I laughed. "That's the gang." I pointed at the cats, who had come to inspect him. Cleopatra was sniffing his shoes, and Antony, who was often more like a dog than a cat, had brought a toy mouse and laid it at Wolf's feet.

"Oh—cats?"

"Yes. Antony and Cleopatra. They're siblings. Throw that mouse; he'll bring it back to you."

Wolf did so, demonstrating a certain athleticism. Antony retrieved the mouse and trotted back, acting like a terrible show-off. "They like you," I said. "Some people come over and these guys go into hiding."

"I love cats," he said. "My building doesn't allow them."

"Have a seat there on the couch, if you want. Can I get you anything?"

"I'm interrupting your meal, I'm afraid. Something smells great."

I hesitated for a minute, then took a plunge, counting on my grandmother's intuition. "I was just about to start. Have you had lunch?"

His face flushed a little. "I, uh—I've been running around, so I haven't eaten much—"

"Sit down here, then." I gestured to the table. "Join me. After interviewing all those Hungarians, I think you should taste their food; my grandma made some and gave me left-overs. They are amazing, I assure you."

"Uh—okay. I guess we can talk over lunch. Thanks." He folded himself into one of my kitchen chairs. I had a plate of *kiflis* on the counter; I set it down in front of him.

"You can snack on a couple of those while I finish cooking."

"Thanks." He took one and chewed it, closing his eyes briefly as he encountered the flavor. Most people responded that way to my grandmother's cooking, or, in this case, her baking. "I wanted to go over the day of the event—the day Ava died. Can you give me a basic rundown of how things happened, in order?" He pulled out his notebook and opened it up.

I shrugged, stirring the chicken and gravy. "We got there about two hours before the event. Did our usual setup. Mrs. Kalas got there about fifteen minutes early, which we expected, because—well, you've met Mrs. Kalas." He smiled at the *kifli* plate. "Then we were pretty much busy from there on out—pouring tea, setting out food, picking up dirty plates and napkins, arranging for my grandma's reading, and then of course I found Ava like—that. I called emergency, and they called the police."

He looked at his notebook. "And after the emergency technicians, you met first responder"—he consulted his notes—"Officer Thomas at the door."

"Yes. And then some other police came, and then you."

He paused for a moment and we looked at each other. Then he took the last sweet crescent and ate it. "Umm. What is this?"

"It's called a *kifli*. That one you just ate had raspberry filling, but it's *málna lekvár*—a thick raspberry jam—not the standard kind of jelly you buy in the grocery store."

"Wow, that's good. How do you stay slim in this family?" His gaze roamed slightly downward, as if to verify my slimness.

"I'm not sure. I know one of my grandma's secret ingredients is pure lard, and my mom and dad have been eating her cooking for thirty-five years—fifty-five for my mom, yet they're both pretty fit."

"Wow." He picked up a napkin I had set before him and wiped his fingers on it. "Okay. We've found no trace of poison except in Mrs. Novák's cup. Do you have any idea how someone could have gotten it in there? The cup arrived with you and was a decoration. You have no memory of seeing anyone looking at it, touching it?"

"No. But I was focused on my work." I put the food on simmer and walked to the table, sitting down across from him.

"So the working assumption is that someone saw your butterfly cup, decided to use it as a vessel of death, took it away somewhere to write that message on it, and then brought it to Ava Novák, who drank it without question."

"I guess that sounds right."

Wolf tapped his front teeth with his pencil, his eyebrows furrowed. "Except that it doesn't. Why did no one see any of this? It was an elaborate process."

"Uh—I don't know—there must have been a time that we were all truly distracted by the tea-leaf stuff. I was in the staff room, talking to François. He got a call from home, saying his father might have suffered a heart attack. We talked about it and then I told him to go home. Ava was at the back of the room, and all of the women had flowed forward. Assuming Ava did have a fight with someone in the bathroom, she might have felt upset, unwilling to talk to other people."

He thought about this. "And the other woman was upset, too. So upset she decided to carry out a plan of murder."

A plan of murder. One of those women who had smiled at me behind her teacup, her sweet little sandwiches, had arrived with the intention of killing Ava. Or had they just wanted to kill *someone*?

"Hana? You're very pale. Do you want some water?" Wolf put his hand on mine.

"No—I just—when I picture it, I feel kind of sick. Can you trace the poison?"

Wolf nodded approvingly, taking his hand away. "We're working on it."

"You're going to ask me now if we have poison, right? My family and me?"

Wolf's green gaze was curious. "I wasn't, but feel free to tell me."

"Well, we don't. Not for whatever reason people might have to possess poison. Kill weeds? Rats? I don't know. We have a landscaper and an exterminator."

"Okey doke." He made another note. I wondered if he could even read his own chicken scratch later, or if all of this note-taking would be a waste of time. Or perhaps it was just a pretension, to make him look official and in charge. Maybe all of the police did it. I watched his hand as it moved with his pen; his fingers were surprisingly long and artistic. I wondered what had made him become a cop; he glanced up and caught me wondering.

"The food is done. Let me get it," I said, leaping up.

I sliced some of the beer bread and laid it on a lovely Herend plate that I'd gotten for Christmas. I walked to the table and set it down, then went back to my stove. "I know you're on the job, but I have some wine that pairs well with this food. If you'd like just a small glass."

Wolf had already broken off a corner of bread. "I'm not officially on duty. I had to take some days off or risk losing them, so I took them. But of course I'm still working."

"Of *course*," I said, pouring him some wine.

I returned to the table and handed him the glass; he looked suddenly concerned. "This isn't that stuff your grandma gave me the other day?"

I laughed. "No, it's not Pálinka. Just wine. And that's *sör kenyér*—Hungarian beer bread, what you're eating now." I raised my own wineglass. "*Egészségedre*."

"And that means?"

"'To your health.'"

He raised his glass, then sipped. "It's delicious."

"Did the Pálinka help? The other day? Your cold seems all but gone."

Wolf's eyes widened. "It knocked me out. Like *unconscious*. But I did feel a lot better when I woke up," he admitted.

I laughed. "Wait until I get the main course—you can eat the bread with it."

I went back to the stove and filled a plate with chicken, dumplings, and gravy, then brought it back to Wolf. "Go ahead, dig in. I'll join you in a minute." I made a little sign of the cross in the air over him and his plate.

"What's that?" he said.

"Oh—just a family tradition. Bless the one you feed. My grandma always did it, and then my mother, and now I guess me. I don't feed that many people."

He nodded, then smiled. "Do you bless the cats?"

"No, actually. I guess it's only an instinct for the humans at your table." I felt thick-limbed again as I walked to the stove. Wolf's smile had been unexpected and glorious. It had transformed his face from something stiff and professional to something—very interesting.

I came back with my own plate. Wolf's eyes were closed again because he had taken his first bite of food and was savoring it. I knew the feeling. "So good, isn't it?"

He dunked his bread in the gravy and bit into it, then forked up some more chicken. "It's amazing. I've never had Hungarian food. I think I may have been longing for it all my life."

"I know." I stabbed a couple of dumplings with my fork and swirled them around in my gravy. "So, did you have any other questions?"

"Oh—yes. Actually I want to show you something." He took another bite, then picked up a little satchel he had set on the floor near the table. Out of that he retrieved a clear plastic bag, which he handed to me. There was a reddish-gray stone inside.

He watched me while I studied it. "Is that the stone you saw on Ava's purse?"

I nodded. "Yes. I'm almost sure it is, yes. How—who—?"

"One of our people found it in the grass outside the tea house."

"Ah." I stared at the bloodstone for a while in silence while Wolf ate his food. Finally I said, "Why would someone steal it just to throw it away?"

"Good question."

I sat up straight. "Did you check it for fingerprints?"

He nodded, sipping his wine. "Nothing usable."

"It really is lovely, although it looks more like a rock than a precious stone. But it has that sort of inner glimmer, and those wonderful red flecks."

Wolf was pushing his bread around his plate, soaking up gravy. "I looked up heliotrope, when you told me about it. Legend says it has healing powers, even magical ones."

"Yeah, well. If you believe in legends, then you would buy into all the stuff my grandma says, with her witches and fairies and fair ladies. She's made me downright paranoid with all of her spooky tales."

"Sometimes legends can influence a person's behavior, though. There were many superstitious people in your tea house on the day that Ava died."

"That's true. Would you like some more wine?"

"No, that was plenty. Thank you. I can't remember ever having such a delicious meal."

"There's something I need to tell you, too. Something I heard the other day."

"Okay. Finish your food first. I ate like a ravenous dog, and you've barely started. I'll go play with your cats for a minute." He got up and walked into my living room, then plopped down on the couch, where my felines were sitting. Antony switched on a purr as loud as an outboard motor and Wolf said something to him in a quiet voice.

I finished my lunch, trying to gauge the situation. Was Wolf just being friendly, trying to get in the good graces of the Hungarian girl so that she would give him more information? Was he just feeling a bit more casual because it was his day off? Or, as my grandmother seemed to think, was he interested in me personally?

I looked again at the bloodstone. It wasn't a manufactured excuse for visiting me; he really had needed me to identify it. I could be reading this all wrong. I finished my food, then got up and brought my plate and his to the sink. Suddenly he was behind me, holding our empty wineglasses. His tallness and his proximity made me slightly dizzy. "Sorry! I should have brought my stuff over here," he said. "Let me wash these out." He set them on the counter and tried to nudge me out of the way, pressing his warm side against mine.

"No, don't be silly." I picked up a sponge to wipe the table, and he clasped my hand, trying to wrest the sponge from me.

He said, "I'll do that." We stood with our hands joined around the warm sponge.

I said, "You don't have to—"

At the same time that he said, "You smell—"

And then we both stopped. Wolf looked miserable, and I said, "Did you just say that I smell?"

He shook his head, still holding my sponge hand. "No—God, no. I was trying to say that you smell good. Whatever that perfume is—I noticed it when I came over here. You—it might be your hair, I don't know."

I pulled the sponge out of his hand and set it on the counter. Then I held up my wrist, and he lowered his head to breathe in the scent. "Yes, that's it," he murmured. His lips were almost touching my skin.

"It's called Éclat d'Arpège. I bought it for my brother's girlfriend, but this morning I decided to sample it myself. It is pretty, isn't it?"

"Yes." His green eyes met mine.

"Detective Wolf?"

"Yes."

Something urgent was building inside me. I didn't know what to say; I shook my head and started to turn away, but his hand shot out and grabbed my wrist.

He cleared his throat. "Erik," he said.

"What?"

"My name is *Erik*. Stop calling me Detective Wolf."

"Why? It's professional."

"You know why," he said.

I was dizzy from indecision. I stood facing the V at the top of his shirt, where blond hairs curled against his tanned skin. Without my permission, my fingertip touched him there, on the little hollow in his throat. It felt electric, that moment of connection. I thought I felt his heart beating against the tentative pressure of my hand.

"Hana."

My eyes moved up, connected with his green ones. We stared at each other in mute amazement.

Then he dove at me and I clasped my arms around him and we kissed each other as though we'd been starved of kisses for hundreds of years. I vaguely felt myself bumping into the counter, then leaning against it while my brain tried to say, *You barely know this man.* Something else in me told my brain to be quiet, and I slid my arms up to his shoulders and then into his hair. I was almost numb with pleasure.

Finally we paused for breath. "Wow," I said.

"Yeah," Wolf agreed, looking as dazed as I felt.

I smiled at him; my hands shook slightly as I removed them from his hair and rested them on his shoulders. "I was afraid you weren't going to kiss me. I would have been very disappointed."

"Me, too."

His lips were gently exploring my ear, my cheek, my hair. I said, "You're actually—sort of terrible at flirting."

His laughter sounded relieved. "I know. I always have been."

"But as you may have noticed, I am, too. We must have real chemistry if we made it past both of us fumbling around." I smiled up at him.

"Hana."

"Hmm?"

"I like you very much."

"Good."

He looked at me again with a strange expression—something between worry and lust.

"Come sit down with me," I said. I led him to the living room and pushed him gently onto my couch. He laughed, and I sat on his lap and kissed him some more.

Finally, he leaned his head back on the couch cushion and said, "I like it here. It's cozy, and your cats are great, and you—" Green eyes looked into mine and I felt a bolt of heat shoot through me. "You are lovely. And soft. And fragrant. And your hair—"

"Mmm. That's much more poetic than before."

He grinned. "Well, you gave me some encouragement. Before, I didn't know, and it made me nervous . . . and I was trying to concentrate on other things."

"You're good at your job, Erik. So focused. And you ask such good questions. It's attractive."

His mouth lifted on one side. "Yeah? So you've been watching me?"

"Observing you. I was forced *by you* into close proximity, watching you interrogate those women. My grandmother says you were watching me, too."

He touched my hand. "I often found I could not look away." We shared another smile—shy, surprised, uncertain.

He leaned back again, and I leaned back with him. We took some time to be silent together; I found that I liked this, too. Eventually I said, "Detective Wolf? I mean, Erik?"

"Hmm?"

"I could iron your suits for you. Not to be a subservient woman or anything, but because I'm good at ironing. I get a lot of practice on tablecloths at the tea house."

His face registered vague surprise. "Do my suits need ironing?"

"Um—yes."

He laughed, and I admired his straight white teeth. "I guess you should teach me how to iron, too, then."

"Okay. And you can teach me some cool interrogation techniques to use on my friends."

He laughed again, then sat up straight. "Wait, you said you had something to tell me."

I pursed out my lips, pouting briefly. "Your timing is problematic."

"I know. Sorry." His expression was appropriately remorseful, but his brows remained raised, awaiting my information.

"Fine. I saw Mrs. Sarka at the mall—she was at the tea event, one of that whole Hungarian group from St. Stephen. You probably interviewed her—she's about a foot tall."

"Okay," Wolf said, smiling.

I started to play with his blond hair, wrapping a lock of it around my finger. "She said that Ava dated her brother Steve before she met Joe Novák."

"What?" He pushed me gently off his lap and dug in his pocket for his notebook. "Steve what?"

"Steve Sarka. Weirdly enough, her husband had the same last name, so Sarka is her married and her maiden name. My grandpa jokes about it, because of the name itself."

"Why?"

"In Hungarian, the name *Szarka* means 'magpie.' Which is a euphemism for thief—you know, because in folklore magpies are the birds that steal jewelry and shiny objects."

"Okay. So what's the joke?"

"Oh, my grandpa just makes some joke in Hungarian about how she went from one clan of thieves to another."

Wolf blinked at me. "Okay, so his name is Steve Sarka." He wrote this down.

"Yeah. He's younger than she is, and more Americanized. She calls him Istvan still, but he's always gone by Steve. He's my dad's age. They go drinking sometimes."

"And your dad's name?"

I frowned. "Jack Keller. He's not a part of this. He's not Hungarian or anything. He teaches history at RHS."

"Uh-huh. Okay." He jotted down some notes. "So maybe your dad can be my contact point for talking to Steve Sarka."

"I suppose. Or you can just show up at his house, like you did to me. Or was I special?"

Wolf smiled a slow smile at me, but it was partly distracted. "You are special."

"You're thinking cop things. It's very insulting, considering this was our first kiss."

"Sorry." He leaned in to kiss my cheek, and his lips trailed around on it for a while. He pulled away and touched my skin with one gentle finger. "So soft. And your eyes are such a beautiful shade of brown—like chocolate."

I laughed. "Domo refers to them as the 'pools of darkness.'"

Wolf stiffened beside me. "Domo?"

"My brother."

"Oh. I thought maybe I had—competition for your affection."

I scooched closer to him. "I think you just got a good sense of where my *affection* lies. And you don't have to worry, anyway. I have a very big crush on you. Even though I don't know you at all."

"Huh." That got a brief smile. "That's going to be the fun part, right? Getting to know each other." Then he sat up and looked at his watch. "Now you're going to be mad at me."

"Why? Do you have to go?"

His eyes were more of a forest green now, deep and limpid, but also regretful. "Yes, but it's worse than that. I can't really pursue this—us—until the case is over. You're a key witness, and someone who's been cooperating with our investigation. I shouldn't even have—"

I glared. "Why did you, then?"

"Because I wanted to."

My scowl was losing intensity under his scrutiny.

He touched the tip of my nose. "Can you wait? Until this case is closed? Please, Hana?"

I flopped back against the couch. "How long do you think it will take?"

"I don't know. A few weeks, a month? More? I'm working hard on it; so is Greg. That's Detective Benton. We might get a break any day."

"It's ridiculous. I didn't kill Ava, and I don't know who did. Now you are free to date me."

"It's policy. And you may have noticed that I am a rule follower; I only broke one today because you—enticed me. With food and kisses." He touched my hair. "Or entranced me, I guess is a better word."

I sighed and stood up. "Fine. You can pretend you don't know me, and that you didn't kiss me. Pretend we didn't share a meal together and look into each other's eyes." I went into the kitchen and began putting food into a bag. I may as well have been my grandmother, who was the master of packing food for a loved one while sending them on a guilt trip at the same time. "You can take the rest of this."

"Stop being mad at me," Wolf said, half laughing.

"Why is this funny to you?"

"Because your face is cute while it's all indignant."

I huffed around the kitchen, putting extra little treats in the bag with the *paprikás* and bread—some of my homemade noodles, some *mákos* (Hungarian poppy seed bread), and the rest of the bottle of wine.

I handed the bag to Wolf. "There. Now you can go."

He set the bag on the table, reclaiming the bloodstone and putting that inside his satchel. Then he moved closer to me. "We can't go back. You've kissed me now."

"Well, we all make mistakes."

He was laughing again as he yanked me against him. "Haniska," he said, before he pressed his mouth against mine.

Chapter 15

Books and Betrayal

There were almost 150 people at the Books and Tea event. My mother and I bustled around with the tea cart, replenishing pots and delivering sandwich trays. The professor, Dr. Caldwell, was on the dais, welcoming her guests and giving a brief introduction to the book before the discussion began.

"Robert Louis Stevenson," she said, scanning the crowd, "had long been fascinated by the duality of human nature. Even as a child he had thought that the potential dichotomy of good and evil in one human being was fertile ground for a story, and it was in fact the theme for more than one of his literary works. Part of the legend of his inspiration for this novel was that he had a dream one night while he was ill; his wife woke him, and he was quite upset with her, because he had been dreaming what essentially became the basis for the book, and she woke him just as Jekyll was about to transform."

The audience oohed and clapped. I scanned the tables, making sure that there were still plenty of sandwiches on each tiered tray. My grandmother, who had been adjusting the sound on Dr. Caldwell's microphone, now moved unobtrusively to the back of the stage and made her way down the stairs. She joined me against the wall and said, "Everything good?"

"Yes," I murmured. "I think they need at least another half hour with the sandwiches; then we can start clearing and bringing out dessert plates. François has some lovely petit fours back there."

She adjusted my apron and studied the Hungarian embroidery on the bib. Then she looked out over the tables. "Ya. The little book covers look good, very good."

"Thanks! I think they add some elegance to the affair. And I—what the heck are *they* doing here?"

Wolf and Benton, wearing dark suits and grim expressions, had appeared in the hall. "No, no—they will ruin everything!" my grandmother murmured.

"Something's wrong," I said as they spied us and walked to our corner of the room.

I should have felt a bolt of joy at seeing Erik Wolf again, but the expression on his face triggered something in me: the misery was back, that general feeling of wrongness, and all I could feel was sick.

I glared at them as they walked up, but spoke in a whisper. Wolf wouldn't look at me; his eyes were fixed on my grandmother. I said, "You can't be here. This is a private event. We do not want these people to know that you're the police."

Wolf still didn't look my way. He spoke quietly but firmly to my grandmother. "Mrs. Horvath, we need to conference with you in the back room. If you please?" He gestured toward François's lair, and my grandmother nodded, seemingly relieved to be able to get them out of the main room, where they were already attracting some surprised glances.

She swept away with the men behind her. I stared, my mouth slightly open. My mother trundled the tea cart over to me and said, keeping a smile on her face, "What's going on?"

"They wanted to talk to Grandma. They didn't look happy."

"What now?" She thought about it for a while, then whispered, "I can handle things out here, Hana. You go see what they want from Mama. I don't want her in there alone with them."

I nodded and made my way to the back of the hall and the little white doorway that led to the kitchen. In the room François, with a furious expression, was icing cakes. He stared daggers at me and I shrugged. "I had no idea," I said.

"They asked me to *leave*," François said. "I will be back in ten minutes to *do my job.* At my *place of business.*" I knew he was truly angry when he spoke in italics. He finished the cake he was icing and huffed out of the room.

My grandmother was sitting at the large table with both Benton and Wolf sitting across from her. I could see her face and the backs of their heads. Benton, who looked rather pale today, had his computer at the ready, and Wolf was studying his notebook. From the back, despite the wavy blond hair that curled enticingly over his shirt collar, he looked nothing like the man who had been in my apartment the day before. This man was stern, unfriendly, suspicious. His posture was unbending.

"Mrs. Horvath, did you ever contact Ava Novák via the mail?"

My grandmother squinted at them. "The mail?"

"As in a written letter."

"No." She patted her curls, which had been shellacked into place with hairspray. "I did not know Ava Novák."

Wolf leaned forward. "Detective Benton spoke with her husband yesterday. Mr. Novák provided all the correspondence that had ever been sent to Ava, or at least all he could find. In it there was a letter from you."

My grandmother looked genuinely surprised. "Must be someone else."

Wolf removed a letter from a file in front of him and pushed it toward her. "Is that your handwriting?"

Even from my spot near the doorway I could see that it was hers. She had a very distinctive and beautiful script that was almost like calligraphy. She had learned it in school. "Looks like," she said, peering at it.

"And is it your signature?"

She nodded. "Ya, looks like mine."

"Mrs. Horvath, I'm going to read this letter aloud. Perhaps you can explain it to us afterward."

"Okay," she said. She looked unruffled, but still mildly surprised.

"'Ava,'" Wolf began in an officious tone, "'You must beware. A dark form is on your path, a determined darkness that lies in wait. You must not drink the cup of happiness without looking behind you. Beware the lovely wings that fly too close.'"

My grandmother's expression changed then; she seemed to be remembering something. Her eyes took on a sharpness that I had not seen before.

"Do you recall writing this letter, Mrs. Horvath?"

She shrugged. "Ya, I write it."

"Can you explain why you wrote it, and why it seems to relate directly to Mrs. Novák's murder?"

"That's ridiculous," I said.

Wolf didn't turn around. "Mrs. Horvath?"

My grandmother said, "This was long ago. Two, three years. There was a party at one lady's house. They ask me to read leaves, and I read Ava's. They—did not show good things. I said something to her, something simple, but she want me to write it down for her. Exactly what I saw in the leaves." She glanced at Benton, then Wolf. "She was nice lady, sad-looking. I felt sorry. So I write it down. I did not mail it, I write it on paper and hand it to her."

"And what did you mean by 'wings'? Coincidentally, she drank poison out of a cup with a butterfly on it."

She shook her head. "No, no. At the time, I see something not clear. Darkness, and cloudy. And something flying above her, something dangerous. I try to put this into words for her."

Wolf cleared his throat. "Mrs. Horvath, I was given to understand that you only read tea leaves as an entertainment. So how is it that you would give such a negative reading to someone? A frightening reading?"

I will always remember that moment because it's when I realized that my grandmother possessed something beyond my understanding. Her face grew calm and somehow smooth. The years seemed to melt away, and I felt that I was looking at her in another time. "I tell her what I see, Detective. I see much. I see that you have not turned once to look at my granddaughter, and yet you watch her with the eyes behind your head. She is all you care about right now, as you look at me with your police face."

Wolf was quiet for a moment. "Please stay on task, Mrs. Horvath."

She went on, as though he had not spoken. "I see that Benton is worried, worried, for someone at home. A boy, I think."

Benton's hands stopped moving on the keyboard. His pale face seemed to grow even paler. He leaned over and murmured something to Wolf. "Excuse us for a moment," Wolf said, and the two of them left the room. Again, Wolf did not look in my direction.

I moved forward and sat across from my grandmother. "You let us believe that you were just doing theater," I said, studying her face. "You said it was just in fun."

She nodded. "Your mama doesn't like me to talk about things. She is afraid people will think I'm a Gypsy."

I sighed. While Americans tended to romanticize Gypsies, with images of nomads who played beautiful violin music and wooed their lovers with sublime singing and dancing, some Hungarians disliked Gypsies with a practiced, centuries-old abhorrence. Traditionally, to call a Hungarian a Gypsy would be to insult them. While my grandmother disliked no one, she was still a product of her culture, and she feared unpleasant associations that might affect her reputation.

"Besides, my gift is small. Nothing like Mama's. Hers was everything. Hers was power."

"What do you mean? Are you saying Great-grandma Natalia was psychic?"

She shrugged. "She saw things. And could talk to nature. Remember the butterflies?"

I summoned up my favorite memory of my great-grandmother. Again, I recalled standing at Natalia's knee while a monarch landed on her hand, bright orange and defining black, impossibly lovely on that summer day. I concentrated on this image. I had been delighted by the experience, because . . . "The butterfly landed on Great-grandma, and then it landed on me," I said, remembering.

"Yes. Because she told it to do so," Grandma said.

"What?" And then it came back, in a rush. I could see her face, smell her paprika scent, feel the softness of her hand on mine. Hear her voice, gentle, sweet, saying, "Go to Haniska now, my friend. Go to Haniska."

And the butterfly rose from her arm in a flurry of color and flew over to my arm—a very tiny target at the time—and the lovely insect settled right in, relaxing its wings. "You are friends now, ya?" she had said, and her eyes creased with pleasure at the sight of us . . .

I looked at my grandmother's luminous eyes. "What—I don't understand—"

The two policemen came back in. I rose from the chair before Wolf could speak to me and went back to stand by the wall.

My grandmother remained serene, composed. Wolf said, "Mrs. Horvath, I think that you have not been fully forthcoming in the representation of your abilities."

"What do you mean?" Grandma asked. "Speak English."

Great burn, Grandma. I felt a bolt of satisfaction as she smiled at Wolf. He sighed. "Are you telling us that you have psychic ability?"

She shrugged. "Just get impressions sometimes. It works well with the tea."

"You just told us about Benton's son. The boy has been very ill."

"Yes. I can feel that inside *him*." She pointed at Benton. "His fear, his upset. It is so strong, it is not hard to pick up."

"What do you see about my son now?" Benton asked. He was trying to be professional, but he clearly couldn't resist asking.

She looked at him with some sympathy. "I feel . . . he will be fine, sir. The tension is less. I feel he is fine now. Call and see."

Benton stood up and left the room.

I stared at the back of Wolf's head as he in turn stared at my grandmother. "Do you remember anything else about the night you wrote this for Ava?"

She studied her hands for a moment, thinking. "I know she had just started dating Joe. I felt the anger—the—what is it, Haniska, when you combine anger and grudge?"

"Resentment," I said.

She pointed at me. "Yes. I feel this resentment of some of the women in the room. But it wasn't all about Joe. There was other resentments, other angers. Crossed wires. This concerned me."

Wolf was writing, writing, writing away in his notebook. I wondered if he were writing an apology to me, to my grandmother, for his coldness. I felt the opposite temperature building in me . . . a heat that grew. My own resentment.

"Anything else you can tell us? Anything else you have withheld from the police?"

A whole new admiration for my grandmother surged in me. She did so well under interrogation that she refused to acknowledge it as interrogation. She said, "I withheld nothing. I am old. I forget. Someday you will be so, Wolf."

His head came up sharply, and they looked at each other.

Benton walked back in and sat down. None of us looked at him; I was almost afraid of what he would say.

My grandmother had leaned forward and was saying something to Wolf in a low voice. He remained stationary in his chair, but even from the back I could sense his surprise. She had his full attention. She spoke to him for at least a few minutes in that voice I could barely hear. Then she leaned back, smiling. She stretched her arms and stood up. "Are you finished? I am at work, as you know. More than a hundred people out there."

Wolf bowed his head. "Thank you for the information, Mrs. Horvath."

My grandmother swept out of the room, but she managed to wink at me before leaving.

Wolf finished making his notes, his back still to me. Benton turned and smiled at me.

"How's your son?" I asked.

"He's better. His fever just broke, for the first time in three days. He's having some lunch. Your grandmother seems to have been—right on target."

"I'm glad about your son," I said, and I left the room. Dr. Caldwell was just finishing her introduction:

"Certainly the novel explores the duality of good versus evil, although this is the most simplistic understanding of the story. Jekyll is a complex character, and even his good side has some problematic moral components. If we apply a Freudian lens, however, we can also think of Jekyll and Hyde as the human conscious and the unconscious. What do we suppress, in the name of being seen as 'good' to our society? And what becomes of suppressed evil?"

François went back into his workspace, still glaring. A few minutes later he wheeled out the first tray of pastries, and the crowd rustled with anticipation. The readers were taking turns at the microphone. Someone was asking, "Did it bother anyone else that there were no women in this novel?"

Wolf came out of the back room and found his way to me. "If you would join me in the parking lot, I have something to give you."

I did not want to join him, or to speak to him. I went, though, following him in silence to his car. Benton came, too, but climbed in the passenger seat, talking on his cell phone. I heard him murmur, "What did the doctor say?"

Wolf opened a door of the backseat and retrieved a bag

which he handed to me. "Here is your teacup. We're finished with it. It hasn't been damaged at all, and it has been cleaned."

"Thank you." My voice sounded frosty even to my ears.

"Hana, I am doing my job. Your grandmother withheld evidence from the police."

"You know that she did *not*. She is seventy-eight years old, and she simply forgot. You treated her like a traitor."

He nodded, looking around the parking lot. "I'm in a very difficult position. I'm trying to be professional. My timing may have been off, with our relationship. I made a mistake," he said.

A moment of silence, hanging there. For an instant I pitied him, and then I just felt disappointed.

"No, you didn't make a mistake, Detective Wolf. I did." I turned and walked away from him, unable for many reasons to rejoice in the reclaiming of my butterfly cup.

I tucked the bag into my car and returned to the tea house; I sat in a chair against the wall, pondering the discussion of the duality of human nature while a group of interested readers drank tea from our fine china and munched desserts carefully frosted by François. Jekyll needed a potion to keep his evil at bay. What else did people hide from the world? My grandmother had apparently hidden a significant aspect of her nature because she feared her daughter's disapproval. Erik Wolf had worn a mask of affection for one day before discarding it to return to his role of devoted policeman (or he valued his policeman mask more than his real feelings). And somewhere out there was a woman, seemingly sweet and harmless, who had deliberately poisoned one of her friends. Had she carried the poison around with her in her purse, just as she had carried the poison of hatred within her heart?

I wanted to walk to the stage and speak into the microphone, to tell the people assembled there that no one could truly be trusted, and that love was an illusion.

Instead I grabbed a cart and began to collect empty teacups.

Chapter 16

Mrs. Sarka's Brother

Before I went home, I stopped at my grandmother's house, where I found my grandfather reading a spy novel and drinking a beer. He took one look at me and said, "Oh-ho! Who made you mad, my little ice queen? My little Zsa Zsa?"

I flounced into a chair. "I'm not mad."

"Yah. Like you weren't angry when your dad threw out the ice."

I shook my head, dismissing this. Family legend had it that I had done something at the age of almost three that convinced Grandpa that I would be tempestuous all my life. As it happened, I was a toddler who loved ice cubes. I loved to feel them, play with them, chew on them, even talk to them. I made up little stories populated with ice cube men, and if they melted I replaced them with new reserves.

This greatly amused my family, but one day my father, not knowing that a glass full of ice on the table was filled with my imaginary ice people, dumped it unceremoniously into the sink, crunching the ice in the disposal. I marched in and demanded to know, in a tiny but imperious voice, the whereabouts of the cubes. My father, seeing that he was in trouble with his two-foot offspring, meekly said that he had thrown it out. Without a word, I turned and went to my room, where I packed a Barbie and five minuscule pairs of underwear in a Curious George backpack and demanded that my father open the front door. I was, I told him, leaving home.

Figuring that I wouldn't go far, my father opened the door, and I walked down the stairs with a very queenly bearing, my father assures me now. In the yard my grandfather was helping my mother plant some perennials. He took one look at my angry face as I glided determinedly down the walkway and burst out laughing. "Who made her mad?" he asked. "You don't cross a Hungarian woman, Jack! Didn't you know that?" Grandpa's laughter followed me all the way down the sidewalk, because he was, in fact, walking right behind me. He finally scooped me up in his arms and asked me what was wrong, whereupon I began to sob out my story of the lost ice family.

"My Hana will have all the ice in the world," he told me. He drove me to the grocery store and bought me a ten-pound bag of ice, then to the Dairy Queen, where he bought me ice cream. They tell me that I was pleased with the compromise, and that in my ice cream–inspired generosity I even forgave my father for his cruel act. That had been more than twenty-four years ago, but Grandpa had called me ice queen ever since as a joke, and sometimes he compared me to Zsa Zsa Gabor, legendary for her excess of husbands, her love of fame and money, and her Hungarian temper.

"That was different," I said. "I was two. And the ice cubes were my friends."

"So what man crossed you this time?" Grandpa asked, setting down his book.

"It doesn't always have to be a man," I said.

He studied my face. "It is, though."

"I don't want to talk about it. Did you know your wife is psychic?"

He laughed. "Ya. We are together because she said I was right, the right one."

"I thought you met at some sort of picnic."

"*Igen*." He had slipped into Hungarian, and he shook his head and switched back to English. "She saw me and knew, she says. She said it felt like being underwater, smooth and calm, and there was a gold light around me. So she walked up to me and took my hand and said she was Juliana. But she didn't let go of my hand. And I didn't want her to."

"Grandpa, that is so romantic!"

"Why are you about to cry, then?" His voice was tender. No one had ever been so attuned to my emotions as my grandfather was.

"I'm not. I have to go."

He stood up and shuffled toward me in his slippers. "Want something to eat? I've got *kolbász*."

"No, not hungry. Thanks, Grandpa." I gave him a kiss and a hug and started toward the door.

"Haniska."

"Yeah?"

"You thought your daddy betrayed you, with the ice, but it turned out you were wrong, ya? And you love him to this day."

"He's my father."

He twinkled his blue eyes at me. “You think about what I said.”

~

My father called me later. “Hey, kid. I have to take Major to the vet for his shots, and Mom and Grandma went off in search of some European market they heard about. Can you go with me? He screams less when you’re there.”

It was true; even though Major glared at me a lot, we were friends, and I had a calming effect on him. “Sure. What time is the appointment?”

“Six thirty.”

I agreed, and at six o’clock I pulled up in front of his house and texted him that I was there. He came out with a carrier; Major was glaring inside, but he was also using his frightened meow. My dad opened the backseat and tucked Major inside. I spoke soothingly to the cat. “It’s okay, Major. We’re just taking you to the vet—you know the drill.”

Major thought about this in silence for a while, but started yowling again when we were halfway there. “Poor guy,” I said.

“Yeah.” My dad fiddled with the radio and found WFMT, Chicago’s classical station. His favorite. “Ah, Brahms. Your mother loves him because of his *Hungarian Dances*.”

“And you like the lullabies. At least you used to sing them to me.”

“Yeah. I was great,” my dad joked.

“How’s school going?”

“Not bad. Not too stressful yet, but give it another month.” He flipped down his sun visor with a casual flick of his hand. “I heard there was some drama at the tea house today.”

"Yes. The police again. Interrogating Grandma about some note she wrote to Ava Novák years ago. She didn't remember it, but then it kind of came back to her. It turns out she has some actual psychic instincts."

"It's true," my dad said, glancing out his window. "Your mother never likes to talk about them. Mom has them, too, but she doesn't explore them. You know what I mean? She has very powerful, instinctive responses, but she shies away from them."

"Why? And why am I only learning this now?"

He shrugged. "Your mom is very practical. She doesn't really believe in the idea that you can have a hereditary trait like deep insight. Or second sight. Or whatever you would call it. Have you ever felt anything of that kind?" He peered at me; his window was open, and his brown-gray hair fluttered in the breeze.

"I don't think so." And yet even as I said it, possibilities were popping into my head. That wall of feeling that had prevented me from entering the tea house on the day of the murder; the gradual misery that I felt when I realized that something evil was in the hall with us on the day that Ava died; that little voice that had told me, against logic, to pursue Wolf; the distress I had felt at seeing Wolf and Benton at the tea house, and the way Benton's worry had seemed to cause physical waves to emerge from him. And hadn't there been other things, little twinges of feeling or insight, going back to childhood, high school, college? These were possibilities I would have to explore at another time . . . like my mother, I found the whole idea intimidating.

My dad cleared his throat. "You and your great-grandma had a strong connection. From the time you were a baby. You seemed to read each other's minds. It was always a beautiful sight—her wrinkled face and your little tiny one. You would look into each other's eyes with these incredibly peaceful expressions. It was—soothing to watch."

"I miss her," I said. Then I poked him on the arm. "Who knew what you were marrying into, huh? Four generations of weird women."

He laughed, then became serious. "Anyway, I hope the police get to the bottom of this soon. It's a terrible thing. What would motivate someone to kill a seemingly nice lady?"

"That's what I've been asking. Major, it's okay, buddy. Shhh." I pulled into the parking lot of Riverwood Pet Care and tucked into a spot. "It seems to be connected to this stone she had on her purse. It's called a bloodstone."

"Oh?" my father said. "What about it?"

So I told him, as we retrieved Major from the backseat and carried him inside, about the purse, and the missing stone, and its appearance in the grass outside the tea house.

"You really seem to have the inside story," my father said as we sat waiting on a bench in the lobby. "I guess it helps to know the police on the case."

I sent him a sharp glance. "What does that mean?"

"Nothing. Just—your mom said you and the detective in charge seemed to have a connection."

"We don't." I made my voice as final as a door slamming, and my father looked at his hands. Major appeared at the bars of his carrier and glared at both of us. I put my finger through one of the wire squares and Major sniffed it.

A woman in a white lab coat appeared. "Major?" she said. My dad raised a hand. "You can take him into exam room three. The doctor is running a bit behind schedule, so we'll have an attendant come in to take his vitals."

We carried Major, who was quiet now, into the room and

set his carrier on the table. We opened the door, and he walked out, unable to resist his curiosity. I closed the door so that he couldn't charge back in when a stranger entered. Meanwhile, he glared at my father and swatted his arm with one paw.

My dad laughed. "I know, bud. You'll be finished soon."

The door opened, and Steve Sarka walked in. I stared at my father in astonishment, and my father said, "Hey, Steve."

Steve Sarka was in his sixties, one of those enthusiastic men who punched people in the arm when he greeted them. "Hey, Jack!" He punched my dad in the arm and then hugged him. He lunged toward me and said, "Little Hana! I haven't seen you in so long!" I winced, fearing impact, but he merely gave me a quick hug.

My dad said, "I forgot you told me you worked at a vet's office now."

Steve had a booming voice, which clearly intimidated Major, whose tail was tucked firmly between his legs. "That was last *year* I told you! We need to have drinks again. But people are all so busy, right?"

"Yeah. So you're what—in vet school—?"

"No, but I went through training to be an assistant. And now I've been doing it two years. I always loved animals." Steve barely had a Hungarian accent, unlike his older sister.

"I saw your sister at the mall a couple days ago," I said.

He swung his gaze to me. His energy was somehow draining. "Yeah? She doesn't go there often. She likes to be in her house, always baking."

"She was getting something for her grandson."

He grinned. "My nephew's son. Bobby."

"Ah. Well, I sent her to the video game store."

"Good idea." He grinned again, then started petting Major's head. "Who is this guy?"

"This is Major," my dad said.

"Let's take a look at you, Major," Steve said. I was glad to hear that when he talked to the cat, his voice became lower, softer, and his big hands became gentle. Major closed his eyes for a moment under Steve's gentle touch, which was currently centered on rubbing Major's ears.

"Oh my gosh, he likes you," I said. "Major doesn't like anyone."

"What a handsome boy. Let's just take a look in these ears. Lovely. And look at those nice white teeth. Very good. A little tartar. Not bad. Maybe we'll clip the nails today, eh?"

I watched as he listened to Major's heart and jotted some notes on a card. Finally he said, "Everything looks good. We just need to give him the rabies and the distemper today."

"Great." My father nodded; he was a brisk and efficient person, and he clearly wanted to move the process along.

"Hey, Steve," I said, attempting a casual tone. "Your sister told me you dated Ava Novák at one point."

Steve stopped smiling and shook his head. "Man, Ava—can you believe that? If you're not safe having tea with a bunch of ladies from the Old Country, then where are you safe?"

Their connection was news to my father, who said, "Really? How long did you date her?"

Steve pursed his lips, thinking. "Oh, maybe a month. Just went out, maybe five or six times. And then I got busy, and next I heard she was dating Joe. We had no hard feelings, though. He was a better match for her."

"Why?" I asked.

"You know me. Kind of a restless guy. I travel a lot, I've had a lot of jobs, I like to move around, go out at night. Ava was more like—let's stay home, sit and talk, drink some wine. More gentle and homey, like. Joe is like that, too. Poor old Joe." He shook his head. He had picked up Major and started petting him, and Major purred, looking at us out of slitted eyes.

I studied Steve's face and decided I could get more information. "What was Ava like otherwise? What else did she like to do?"

The men both looked surprised, and I said, "She died at my tea house. And I'm trying to figure out how someone like her could have enemies."

Steve nodded. "I couldn't believe it when I heard."

"Who did you hear it from?" my father asked.

"From Father Istvan, at the church. Father Steve. Like me. I went to morning Mass, and he said, 'Have you heard?' I couldn't believe it."

"Was she unhappy?" I asked.

Steve sighed. "It was hard to tell. She was so nice, but that's not the same as happy. I know she had a lot of sadness. She grew up in Hungary, lived there until she was eighteen. Then she lived in Vienna for quite some time, and other parts of Austria. It's not clear why she left her family. She had two sisters, and one of them had been very sick from birth. She died, this little sister. Ava didn't forget her, not ever. I think that sadness stays with you."

"How terrible," I said.

"The sisters loved Ava very much. The little one, the sick one, gave her this special stone, something she'd gotten as a gift. And she—what is it?—bequeathed it to Ava. So Ava took it with her everywhere. It was really neat. She let me hold it. They say sometimes that these rocks and stones can calm you down, stuff like that. I always felt like her rock did that. Felt good to hold it."

"Was it a bloodstone?" I asked. My lips felt numb.

"A bloodstone. Yes. Had some fancy name."

"Heliotrope," I said.

"Yes!" Steve boomed, and Major wriggled in his arms.

"So this bloodstone came from her family. What was her name, before she married Joe Novák?"

Steve set Major down with a final pat. "Fodor. Ava Fodor. That's the lady I dated."

"Was she married to anyone else, in Hungary or in Austria? Or was that her family name?"

My father was staring at me with a bemused expression.

Steve didn't seem to mind my interrogation. "No, she never married. I was surprised when she married Joe. She was flirty, fun, but at the same time she seemed—solitary, you know? Even when she was with me, she seemed alone."

This comment brought a palpable sadness into the room. "Did she ever say anything else about Hungary, Steve? Anything about her family?"

He shrugged. "Just that she always had wanted to leave, but she stayed for this sickly little one, the sister. But finally it was the little sister who told her to leave. She said, 'Go live for us both,' or something. That is when she gave the stone, I guess. Ava said it was like a blessing. She did this for her sister."

I nodded, thinking this over. Steve said, "Let me go get the shots ready. The doctor will come in soon to look over this little guy." He shook my dad's hand and punched his arm, more lightly this time, and then he blustered back out the door.

"He's intense," I said.

My father said, "Look who's talking. When did you become a cop?"

I shrugged. "I heard a lot, when they asked us to read all

those transcripts. I guess I learned some facts and some—interrogation techniques."

He laughed. "A new career for Hana."

"My career is fine." Major had edged toward me and was butting me with his head. "And it seems like Major is fine, too."

"Yeah. We should be out of here in ten or twenty minutes. Do you want to come for dinner?"

I pretended to punch his arm, Steve Sarka–style, and my dad laughed. "No—I have some stuff I have to do tonight. But I'll take a rain check."

"Good. I haven't had a chance to really chat with you in a while."

I knew this meant he was still curious about my love life, and I sent him a suspicious glance, which made him laugh again. Then he shrugged. "You can tell me, or I'll have to get my information secondhand from your mother and grandmother."

"Good point. I'll come by on Friday."

This pleased him. When we left with Major, he slung an arm around me and said, "Things will get better, my baby Haniska."

I drove home in the dark, tucked into my parking spot, and sat in my car for a while, looking at the stars. I had information, but I was not obligated to give it to the police. It was Wolf's job, and Benton's, to find this out. Maybe they had already spoken to Steve Sarka. They should have, if they were doing their jobs. And I knew firsthand that Wolf asked very thorough questions. So there was no need for me to call them.

And yet. Ava had been murdered, essentially under my

nose. And if I could help to catch the person who had done it, then I should certainly embrace that responsibility. I sighed and dug out Wolf's card. I didn't dial his cell number, but the one at the station. It rang and rang, and I got his voice mail. I ended the call. I looked up the main number for the police station and asked to speak with Benton; I got his voice mail as well.

I leaned my head back on my seat and closed my eyes. Then I opened them and looked at the stars again. They really did twinkle. What created that effect?

I thought of Ava Novák and her ailing little sister.

I dialed another number. He picked up on the second ring. "Hana?"

"Yes. I tried the station, but no one was available."

"Hana, I'm so glad you called—"

"I have some information, Detective Wolf. I am not calling for any other reason."

A silence. "What information?"

"I spoke with Steve Sarka. He works at the vet, and I was there with my father's cat. Steve said that Ava's maiden name was Fodor, which you probably already know. He said that she had two little sisters in Hungary that she loved, and she stayed around for their sake when she really wanted to leave."

"Okay." Somehow I knew he was jotting this down in his ubiquitous notebook.

"Her younger sister had some terrible ailment, and she died. Before she died she gave Ava a stone. I asked Steve if it was a bloodstone and he said yes, heliotrope. He said Ava took it everywhere as a remembrance of this sister."

Wolf inhaled loudly. "And someone at the party got angry with her because of the stone. You said there was another sister?"

"Yes, Steve said two sisters."

"But Ava had no sisters at the event, did she? Or even sisters in America?"

"Not that I know of, no."

"This is very interesting. Did he say anything else?"

"Only that she was very private, liked being alone. That she seemed alone even when he was with her. That she was shrouded in sadness. Oh, and that she had never married before she married Joe."

I heard the scratching of his pen on paper. I wondered what his home looked like, what sort of visitors he received there, what family he had.

His pen stopped scratching, and he said, "Hana."

"What?"

"I think you misunderstood me today. When I said I had made a mistake—"

Anger flared in me. "I understood. You found evidence that you thought implicated my elderly grandmother in a murder, implicated our whole family, maybe, and you thought, 'What have I done? How could I have been so unprofessional? I'm a police officer first and foremost. And now I may have gotten involved with some sort of criminal seductress who distracted me from her guilt as a poisoner by feeding me lunch and kissing me with significant passion. I need to put things right. I'll pretend I don't even know Hana Keller. I'll refuse to make eye contact with her so that my partner believes I'm a humorless police officer who would never do something as foolish as become attracted to a woman.'"

Silence. Then he said, "I didn't handle things well, Hana. But that's not how it was."

"I have to go. Good luck with the case."

"Hana—"

I ended the call and looked back at the stars.

Chapter 17

The Witch with the Iron Nose

The next morning I lay in bed, contemplating the rain outside my window. We had planned to use a day free of events to mop the floors and wash the draperies in the tea house, but my mother had called to say Grandma felt under the weather, so we would postpone the tasks until the next week.

I let my eyes linger on the things I loved: Isabella and Fairy on my windowsill, the stacks of books on my shelves, the family photos in green and blue metal frames, the bits of porcelain I had collected over ten or so years. My room was a beautiful place, and beauty was important to me, had always been so, as a way of replenishing my soul. I reached for my iPad, which sat on my little white nightstand, and went to my music library. I pulled up Brahms's *Hungarian Dances*, the ones my mother loved, and played them softly as I looked at the rain.

In less than a week my life had been drastically altered.

I had seen death, literally looked at its face when I had never expected to do so, and I had fallen prey to what my grandmother had always feared: a wolf. My eyes went to a bag in the corner of my room. It contained the butterfly teacup, the prize that had brought me such joy and excitement, and I hadn't summoned the courage to unpack it.

I picked up Fairy and ran my hands over her smooth, cool glaze, absorbing the loveliness of her peacock blue exterior. When I held something beautiful in my hands, I always thought of John Keats's words: "Beauty is truth, truth beauty,—that is all / Ye know on earth, and all ye need to know." In college, studying those words in Keats's famous poem about a Grecian urn, our class had struggled to understand Keats's intention, and what the final words, spoken by the urn itself, could have meant. But the older I got, and the more I immersed myself in an appreciation of artistic creations, the more I understood why Keats gave the urn its own voice. Of course art spoke to us, all the time, and it told us in its silent message that it was everything, everything we needed to sustain ourselves.

I sighed. Antony and Cleopatra, already on my bed, moved closer to me and snuggled against me. Really, this was what rainy days were for. I closed my eyes and listened to Brahms and the rain.

Katie called me an hour later, accusing me of severing her from my life. Katie was melodramatic, always, mostly because she thought it was funny. She lived in downtown Chicago, a good hour from me, and we had less opportunity to see each other than we had assumed we would when we left college. Katie worked at an advertising firm which paid her a crazy amount of money but also demanded crazy hours.

We kept in touch mainly via texting and Facebook and Snapchat photos. She had sent me one the night before, a picture of her at some jazz club in the city. She had captured her current boyfriend, Eduardo, in the background; he was obviously enjoying the music, while Katie's face had been less than enthusiastic. It had made me laugh.

"I'm not severing you from my life. In fact, I need a good old girls' night so that I can talk about men and their endless perfidy."

"Ooh—this sounds bad. But also sort of exciting," she said.

"Are you eating popcorn?"

"Yes." It was Katie's favorite snack.

"Stop chewing into the phone."

"Okay, I'm putting it aside. Now tell me. Who is the new guy?"

"There is no new guy. There *was* a new guy for literally a couple of hours. He managed to ruin things the following morning by being incredibly rude to my grandmother and ignoring me."

"Oh no. Did you Zsa Zsa him?"

"*No*. He is the guilty party here, Katie."

"All right, geez. For him to get you so hot, he must *be* hot."

"No comment."

"Come on! Do you have a photo?"

"No, I don't have a photo." I glared out the window. "But I happened to be looking around online, when I first met him, and I found a picture of him getting some sort of award a couple years ago. Google 'Detective Erik Wolf, Riverwood Police Department.' That's Erik with a *k*."

"Awesome." I heard Katie rustling, probably reaching for her phone and typing away. Then she gasped. "Oh, wow.

Oh, man, Hana—that is one good-looking betrayer. A little bit wrinkled in the clothing department, but very good-looking."

"*Anyway.* How are you and Eduardo doing? It's been what—three weeks now?"

"Yeah. He's okay. He's no *Detective Wolf*," she joked.

"Stop it. I'm still feeling murderous." I froze then, my eyes on the branches of a tree that waved gently outside my window. Katie was talking, but I didn't hear her.

"Hana?"

"What? Sorry, I was spacing out for a minute. Katie—do you think a woman would kill over a man?"

"Do I think she would? I *know* she would. Because I read the headlines and watch true crime. Women kill out of jealousy all the time."

"Yes, yes. I wonder . . ."

"You're talking like someone in a movie. What's going on?"

"You know that someone died at the tea house."

"Yeah—you texted me. It's so bizarre. I would have bet good money that if anyone was going to die at one of our jobs, it would be someone at Imperius. Advertising is a cut-throat business."

"And you would think tea parties would be pretty safe. But no one is safe from jealousy, right? How long do you think a woman could hold a grudge?"

Katie laughed in my ear. "You're seriously asking me that? You, the woman who can't forgive her first-grade teacher because she wouldn't read the book you wanted at story time?"

"It wasn't just any book. It was *Alice's Adventures in Wonderland*," I said, indignant.

"You're proving my point."

I sighed noisily in her ear. "Anyway, I might not be available for about a week yet. We have a lot going on at the tea house."

"Yeah, and I'm on a project that is ridiculously time-consuming."

"Is Eduardo on it with you?"

"Yeah. This is how we met, silly."

"So is he distracting you with his sexiness?"

She sounded disappointed. "Not really. He occasionally distracts me by being wrong, and then we have to argue until he sees it my way."

"And people think *I'm* controlling."

"Maybe all women are," she said.

Even after we said good-bye and I put the phone down, I pondered that idea—controlling women, and how angry they might get when things didn't go their way.

~

Two hours later I called my grandmother. "How are you feeling? Is Grandpa taking care of you?"

"He will, when he comes back. He pick up something we order at the store. New TV—very big." Her nose sounded stuffy, even over the phone.

"Wow! Remind me to come and watch movies at your house."

"Yes, we would like."

"Anyway, I'm going to come over and make you some lunch. If you have a cold, you should have some chicken soup, right? And we already made the noodles. I'll just come and make the broth."

"Good girl. Tank you, Hana." She gave in so quickly I knew she must be genuinely under the weather.

I packed up some ingredients for the soup and fed the

cats, then locked my apartment and drove to the Fair Price Grocery on the edge of Riverwood. I picked up a few things that I needed at home, then got a box of chocolates and a couple boxes of lotion tissue for my grandma and proceeded to the checkout lane. I knew Maria, the checkout girl, so well that I almost considered her a friend. I had seen her once at one of the Hungarian events—some picnic or wedding or party where I was the guest rather than the hostess. Since then I'd always said hello to her at the store. We had discussed many things across the conveyor belt, from food to men to movies to the meaning of life. Today, with her dark hair wrapped up in a bandanna, she reminded me a bit of the Gypsies my grandmother so greatly feared.

"Hey, Maria."

"Hey! Looks like someone's sick," she said, her voice sympathetic.

"Yeah, my grandma. I'm going to go make her some soup."

"Well, you could not be a more ideal grandchild," she said, grinning. "I might buy my grandma some Campbell's, but that's about it. I don't have the magical touch in the kitchen."

I smiled. "Are you having a nice fall?"

She shrugged. "It's not officially fall yet, right?"

"I think it was the twenty-first. So it's been fall for about a week."

"Who knew? I'll have to start putting out some pumpkins. Okay, that comes to thirty-four fifty-three." We chatted while she got my change and bagged my groceries, about a Netflix show we both liked, about cool weather, about cats versus dogs (she had both). An elderly man pushed his cart into her aisle, so I waved and said farewell.

"I'll check in to see what you think of that series when you finish it," I said.

"Good! I need someone to talk to—no one else I know watches it!" she called.

I went back to my car and drove across town to my grandparents' house. It was a small brick building with impeccable landscaping (my grandfather's touch) and, inside, the amazing smell of food (my grandmother's touch). I found Grandma sitting in a big living room chair; she was wrapped in one of her own crocheted afghans.

I patted her hair and felt her forehead.

"Not a fever," she said, sniffling. "Just a cold. Maybe I caught from the policeman."

"Do you want some Pálinka?"

"No. Make the good Hungarian cure."

"That's kind of strong."

Her voice was raspy. "Ya. Probably good."

"Okay, Grandma." I went back to the kitchen. I found a lemon and sliced it up on a cutting board. Then I poured a cup of water into a small pot and turned on the heat; to this I added the lemon and two teaspoons of sugar (when I was the patient and still living at home, my parents had sometimes replaced this with honey, especially if I had a sore throat). While this mixture softened, I went to Grandpa's liquor cabinet and pulled out a bottle of his J&B. I poured a shot glass of the whisky and added it to Grandma's cold mixture. Stepping away from the pot, I lit a match and ignited the contents. Blue flame shot up, spectacular in the shadowy kitchen, and eventually burned away the alcohol. I poured the hot whiskey and lemon, rinds and all, into a cup for Grandma, and brought it out to her.

"Let's get you to bed first," I said. I helped her walk into her bedroom; of course her bed was made with almost military precision, with Grandma's favorite soft doll in Hungarian traditional dress sitting against some colorful crocheted pillows. I tossed all of these onto a chair by the window and helped her climb under her covers.

I handed her the drink and said, "This is very hot."

"Yah." She inhaled it for a few moments, her eyes closed. Then she took little sips, as much liquid as she could get down without burning her tongue. "Good for da cold," she said. "Even ven I vas little."

Her accent had grown stronger as her body had grown weaker. I watched her drink almost the entire cup, and then she smiled at me and closed her eyes.

I returned to the kitchen and cleaned up my dishes, then got to work on the chicken soup I had planned to make her.

Grandpa got home and smiled at me. "Hey! You want to help me carry a big box?"

I went out to the driveway, where his trunk stood open to reveal his exciting purchase, and together we managed to wrestle the new television box into the house. He had already given away his old TV, so I helped him remove the flat screen from its protective foam and set it on their entertainment console. Grandpa looked pleased. "I set it up later. Your mama says we will like Netflix."

"You two are just so modern," I said with a grin, smoothing a wayward tuft of his white hair. I checked on the soup, put it on simmer, and then sat on the couch with my grandfather, who had found himself a beer.

"Grandpa."

"Yah."

"What can you tell me about the witch with the iron nose?"

"*Boszorkány* is 'witch' in Hungarian. Lots of witch tales and stories, I guess. The witch is sort of the dark fairy, the creature who push out of the—what? Under earth. Underworld. Vasorrú Bába is more like saying 'the bad old woman,' the opposite of the good fairy," he said.

"Yes. What did you know about her, growing up?"

He shrugged. "Just stories, at home, at school. In some, she is just an old witch, sometime even kindly. But in the worse ones—she is horrible. Full of teeth, waiting in the forest to bite, bite at you. Or as an invisible soul that absorbs your soul and all souls. Sometime she eats children, or boils the water to cook the child."

"That's hideous. What sort of parents told folktales like that?"

"*Grimm's Fairy Tales* are cruel, ya?"

He had me there. "So—she's cruel to children, especially?"

"Ya, I suppose, like all those witches in tales."

I thought of Ava's little sisters. If Ava's murderer had been the woman who yelled at her in the bathroom, then that person had been particularly offended by the stone. Had that person known Ava's family? Had the person thought Ava was cruel to her little sisters? Is that why the killer would compare Ava to the witch?

My grandfather got up and moved behind the TV, studying the various wires and plug-ins. Their mail carrier, wearing a yellow rain slicker that made him look like a New England fisherman, appeared on the porch. Their mail dropped into the box with a plunk. The mailman, through the little window next to their front door, saw me and waved, then pointed at a package on their stoop.

"Grandpa, your mail is here. I'll grab it before it gets all wet."

"Good," he said, his face hidden behind the television.

I pulled their few letters and bills from the box, grabbed

the package, and came back in. The rain, which had briefly pelted me, had felt cold on my skin; I was glad to think of my grandmother, warm under her covers with whisky coursing through her veins.

I set the mail down on the dining room table and contemplated my grandpa, who had already gotten the television to go on, and was now fiddling with the new remote. "Wow, you're almost as good with electronics as Grandma is."

"Yes, she teaches me," he joked.

"Grandpa, do you know Joe Novák?"

He set the remote down and looked mournful. "Ya. We were the two who run the whole Christmas coat drive last year, down at the church."

"But isn't Joe a member of St. Stephen's? You and Grandma go to St. Anthony's, don't you?"

He nodded. "But the drive was three parishes. So we work together. Good leaders." He held out his arm and made a muscle for some reason.

"Have you talked to him, since Ava?"

He shook his head. "Still too soon. In a few weeks, I'll take him for a drink somewhere. She was good for him. I hope he is okay, knowing she is in heaven."

I plopped on the couch. "What made them good together?"

My grandfather looked out at the rain for a while. "She was quiet, sad. He is the kind of man who can let someone be herself. He didn't try to change her. He loved her for what she was."

This moved me, and made the rain outside seem more like tears running down the window. "And what did she do for him? What made him so sure he wanted to marry her when every Hungarian lady in town was after him?"

"She was talented. She sang, played the piano, entertained him always. He said it was like hearing an angel sing."

I stood up. "I have to check on my soup." I walked back into the kitchen and stared down into the fragrant broth, full of Grandma's fresh noodles. As I inhaled the healing aroma, I could think of only one thing: who would want to kill an angel?

~

My grandmother woke up an hour later and looked much brighter around the eyes. She scuffed to the table and ate a whole bowl of soup, praising my efforts. "Delicious, Haniska."

"I have to get going soon. Grandpa has almost got your new TV working, and he and I had a nice talk."

"About what?" she said, sipping soup from her spoon.

"Vasorrú Bába. Joe Novák. Ava's musical talent. Stuff like that."

Grandma looked at him, smirking. "What you know about Vasorrú Bába?"

He shrugged. "Everyone knows a little. And now Hana does."

I pushed the letters toward Grandma. "You got mail. Something to look at while you're resting."

She made a *pffft* sound and said, "All bills, I guess." She started going through them, tossing some of the junk mail into a wastebasket and opening others and setting them aside.

"Do you think you'll be well enough to go to work tomorrow? We have the tea party for that St. Stephen's fundraiser. Your Hungarian friends will be back for more of François's delicacies."

She nodded. “First day of cold is the bad day. Tomorrow I’ll be fine.” She pulled the package toward her and said, “I think your mama and dad come tonight, so I have many caretakers.”

She turned in her chair and opened a drawer on her sideboard to retrieve a knife. Something happened then—it wasn’t like movie slow motion, but it was as though time paused and gave me long moments to reflect on what was before me: the square package wrapped in brown butcher paper, the multitude of stamps in the upper-right corner, the typed label with my grandmother’s name and address. The lack of a return address.

She turned back around, holding a letter opener, and my hand reached out to cover hers before I had a conscious thought to protect her. “No, Grandma. Don’t open that.”

She looked at me, and her hazel eyes did that thing they had done when Wolf interviewed her: they seemed to grow luminous, full of knowledge. “No,” she agreed. “I should not.” She put the knife down and I went to my purse to retrieve my phone. Once again I pulled out Wolf’s card, and once again I dialed the police station number. This time he answered at work.

“Detective Wolf.”

“It’s Hana.” I heard fear in my own voice.

“What’s happened?” he said, his voice urgent.

“My grandmother has received a package. We both feel wrongness around it. I don’t want her to open it.”

“Put it outside, far from the house. Give me her address,” Wolf said. “I’ll be right there.”

Chapter 18

Good and Bad Fairies

The package sat on the sidewalk, in the rain, like a sad neglected bundle dropped from someone's grocery bag.

Grandma, Grandpa, and I sat inside, fascinated by the police cars and the interesting outfits of the people on the bomb squad, who approached the box with bizarre equipment and started to open it inside a protected container.

Wolf and Benton finally came in, looking damp, and began their barrage of questions. What had alerted us to a problem? Did we have any idea who sent it?

"It was all the stamps," I said. "You put on stamps like that when you don't get something weighed at the post office. When you're guessing at how much it will cost. I thought, someone wanted to mail it without being seen, or make it look as though it had been mailed. That's why there's no return address, nothing to trace it to them."

Wolf turned to my grandmother. "What made you suspicious?"

She shrugged. "The feeling of it. A burden. Heavy. Wrong."

Wolf's pen hovered over his notebook, probably trying to figure out how to quantify her instinctive response.

"They've got it open," Benton said. "Hang on." He went outside and conferred with the men on the sidewalk. He brought the box back in and showed us its contents. "Don't touch, just look," he said.

Inside the box was a little wicker basket with a pretty pink teapot/teacup combination, one of those single-serving things you can buy as a gift, along with a tea bag and a little note, also typed, that said, "Thank you for hosting the Magyar Women's Monthly Tea Gathering! With gratitude, the women of St. Stephen's Parish."

"All typed, and no signature," I said.

Wolf nodded. "Have you ever received a thank-you gift, or card, from the group before?"

"No," Grandma said.

Wolf prodded the contents with his pen. "Normally, if you get tea as a gift—don't the tea bags come wrapped in paper? Or in a box of tea bags?"

I leaned in and looked at the tea bag. "The tag says 'Lipton.' This is just taken from one of those big standard boxes of black tea. They just grabbed one rather than give a whole box. Which is either really cheap or really weird."

"Maybe more sinister than that," Wolf said. "We'll need to take this, have it tested."

Benton said, "Do you have security cameras?"

My grandfather sat with us at the table, and he laughed. "Why would we?"

Benton nodded. "Okay—did anyone see this get delivered?"

I raised my hand. "I saw the mailman come, in his yellow

slicker. He dropped the letters in the box, and he saw me and pointed to the box on the ledge, because it wouldn't fit through the letter slot. But—I don't know if he actually put the box there."

"We'll find out. Do you know the name of your letter carrier?" Wolf asked my grandparents.

Grandpa said, "I just know William. That's what I call him."

"William is great. Thank you." Wolf stood up and smoothed down the sleeve of his rain-wrinkled shirt. "We'll get out of your way; I'll notify you when I find out about the contents of your box. Meanwhile, don't open anything else that looks suspicious. Luckily, it seems that your instincts are strong enough to protect you."

My grandparents nodded. Wolf's green eyes met mine. "Hana, if you could come with me, I have something to give you."

I followed him, wondering if he had lost his memory with the stress of the case. We had just done this in the parking lot of Maggie's Tea House. Had he forgotten that he already gave me back the teacup? I certainly hadn't forgotten that moment—the crushing disappointment of it, the terrible plunging hopes.

I paused on my grandparents' front porch. Benton had already moved outside to talk to the remaining techs out on the lawn. "You already gave me the butterfly cup," I said. "I have it at home. I haven't had the courage to open it."

"This is something else," Wolf said. He searched in a corner of the porch and handed me a green bag that I recognized; it had the name of Falken's store on the outside—the words "Timeless Treasures" with the little antique clock logo. I had several of those bags folded up in a drawer at home, recycled from my frequent visits to the store.

"What—did I leave this somewhere?" I asked, confused.

"I have to run. Call if anything else seems odd. We'll have a patrol car keep an eye on this house for the next twenty-four hours." He waved and moved swiftly out the screen door of the closed-in porch.

I went inside to find my grandfather tucking his wife into her chair with her blanket and a piece of chocolate. "You're sweet," I said. "And I'm going. I'll see you tomorrow, Grandma."

"Enough excitement for one day?" she asked.

"Yes. More than enough. Wolf says the police will be watching the house. So you're safe."

She gestured toward my grandfather, white-haired but solid with railroad muscle. "I was already safe."

I waved and went to my car. Once again I sat in it for a while without starting the engine. Had someone in fact sent something harmful to my grandmother? If so, why her? The box had been specifically addressed with her name. So either someone from the Magyar Women was genuinely sending her a thank-you, or someone was specifically targeting her in a way that seemed friendly and even generous.

The Jekyll and Hyde discussion came back into my thoughts. The lovely pink teapot, so alluring to anyone who enjoyed fine gifts, or tea, or both, could merely be the happy face over an evil intention.

I turned to look at the Timeless Treasures bag on my seat. Too curious to wait now, I pulled open the bag to find a white envelope and something wrapped in tissue paper. I opened the envelope, and then a card with a reproduction of a painting by Albrecht Dürer, a dozing cat sitting outside while a mouse sits behind him, and looked within to see Wolf's handwriting, which I recognized from the jottings in his notebook.

The card said:

Dear Hana,

When I said I had made a mistake, what I meant was that I had allowed myself to like you so much that I couldn't look at you without giving myself away. That's why I avoided your gaze, and I realize that is a paltry excuse, and that as usual I did a terrible job of explaining myself. I don't seem to find the right words when I'm in front of you, especially not when you're looking at me with those dark eyes that can destroy me before I even begin.

Your grandmother sent me to this store, and your friend Falken suggested you might like this. I hope you will accept it, not only as an apology, but as a gift from someone who would like to earn the right to give you more gifts in the future.

—Erik

I felt hot inside then, as though I had drunk my grandmother's whisky cure. I lifted the tissue paper, unwrapping it carefully to find a blue Herend porcelain rose, nestled into three green porcelain leaves. I had seen these before in the Herend catalog, had watched videos about how they were crafted by hand, layer by layer, then colored with the deep, rich blues and greens, then glazed to shining perfection.

I held Wolf's blue flower in my hand and felt as though bolts of light were shooting through my limbs. I wrapped the rose tenderly in its protective paper and tucked it back in the bag.

I started my car and drove home, smiling at the darkness.

After tending to the cats and giving a cursory cleaning to my apartment, I returned to my room and flipped on my table lamp so that the whole space was bathed in a warm, cozy glow. I took out the Herend rose and placed it carefully on one of my white shelves, in a spot where both sunlight and lamplight would illuminate its beautiful, shining blue surface. I tucked Wolf's note beside it.

I glanced at the book of fairy tales I had read earlier, and on a whim I grabbed it again. My grandfather hadn't given me much input about the witch, but perhaps I could learn more about fairies to help add some cultural insight to the police investigation. I flopped on my bed with the book in my hand and began paging through it. I caught a glimpse of my phone and found I couldn't resist it.

I picked it up and dialed Wolf's cell number. "Hana?" he said after one ring.

"Hello."

"How are you?" He sounded casual, but nervous.

"Erik—that was a very generous gift. I'm probably not worthy of it, but I loved it and I've given it a special place on my shelf. Thank you very much. You shouldn't have spent—"

"I don't care what I spent. I just needed you to know—I wasn't trying to be cruel, or rude, or heartless."

"I understand. You said you were in a difficult position, and I get that."

He cleared his throat. "And in all honesty I wasn't pleased to find what seemed like incriminating evidence about your grandmother in Ava Novák's papers."

"I know. I was a little shocked myself, at first. It's been a very stressful couple of days."

"We're working hard to end this for you."

"I—thank you for that."

He cleared his throat. A moment of silence. Then he said, "Hana. Give me a second chance?"

I stared at Isabella, counted fronds on her gentle branches, trying to make the moment last. "I think I can do that."

He exhaled his relief and said, "Thank you. I'm glad."

I turned a page and looked at the face of a vengeful fairy. "I don't recommend giving me the silent treatment again."

"Point taken," Wolf said. Then, his tone lightening, he said, "How are my friends Antony and Cleopatra?"

I laughed. "Lazy. Sleeping on my feet. I'm in my little kingdom, my room, which is where I like to hole up when it's raining."

"I'd like to see your room," said Wolf in what could be construed only as a suggestive tone.

"I'd like that, too." I smiled and turned another page. "Oh—there's something I forgot to tell you. My grandpa told me that a lot of the old witch tales were about her cruelty to children. She lured them into the woods and bit them with sharp teeth, or she devoured them or cooked them—"

"Good God," said Wolf.

"But I was thinking—whoever called Ava 'Vasorrú Bába' might have been thinking of cruelty to a child. And then I thought—Ava had that little sister who was ill. What if it had something to do with that?"

"That's good, Hana. Let me write that down." He scribbled something. "But you said that Sarka told you Ava loved her little sisters."

"Yes, he said she lived for them. So it doesn't seem to mesh, and yet the only link I've heard between Ava and children is about the little siblings. Ava must have been significantly older if she was already contemplating leaving home and these little girls were still so young. Maybe the mother or father married twice? Maybe they were half sisters? In any case, Steve said Ava left home at eighteen, so the sisters were much younger than that."

"If they're half sisters they might have a different name," Wolf said, still scribbling.

"In any case, I just thought you should—oh God. Oh no."

"What's wrong? Are you all right? Is someone there?"

I had turned a page, and an image flashed up at me, horrible and familiar. A woman with a teacup; a butterfly on the rim; a witch with a vengeful expression . . .

"No. Erik—I'm looking through this book of Hungarian tales about fairies, both good and bad. I've had it since I was a kid, but it was probably something my grandmother had when she was tiny. I read one the other night, and I thought I'd read some more, and one—there's a story here, with an illustration of a girl drinking tea."

"Yes?"

"It's called 'The Woman Who Angered the Witch.' There's a picture of a girl drinking out of a teacup, and there's a butterfly perched on one side of the cup, and another in the girl's hair. But the witch is standing behind her and has wrapped her own long hair around the girl's neck, and she's about to pull it tight with one hand, and the other hand is dropping something into the girl's tea."

"Whoa. Bring that book to me tomorrow, can you? Or should I stop by your place and get it?"

"You can do that; I'm leaving at about ten o'clock."

"I'll be there at eight," Wolf said.

"This is bad, very bad," I said.

"Why?"

"Because a woman might have based her revenge, or whatever it was, on this detail. But also because that day, the day Ava died, my grandmother saw a fairy in the cup. You see? It was Mrs. Kalas's cup, but that doesn't necessarily mean anything. It's just that the fairy emerged at all and Ava died. This is a terrible omen."

Wolf's voice was staid and practical. "Only if you believe in witches and fairies."

Chapter 19

The Woman Who Angered the Witch

Wolf showed up the following morning at eight. I was already wearing my tea house white blouse and black skirt and trying to tame my thick hair, still damp from the shower, with a fragrant smoothing mist. I buzzed him up to my apartment and went to the door. I had been prepared to be very detached and professional so that Wolf could see I was adhering to his guidelines, waiting to show affection until the case was solved. I was going to show him the picture, hand him the book, and wish him a friendly good-day.

Instead, I opened the door and got one sight of him and his intense green-eyed stare before he pulled me against him and kissed me. I kissed him back, twining around him instinctively. "Hana," he said softly. "I missed you."

"Good," I said. Then, "I missed you, too."

His smile was half wince. "I thought you'd never speak to me again. I can't tell you how bad I felt in the parking lot outside your tea house, watching you stalk away. I didn't know a human body could be that rigid."

I laughed. "You deserved it. But I'm sorry if I—jumped to conclusions. You *appeared* extremely rude and thoughtless."

"I know. I'm sorry." The cats were milling around below us, and Wolf bent to pet them. When he stood up again, I was ready with an admission. "I have sort of a reputation in my family, with my temper. It's not deserved, I don't think. Just based on something I did when I was a toddler. But they call me Zsa Zsa, you know—for Zsa Zsa Gabor."

Wolf frowned. "I don't really want to face Zsa Zsa again. I like Hana."

I put my hands on his chest. "Hana likes you."

"I've been eating that food you gave me. I think I have an addiction."

"That's fine. I'll be your supplier."

He smiled at that. "I guess you'd better show me this book."

"Sure. Come on." I led him to my room, where the book still sat on my bedside table. He became immediately distracted by my amazing bookshelves.

"Wow—this is fantastic! Did this come with the apartment?"

"No. My dad made them, with help from my grandpa and grandma. She did the electrical work—see how two of the shelves have lighting? And Dad designed the whole thing. Grandpa is a great carpenter, so it was a family endeavor."

Wolf was looking at the photographs; he smiled at the picture of Domo and me holding hands. He picked up the photo of my great-grandmother and said, "Who is this?"

"That's Natalia. Grandma's mother. She's in Hungary there, Budapest, but she came over here in the 1980s, with

Grandma and Grandpa and their little children. Grandma says Natalia was the one, really, who had—you know—abilities. Grandma says she could talk to nature, and that she understood things about people."

"Huh." He studied the photograph for another five seconds, then set it down. He spied the blue rose and turned to smile at me. "That looks good here, on Hana's shelf of treasures."

"It does. I love it." We were silent for a moment, looking into each other's eyes across a distance of about five feet. I broke the spell and said, "Speaking of treasures, how did you happen to talk to my grandmother about Falken's store?"

"I called her." He folded his arms and looked down at his shoes. "After you gave me that—deep freeze in the parking lot. I knew I was doomed unless I got help. She was a bit reluctant at first—"

I could only imagine. A wolf calling her on the phone.

"—but then she said I might want to look at the store, to ask the owner about your preferences."

"You couldn't have found anything more beautiful."

"Yes I could," he said, his gaze lifting to look at me.

That whisky feeling was back in my veins. "Anyway, I love it, and I will always treasure it. Here's the book."

He took it from me and studied the cover.

"Page eighty-five," I said.

He flicked pages until he reached the story about the woman drinking the fairy's poisoned tea. His face actually paled. "Oh, wow. I see what you mean." He sat down on the edge of my bed, a bed which I had made the moment I jumped out of it at six thirty that morning because I am my grandmother's granddaughter. "We did some research on Ava's family. She did have two sisters, Vera and Magda. It was Magda who was very ill; we think she had tuberculosis. What I need to find out is if this book in particular—what's the copyright?" He flipped back and looked. "Yes, it's old. Published in 1958. I need to determine whether or not her family would have had access to a copy of this book in particular, with these illustrations. And maybe whoever did this knew of the book, too. Which would mean, if we follow that hypothesis, that the two women knew each other long ago."

I sat down beside him. "And if that's true, then when the murderer, who was already planning to kill Ava, saw the butterfly teacup, she saw an opportunity to get some poetic justice. To make the fairy story come true. And Ava would have realized it too late, when she saw the writing on the cup. If she saw it at all. Did she—suffer?"

Wolf shook his head. "She ingested cyanide; it killed her very quickly."

I stared. "Where would a little old lady get cyanide? Or know anything about it?"

"You're falling prey to an illusion. They're elderly, and they have accents, but they're not automatically harmless."

My stomach felt sick. "Jekyll and Hyde," I said.

"You bet. And it's my job to find Hyde. In everyone." His face was solemn.

I took his hand in mine. "That has to be depressing."

"It is, some days. Other times it's a challenge, even a moral obligation. I owe this to Ava and to anyone else who might be threatened by this person." His phone rang and he touched the screen. "Wolf," he said.

I moved out of the room to give him privacy; I went to my kitchen and looked out at the grassy hill; green- and wheat-colored blades waved and bowed in a gentle breeze. What a strange September it had been; what a strange world we lived in now . . . Wolf joined me moments later, and his face was grim. "Hana. You and your grandmother had good instincts."

I gasped. "The tea bag?"

He nodded. "I have to go."

"Before you do, you should know that we have an event today; it's some sort of fund-raiser for St. Stephen's. A lot of the same ladies will be in attendance."

"If I have time I'll stop by, but it might be better if I'm not there. Just keep your ears and eyes open and tell me anything that seems amiss. Based on what happened to your grandmother, I think someone is getting desperate, and that means they'll make mistakes."

"Why would they target Grandma, anyway?"

He started to shake his head and move away, but then he turned back. "How many of the Hungarian ladies know the rumor that your grandma's reading of the leaves is based on a real—ability?"

I shrugged. "I mean, it's not exactly talked about, but I've heard murmurings. Murmurings I didn't believe until recently, by the way. I thought it was just those ladies being melodramatic. Now—I see that they've probably had some experience with Grandma. So probably quite a few of them know. In fact—do you remember the testimony of Mrs. Kalas? You can look it up. She said something about how Grandma's whole family had 'the gift.'"

"And if Mrs. Kalas knows, how likely is it that everyone else knows?"

I didn't have to think about that one. "Very likely."

"In which case, whoever did this would want to silence your grandmother, who may have seen the truth in the leaves."

I thought about this, chewing on my lip. "But Grandma

has already talked to you. So if she knew something, she would have told you about it."

"Except that she didn't. Your grandmother didn't even tell me what she thinks she saw that day. Apparently she's gotten into the habit of keeping her instincts to herself."

I thought of my mother, frowning whenever Grandma mentioned a feeling. "That's true."

He pulled me into a sudden warm hug. "Don't worry. And don't be afraid to call me, if you hear anything suspicious."

He tucked the book under his arm and left my apartment, throwing one quick green glance over his shoulder.

~

The speaker at today's tea was Father Istvan, the pastor of St. Stephen's. He led all the assembled parishioners in a prayer and then told them why they needed to raise money for a sister parish with many parishioners in need. Then he moved aside and someone else came to the podium to explain the prizes they could win by buying today's raffle tickets.

I tuned them out and concentrated on my task of pouring tea and delivering sandwiches to the tables. François's work just got better and better, and today's food looked so delectable I felt tempted to steal one from a tray and eat it. This one, a tiny pumpernickel square, seemed to contain cream cheese, cucumbers, turkey, and sprouts, with the obligatory paprika sprinkled across the sliver of egg on top.

"Hallo, Haniska," said one of the women as I passed her table. She smiled at me, but I had trouble smiling back. Which of these women had killed someone? Which had sent a package to my grandmother, hoping that she would fix herself a cup of poisoned tea? I forced a pleasant expression onto my face and continued to the next table. A quick glance at my family members told me that my mother and grandmother faced the same challenge; their hostess faces were less bright than usual.

After the threat to my grandmother, both my father and grandfather had decided to attend today, and they sat like sentries in opposite corners of the tea house, observing the event in silence. There were men mixed in with the crowd, too, and their deep voices sounded unnatural in a room that was generally filled with the happy chatter of women.

Remembering what François had overheard from the bathroom window, I purposely visited the bathroom several times that day, lingering in a stall and looking at my cell phone, or elaborately checking my makeup at the mirror over the sinks. Most of the conversations I heard were about church things, or family updates, or gossip about someone's broken engagement or unexpected pregnancy. On the fourth visit to the bathroom, though, I happened to hear a conversation between Mrs. Kalas and Mrs. Sarka, and they seemed to be discussing Ava when they walked in the room.

"Joe is doing a little better, Father says," said Mrs. Kalas's recognizable voice. "He comes to morning Mass again. And he's eating better. People are taking turns making him dinner, lunch. He has a fridge full of *hurka*, *kolbász*, *paprikás*."

"Poor man," said Mrs. Sarka's voice. "He loved her so. You know she was so talented, yes, with music, singing, piano. She only just started singing again with Joe. Before, she was too sad. That's what Mrs. Toth said."

"Sad about what?" asked Mrs. Kalas. This was strange to me, since she must have heard all the rumors by now about Ava's life and death.

"Oh, family things. Steve said there was a lost sister, a dead sister. Not something you can forget. My own sister and brother are so dear to me."

"Yes," said Mrs. Kalas. "And what did she do for Joe? Sing and dance in their house?" She laughed a little, as though this was a ridiculous notion.

"She was teaching piano. Mrs. Toth says that she joined a local theater group. Played piano for them, for these shows where they sing."

"Musicals?"

"Yes, for musicals. She played for them and was taking part more, like."

This made me think of Margie; again I felt sad, for her and for Ava and for everyone in the world. People had such trouble connecting, such trouble loving one another.

"Steve said he went to see her show. She invite him, I guess."

"What show?"

"It was called *Freddie* and Something. Two names. I forget. She play the piano, like I say . . ." They had finished washing their hands and had wandered out the door. I left the stall and washed my hands for no reason, then went back out to the party.

François leaned out of the back room, spied me, and beckoned. He looked disturbed, so I made my way quickly to the kitchen and sat down on a stool near his workspace. "What's up?"

He went to the black messenger bag that he carried from work to school and pulled out the *Riverwood Star*. "Did you see the story about the lady who died here?"

"Uh—they printed one the day after, saying police were investigating a death . . ."

He shook his head, impatient. "No. This is worse." He handed me the newspaper and showed me the story, with the byline of Thomas Brayburn. The headline said "Tea Party Murder Raises Disturbing Questions."

"Oh no," I said.

"Read," said François.

I focused on the story, despite a horrible twisting feeling in my stomach.

A woman died of cyanide poisoning at Maggie's Tea House Thursday, police say. While the origin of the poison remains unknown, it is clear that tea was served to the dead woman, Riverwood resident Ava Novák, by someone other than tea house staff. Police are investigating any possible motives that would center on Novák, but they are also leaving open the possibility that this was a random crime, according to Riverwood Police Detective Greg Benton.

One of the store's owners, Maggie Keller, assured the press that this was a random, isolated, and tragic incident. "No one could have predicted that anything like this would happen," Keller said. "We have run this tea house since 1989 with not one negative incident, and we are filled with sorrow for Mrs. Novák's family and friends."

What Keller did not address was how a guest at the tea house was able to serve food or drink to another guest without being noticed, or what steps they might be taking to ensure that nothing like this could ever happen again. The Riverwood health inspector could not be reached for comment.

Novák's funeral services will be held at St. Stephen's Church on September 29.

"This seems slanted," I said. "It has an objective sound, but under that is this tone of judgment, judgment of my mother and of Maggie's Tea House."

François nodded, looking grim. "It is not good. It reflects on us all."

I touched his arm. "Oh God—you're not going to quit, are you? We love you, and we couldn't run this place without you."

His mouth curled in a pleased smile. "No, no. But I am glad they did not mention me by name, to tell the truth."

I sighed. "I get it. All we can do is hope this blows over. Or that the police will catch this person and then the story will be about her. Or him."

I took another look at the name: Thomas Brayburn. I would be getting back to him. "Do me a favor, François. Put that away and don't show it to the others. They have enough going on."

"Okay, *oui*," he said, slipping into French.

I returned to the main room, grabbing a cart for busing tables. My grandmother walked past me, looking pale. I tugged on her arm and pulled her into the little foyer where the restrooms were. "What's wrong?" I asked.

She looked into my eyes and seemed to read them like a text. Then she nodded. "Just my cold, I guess. Also that table in the center. Make me feel bad." I looked past her at the table in the middle of the hall. Seated around it were the people who had initially been Wolf's most likely suspects: Mrs. Kalas, Mrs. Pinkoczi, and Mrs. Guliban, along with Mrs. Sarka, her brother, Steve, and Father Istvan from St. Stephen's parish, and then two people I didn't recognize.

"You're probably exhausted; that can affect the emotions. Don't worry; they're finished eating. I'll bring their cakes when the time comes. You go sit in the back for a while and rest. Your cold has you feeling weak."

She nodded and walked away, toward the back room. Normally my grandmother would have put up a fight, lifted her chin, and said she felt fine. With a pang I wondered if her age were finally weakening her, allowing illness to have a bigger impact on her system.

I sighed and moved among the tables, collecting discarded napkins and empty sandwich trays. Various women said hello to me or asked how I was "holding up" since the event at which Ava had died.

As I pushed a cart toward the kitchen, my father appeared next to me. "Is Grandma okay?"

I shrugged. "She's got that bad cold. And of course—you know what happened yesterday. I think it has her feeling off-balance."

"Yes. How much longer is this thing?"

"They're getting dessert now, and I guess they'll call out the raffle winners. Then they'll start leaving after that. Once the chance to win is gone, people head home. And then we clean up."

"Good." He looked at his watch. "I have papers to grade, but I just wanted to keep an eye on things."

I lowered my voice, despite the loud chatter in the hall. "Have you seen anything weird?"

He smiled a little. "Everyone in here is a little bit weird. With their rosaries and saints' medallions and church gossip."

"Dad, your agnosticism is showing."

He grinned. "Hey, I bought a raffle ticket. That counts for something."

And in the final moments of the gathering, while people devoured François's pastel-glazed petit fours, the priest announced the raffle prizes: Steve Sarka won the grand prize iPad; a woman in an orange dress won one hundred dollars of free groceries; a man in a plaid suit won a month of casseroles made by church ladies; my father won a bottle of Pálinka.

After everyone left we all cleaned up together: my parents, my grandparents, and I. François left first, having polished his kitchen countertops to their usual gleaming state. He told me he had a date with Claire and wanted to get her some flowers.

My father hurried my mother out the door because he needed to do his schoolwork. My grandparents were close behind because my grandmother needed more rest. I walked out with them, and we locked the door together.

"No event tomorrow," my grandfather said. "So you will rest. No arguing." He pointed at my grandmother, who shrugged.

The two of them rarely displayed affection in public, so when my grandfather slung an arm around her as they walked to their car, I felt the surprising prick of tears in my eyes. I went to my own car, climbed in, and locked the doors.

Wolf came by that evening to return my book. It was storming outside, with dramatic flashes of lightning occasionally illuminating the dark corners of my apartment. I buzzed Wolf up and opened the door to find him looking slightly damp and shaking out an umbrella. The book was wrapped in a plastic bag to protect it from the weather.

"Come in!" I said. "I'm so sorry you had to drive out in the rain."

He stepped across my threshold, shook himself slightly, and smiled at me. He handed me the bag. "Thank you," he said. "We got everything we needed." His cell phone rang and he held up a finger so he could answer it. "Wolf."

He listened for a moment, and his eyes widened. "Okay, thanks. I'll be right there, Dave." He ended the call.

"Dave?" I said. "Is this about the train?"

"He saw it running tonight, just before the storm."

"I'm coming, too."

He opened his mouth, then shut it again. Then he said, "Okay. I'll drive."

I grabbed an umbrella from a holder near my door; we ran out to Wolf's car, huddled under the umbrella together. When we were on the road, he said, "Dave says he ran across the street and gave chase to someone he saw on your lawn. The person dropped something. He said he didn't touch it in case I wanted to fingerprint it. I think Dave feels like a secret agent," Wolf said, smiling slightly.

"What could he have dropped? Is this related to the coal car? The one that opens? You seemed so interested in that."

Wolf shrugged. "I'm not sure. But let's say someone wanted to sell something illegal. He could go to your tea house in the middle of the night—it's relatively isolated, aside from Dave's house—and put whatever he was selling in the car. Then he could turn on the train, a signal that he had made the drop. The other guy could retrieve it and leave his payment."

I turned in my seat. "You mean *drugs*? You think *drug dealers* are using the *tea house*? Oh God, murderers and drug dealers."

Wolf covered my hand with his warm one. I leaned back and stared at the windshield wipers, flicking rain from the windshield with every rapid movement. He said, "Take a deep breath. You sound like your grandma when she hears the word 'wolf.'"

"Maybe you're wrong."

"I may be. It's just a theory. But it would explain why the guy was there when the train went on, and why he wanted to get away from you as fast as possible."

I sighed. "What is going *on*?"

"Here we are. I can see Dave. We'll sort this out; it even seems like the rain is slowing down." Dave stood under the awning of our entrance; we jogged through the drizzle to meet him there, protected from the weather. The train made its ghostly rounds again, its lights glowing weirdly in the rain.

"Hey!" Dave said. "I didn't get a good look at the kid, but he did seem to be a kid. Like a teen, you know. Sort of tall and lanky."

"Where's the thing he dropped?" Wolf said.

Dave pointed to the center of our front lawn, where a small square lay in the grass, glowing white. Wolf jogged out to the spot and bent down to examine it. I heard him mutter something under his breath. He sounded angry. He picked the white thing up and stalked back to us under our roof, holding up a little box that said "Newport." "A pack of cigarettes?" he said in disbelief. "This kid is going through all this nonsense to get *cigarettes*?"

Dave tried hard to hide his disappointment. "Maybe there's something inside. Like microfilm or something."

Wolf shook his head. "Just cigarettes inside. I guess we can go through them at the station, see if they're anything more than that, but I need to rethink this. Figure out what this means, why here, why this." He stared at the pack with something like hatred, his hair wet and matted on his head.

I patted Dave's arm. "Thanks so much for calling us. I'll go turn off the train."

Wolf's hand shot out and grabbed my arm. "Not alone. Hang on." He shook Dave's hand and asked him to call at any time if he saw anything suspicious. Dave agreed, looking pleased, then loped off under a dark umbrella, bound for home.

Wolf faced me in the dark. "Who else knows about that outlet? Besides you and your dad?"

I shrugged. "I mean, just the family. Mom, Grandma, Grandpa, Domo. And of course Grandpa's friend."

Wolf pushed some wet hair out of his eyes. "Who is 'Grandpa's friend'?"

"Some guy who does our landscaping. He's a Hungarian friend of my grandfather's. Grandma always looks like a mobster, paying him with a white envelope on the side of the building."

"I want to talk to him," Wolf said.

"Now?"

"Tomorrow is fine." He stuck out his hand. "Let's go turn off your little mystery train and get you home."

~

In my apartment I sent Wolf to the bathroom to dry off and gave him a pair of gray sweats that Domo had lent me once when I was at his place, and which I had washed with the intention of returning to him.

Wolf emerged looking casual, comfy, and huggable. I smiled at him.

"Can you stay for a while? I can make some dinner."

"I actually want to run back to work," he said. "I'm going to burn some midnight oil." For the first time I realized he was tired. There were lines around his eyes, and his shoulders looked tense.

"Oh, okay."

My face must have looked forlorn, because he smiled. "I can spare half an hour," he said. "But don't bother cooking. I had a burger earlier. Let's just sit in your cozy room here."

He led me to my couch, sat down, and pulled me against him so that we both faced outward, looking at my white faux fireplace draped with Italian lights. I let my head fall back against his chest. His voice rumbled in my ear. "I'll want to speak with the landscaper tomorrow. Meanwhile, I spoke with Joe Novák again today. He was a bit more forthcoming this time."

"Good."

"He said Steve Sarka was quite upset when Ava broke up with him."

I turned and faced him. "What? Steve told my dad and me that there were no hard feelings. That he traveled a lot and it was just a natural separation."

Wolf raised his eyebrows. "He lied. And that is very interesting."

"I'm learning so much about people. And it's not good information." I flopped back against him and closed my eyes.

The silence wrapped around us, occasionally punctuated by muffled thunder. The cats ran past with tails high, frightening each other. Wolf, by contrast, seemed serene. He studied my apartment and said, "You have a gift for decorating. You love beautiful things, don't you?"

"I do. Someday I think I'd like a shop like Falken's, where I can discover treasures and brighten people's lives with art. With the work of other people's hands."

"Hmm. You'd be great." We sat quietly for a moment, and he said, "You seem a little sad tonight. Why didn't you go to your family this evening?"

I shrugged. "I think Grandma wanted to be alone. Although I know she's cooking up a storm. It calms her down. But I called a while ago and Grandpa said she made *kocsonya*, so that's one reason to stay home."

"What's kuh-chon-ya?" Wolf asked.

"It's a Hungarian staple. Pig's feet in aspic. It probably

emerged from the Depression, or just poverty in general, but Grandma always made it because her mother always did. When Domo and I were kids, we wolfed it down like it was no big deal. Now I can't even look at it for too long."

"Sounds great," Wolf joked.

"As you've learned, most Hungarian food is delicious."

"Yes."

I leaned against his shoulder. "I don't know why, but I've been sad all day. Angry, too, but mostly sad. I feel like I just want to get away. Somewhere I don't have to think about anything at all. Do you ever feel that way?"

"Sure."

"I picture an autumn wood, full of tall trees. I could walk in there and inhale the scent of pine and be one with nature."

"Sounds good."

"My grandparents have a place in Michigan—twenty acres of forest and a little house. Grandma rents it out now, but we used to go there every summer, the whole family, and just enjoy the woods, visit the lake. And Grandpa would do a bacon fry over a campfire—I can smell it now."

Wolf straightened his back and leaned into the couch, tucking me more securely against him. "What's a bacon fry?"

"Oh, it's an old Hungarian treat. Probably goes back to the Gypsies or the Hussars or something. Grandpa says it was a shepherds' tradition, so they could have their lunch or dinner out in the field while they were tending the sheep. It's called *szalonnat sütjük*—means 'bacon fry,' or 'we fry bacon,' or something like that. You take a big old chunk of jowl bacon and find a likely stick—something fresh and green that won't burn, like willow or birch—then you hold the bacon over the fire until it sizzles. Grandpa says the fire should be made with hardwoods, so that it burns more slowly, and you get beautiful embers instead of ash. Then you can keep roasting the bacon over those hot embers until it's dripping with grease. Someone lays out slices of rye bread. My grandpa would take his bacon and let the grease dribble all over the bread, till it was soaked."

Wolf craned his head to look at me. "How are you still alive?"

I giggled. "That's not all. Then he had sliced raw onions and peppers and tomatoes ready to sprinkle on top of the grease. No paprika this time, but a touch of salt. Some people put other things—red peppers, radishes. But ours was just onion, tomato, green pepper, and bacon grease. You wouldn't believe how good it tasted."

"You're right, I don't."

"Erik, it was amazing. It tasted like a campfire. It tasted like my grandparents' homeland."

"Make it for me sometime."

"I will."

We looked at each other for a minute, and then I leaned back against him again. "Thank you for being here, and for always coming when I call. Never mind the crazy train incidents—I can't get over the idea that a person sent poison to my *grandmother* . . ."

He grunted. "I still have a car watching her house, just in case."

"I read a piece in the *Star* today about Ava's death. The reporter—Thomas Brayburn—implied that we were careless at Maggie's Tea House, that somehow she died because of us."

He petted my hair with a soothing gesture. "I read that. The guy was purposely misleading. You need to call and complain."

"Meanwhile our establishment will suffer. I never knew a person could be so callous."

"I have known plenty."

"My grandma has some old expression from Hungarian mythology about how some evil demon should eat him. I wish I knew it in Hungarian."

His stroking hand was becoming hypnotic. "There's a whole Hungarian mythology? Besides those stories in the book?"

"Oh yes. Some of it is a sort of origin story of the Huns and the Magyars. And it's like lots of other ethnic mythologies—there's an upper world, a middle world, and an underworld, and all sorts of creatures in each."

"Yeah? Tell me about some beautiful women in mythology."

I laughed, feeling suddenly drowsy. "There's the Fair Lady, you know about her. She's called Szépasszony. She emerges during storms—maybe a storm like this—and she dances. She has long hair and wears a white dress, and she seduces young men."

"Nice."

"But she's a demon, so she cannot be trusted. I suppose she's sort of like the sirens. She can hide in a puddle or in the drops of rain and surprise the unsuspecting."

"Ah. Who else?"

"There's Forest Girl. She is a seductress of shepherds; some of the stories in that book are based on her, or that model. Vadleány, they call her. She is always naked, and her long hair reaches to the ground, like Lady Godiva."

"Is she a demon?"

"No—she's a forest sprite. When she lures the shepherds, she kisses them and then steals their strength, and she uses it to make the leaves rustle, or some other event that we attribute to nature. But sometimes she can be caught, too. The shepherds learned that if they put out one boot, she would try to slip both of her feet into it, and then they could seize her."

"Ah. I think Forest Girl sounds like more fun than Fair Lady."

"They are both quite dangerous. They are beautiful, but they cannot be trusted. They are vengeful, especially Szépasszony. But also especially Vadleány."

He laughed.

"You know what scared me the most, hearing the stories as a kid? They can fly, both of them, all the fairies can. And they sing as they fly. It gave me the creeps, trying to imagine what that singing would sound like, you know?"

It was very quiet in my apartment, aside from the occasional gust of wind against the kitchen pane. Wolf still had his hands on my hair.

"I know you want to go," I said. "Thank you for sitting with me."

He turned me to face him. "Of course. You don't have to worry, Hana. I *will* take care of this."

"I know."

He studied my lips, and I leaned away with a burst of playfulness. "You said we had to wait, remember? So don't even try to kiss me."

His mouth lifted on one side. "I'm not going to *try* to kiss you. I'm just going to kiss you." He pulled me back to him and lowered his mouth to mine. Something relaxed inside me, and I felt the rightness, the naturalness of Wolf in my life. This was the opposite of The Misery; it was The Happiness.

Finally, I moved away from him. "That was pretty good,

what you just said. Not awkward at all, like the 'you smell' incident."

He grinned. "I think I'm getting the hang of it. It's easier when you're not glaring at me."

I smiled. "You're worth waiting for, Erik."

He looked pleased and surprised. "So are you, Hana."

"Now go. I have TV to watch."

He laughed and got up, giving me one last kiss on the top of my head. "Keep in touch," he said.

After he left I turned off the lights, except for the little white ones that lined my fireplace.

Cleopatra jumped up beside me and nuzzled my hand. "Never mind television. We should go to sleep," I told her. "Things will look better in the morning."

I put on pajamas, brushed my teeth, and placed the Hungarian storybook back on my shelf.

I climbed into bed. Across the lightning-illuminated town my grandmother was probably fast asleep. She still prayed in Hungarian, and I was sure that recent events would not alter her prayers for all souls, even the soul of her would-be assailant.

My own thoughts were a bit less forgiving, and I saw justice in the actions of the vengeful Szépasszony, the dangerous spirit. Eventually, someone would be caught for the crime of murder. Eventually, someone would pay. And since the evil intentions had extended to my family, my blood, I hoped that I was a part of that person's apprehension and could look them in the eye as the authorities led them away in shackles.

Chapter 20

The Witch with the Wild Hair

My mother called the next day to tell me that our clients had canceled. Her voice was carefully toneless. "There was an article in the paper; I didn't want to mention it to you—"

"I saw it," I said. "So did François."

"Oh no. I have to call him next; I'm not looking forward to that. And I had to return their deposit, of course."

"It's not a big deal," I said.

"No. Not if this is an isolated thing. But if people talk, and fear spreads—we could be in big trouble, Hana."

My mother had never been much of a worrier, but I heard traces of real concern in her voice.

"They just need to catch this person. You wait and see—once they expose a murderer, it will give us notoriety for a while, and people will want to come just for that. Just to be where a murder happened. Because people are weird and horrible."

"Don't be so dark." She sighed. "Meanwhile, we can use the day to polish cups or clean the floors and the kitchen. We've been meaning to do that, anyway."

"Oh, Mom! I need the phone number of our landscaper. Grandpa's friend. Wolf wants to talk to him."

"What? Why?"

I told her about the train, both the evening that I was knocked down and last night, when Dave called Wolf.

She listened in silence, then said, "So—Detective Wolf was at your house?"

"That's what you took away from those two stories?"

"All right, so why does he want to talk with Janos?"

"That's his name, Janos?"

"Yes. I think his last name is Kalmár. Does Detective Wolf think he turned on the train? Because Janos would never do that. He's very particular about our grounds, and he's quite protective of your dad's train."

"Yes, well. Can you give me his number?"

She sighed. "Tell Detective Wolf to come to the hall today. I'll have Grandma ask Janos to come by. Let's say two o'clock. Then we'll still be cleaning and can find out what's going on."

"Okay, great. And there's one good thing about this being a cleaning day: I can wear jeans," I said. My mind drifted back to a previous resentment. "I'm tempted to call and give a piece of my mind to that reporter. I'm going to tell him I'm a Gypsy and that I put a curse on him."

"Hana! Don't say that around your grandma." Then, with a little smile, she added, "Did he make our little Zsa Zsa angry?"

I snorted. "Tell me you're not angry, Mom."

"I'm unhappy, that's true. Your father made crepes for me before he went to work. Isn't he sweet?"

"Yes." I wondered if Wolf would do something like that for me . . . I thought that he would, given a similar situation, but then again we were only on the verge, the precipice, of a relationship. Everyone was wonderful at the start . . .

"I have to go, sweetheart. I'll see you at the hall."

"Bye, Mom."

Later, as I scrubbed the counter in the kitchen of the tea house, I thought about the day of the crime. First, Ava Novák sitting essentially alone, although at least one woman had chatted with her, the woman in a blue dress, someone I didn't know, but who my grandmother had said was named Szilvia and who had just been introduced to Ava that day . . . Then Grandma reading tea leaves, and Mrs. Kalas reddening when she learned her results. Then Ava's seat empty, Ava rushing away, Ava slumped against the wall, her red purse left behind on the table, the stone gone. Me in the hallway, trying to wake her; calling the police . . . the ambulance arriving . . . the terrible reality of the stretcher.

And then police. Wolf and Benton, in their suits. Grandma's shock at Wolf's name, Benton's offensive mustache. And the statements. Mrs. Kalas, so brash and confident and defensive. Mrs. Pinkoczi, nubby and sweet and elusive. Mrs. Guliban, attacking to avoid being attacked.

My rag paused in its movement. Mrs. Guliban had a sister, Mrs. Cseh. But they never really sat together at the events; why? Were they estranged? This made me think of Ava and her sisters. What had become of them?

Was Mrs. Pinkoczi really fine with her husband dating Ava?

And Mrs. Kalas—I paused, thinking back to her statement. She had told Wolf that Ava stopped dating Mr. Pinkoczi because she had met Joe Novák. But that wasn't true, because Steve Sarka had said that Ava met Joe right after dating *him, Steve.* And Mrs. Kalas would know this, because she was the one who had introduced Ava to Joe Novák. She had left Sarka out of her statement entirely.

I pushed the rag aside and grabbed my phone. I texted Wolf: A thought: look at Mrs. Kalas's statement. She said Ava went from Pinkoczi to Novák, but she didn't. She dated Sarka first. This is the second lie told about Steve Sarka. I wonder why?

I sent the message, then typed another one: I mentioned the sisters to you once before, but Mrs. Guliban and Mrs. Cseh never sit together at events. Important?

I sent that one, too.

I didn't expect a response, but a moment later my phone beeped. I grabbed it and read what Wolf had written: You should consider becoming a cop. I'm not kidding.

And then he sent about ten heart emojis.

My grandmother walked in and said, in her husky cold voice, "Why are you smiling, Haniska?"

I met her gaze and saw that she already knew.

~

Wolf arrived about an hour later, just after Janos. My grandmother introduced the two men with the formality of a foreign ambassador. Janos shook Wolf's hand and said, "Nice to meet you."

Janos was a tall, white-haired man with a narrow white mustache. He was also a man of few words. Wolf explained about the train incidents; Janos looked grave and concerned. "Was the train damaged?" he asked.

"No," Wolf said.

"And the mulch—was it disturbed?"

Wolf was having trouble suppressing his impatience. "The mulch is fine."

"Did the cars sit out in the rain?" Janos asked. He looked distressed.

"No—Hana put them back in the Alps both times."

Janos spared an approving glance for me.

I caught Wolf assessing Janos. "Does anyone ever help you with the groundskeeping?" he asked.

Janos looked surprised. "Not usually. Mark sometimes. My grandson. A strong boy."

Something flickered in Wolf's eyes. "How old is Mark?"

"Fifteen," Janos said. "Youngest of five."

Wolf nodded. "And Mark knows where the switch is? For the train?"

Puzzled, Janos nodded. "Yes. But he has no reason to turn on a train in the middle of the night. He is not interested."

"I wonder," Wolf said, acting as though an idea had just occurred to him. "Is Mark allowed to smoke cigarettes?"

Janos scowled. "Was he smoking here on the grounds?"

Wolf's eyebrows went up. "Would that bother you?"

"His father is bothered. My son. He has caught Mark with cigarettes and forbidden it. He does not want the boy to develop a habit." With his white mustache, Janos looked as grim as a king on a playing card.

"I think he already has developed a habit. And I think he has a friend who was selling him cigarettes—using the train as a system."

Janos turned stiffly to my grandmother. "I hope not is the case. If it is, I deeply apologize."

Grandma patted his arm. "He is a boy. This will be good lesson."

"Call him. Ask him to come here," Wolf said. "I want to talk to him about these nighttime train routes."

Janos, solemn and hesitant, studied Wolf's face, then he pulled out a battered phone and walked to the window to make his call. I went back to cleaning with my family, and Janos eventually toured the grounds, frowning at hedges and poking shrubs with the toe of his boot; Wolf sat in a corner and made some notes in his notebook.

Half an hour or so later a thin, dark-haired boy with freckles appeared in the doorway. He looked around uncertainly and my mother waved at him. "Hello, Mark. Come on in." She moved forward, apparently familiar with this person I'd never seen before. "A friend of ours would like to ask you some questions."

Wolf strode into view from the corner where he had been texting. He looked grim and intimidating; I found it weirdly exciting.

He waited until the boy made eye contact, then said, "Mark, I'm Detective Wolf from the Riverwood Police."

"Okay," said Mark, trying to look uninterested.

"I'd like to know if you have been showing up here at night and turning on the outdoor train."

Mark's skin paled, but he lifted his chin. "The one in the front flower bed? Why would I do that? I have a life."

Wolf nodded. "How about if you tell me now, and I don't have to study the footage to determine if it is you."

Suddenly Mark's freckles became more apparent on his face. "What footage?"

Ignoring this, Wolf said, "Is your family pretty strict about cigarettes?"

Janos had come in from outside; Mark folded his arms defensively. "Smoking's not a big deal."

"It is a big deal to trespass, though, and to use other people's equipment with malicious intent."

Mark's eyes widened. "It's not malicious intent! It's just a train! He puts in the pack and flips it on, and I pick up the cigarettes and flip the switch off. It's no big deal!"

"Who is *he*?" Wolf asked with a smug expression.

Mark sagged. "My friend Will. He's old enough to buy cigarettes." He turned to my mother. "I'm sorry I touched your train."

She moved forward and patted his arm. "It's not a big deal, Mark, but you probably shouldn't do it anymore."

Janos frowned at him. "How many times have you done this?"

"Just a few. I didn't even want to come back last night, after the last time, but I was sort of craving a cigarette."

Wolf's cop antennae seemed to be quivering again. "What happened the last time?"

"It was a few days ago. The day we heard that lady died here. I thought it might be her ghost."

The room had already been quiet, but now it was silent with dread. "You thought *what* was her ghost?" Wolf asked.

"I had just flipped off the train, and I was coming back around to the front to get my bike. This lady came running out of nowhere, just weirdly running back and forth, with her hair all wild. It was freaky."

"How was her hair all wild?" I asked.

His eyes drifted to me. "It was all around her head; I think it was gray, or white, but it looked silver, like unnatural, and her eyes were like craters in her head. She looked like a witch."

My grandmother moaned. "Vasorrú Bába," she whispered.

Mark looked at her, uncertain, and Wolf said, "Did she see you?"

The boy shook his head. "No, she was too distracted.

She was just running around, back and forth. There was some sort of light that she had, but not a flashlight. She was shining it on the ground, just sweeping it like this." He moved his hand from left to right in a rhythmic motion. "She was crying or moaning, too. I was scared; she was, like, really scary. And sometimes she dropped down and dug around in the dirt. One time she looked up at the sky and, like, screamed."

The chill in my spine had extended to my fingers and toes. "What did she say?"

Mark suddenly seemed to notice that we were all hanging on his every word. He warmed to his story, realizing that this might overshadow the cigarette incident. "I don't know; she seemed to be saying the same words over and over." His gaze met mine. "It sounded like she was saying, 'Fear, murder, fear, murder.'"

The teacup my grandmother had been holding fell to the ground and shattered. My mother ran for the broom, but Grandma stood still, transfixed, her eyes not on Mark, but on nothing. It seemed she was looking inside herself. "Guilt, guilty," she said. "She is the guilty one."

"Did you recognize this woman?" Wolf asked.

Mark shook his head; even in his awe at the remembered horror he showed some enthusiasm for his story. "I didn't even think she was human, like I told you. She looked like one of those witches from a fairy tale. I was shaking when I rode home."

"Who left first, you, or this mystery woman?"

"She did. I wasn't going to show myself while she was there."

"And how long was she there?"

"I don't know. A long time, like maybe half an hour. When I tried to stand up, my legs were numb."

"Did she have a car?"

He thought about this. Even his stern grandfather had become interested in the story. He had taken a few steps forward and now leaned in to hear Mark's response. "No, she didn't. I remember because I was surprised that she walked out to the road. That's when I really thought she was a ghost. Like Resurrection Mary."

"Who?" Janos asked.

Wolf, who had been studying Mark's face with great attention, said, "She's a famous Chicago ghost legend. People said they saw her on the road. Sometimes they picked her up as a hitchhiker."

Mark said, "I don't know where she went after that. It was even a little foggy, like a horror movie. And by then she wasn't running around, but walking kind of slow, with these weird, lurching steps." He moved toward us in a Frankenstein pose.

"Thank you, Mark." Wolf stuck out his hand, and the boy, surprised, shook it. "This has been very helpful information."

When Mark left, his grandfather seemed less upset with him than he had at the start, although I overheard a whispered conversation about cigarettes that contained the words "tell your father if it happens again."

My mother and grandmother had retired to a corner to speak to each other in Hungarian; the story had not sat well with either one of them.

I turned to Wolf. Fear and skepticism were at war within me. "Do I have to be afraid that a witch comes to this place at night, digging her claws into the dirt and screaming at the moon?"

He shook his head; his eyes were bright with excitement.

"No. She only came once, Hana! Because the next day our people found the stone."

I stared at him for a moment, then realized my mouth was open and snapped it shut. "She didn't throw away the stone when she left the tea house. She lost it."

"And she tried to search for it in the dark. That would explain her distress, her wild appearance. If it had value to her, it would be important to retrieve it without being seen."

"But what about the stuff she was saying? 'Fear, murder, fear, murder'?"

Wolf shook his head. "I can't explain that, unless she was processing the guilt your grandmother speaks of." He glanced over at my grandma. "She felt something, right? She sensed that this was our murderer."

"Well, clearly, since she came back for the stone and was highly emotional. It would take some strong emotion to make you kill, wouldn't it? This is a crime of passion, isn't it?"

Wolf nodded. "But which of those old ladies was concealing that kind of drama? I didn't see it; not in any of them. Someone is good at hiding."

I said good-bye to him soon afterward. He squeezed my hand with a surreptitious gesture, conscious of my family nearby, and I watched him stride out to his car, deep in thought. Wolf had put it in perspective: the weird scene that Mark described had a perfectly plausible explanation. So why was it that I couldn't shake the connection to my book of bad fairies and the tales of Vadleány, who waited in the farmer's fields, her hands digging rhythmically in the soil as she anticipated the strength she would steal from the unsuspecting man, out in the darkness tending to his last jobs on the farm?

That man, like Mark, looked up to see a wild woman, silver hair flying, looming up in front of him before he had a chance to cry out. She was vengeance and judgment, she was envy and cruelty, she was hunger and greed. She fed off of him and used his power to glorify herself.

Here was another duality that troubled me long after I left the tea house: a guilty woman's actions, explainable on the surface as a search for something lost, yet mythical in their resemblance to the folklore of centuries—how likely was it that somehow, one interpretation was rooted in the other?

Chapter 21

Revelation in a Blue Room

That night I went to Margie's apartment for pizza with her and Domo. Her place was as cozy as mine, with an emphasis on blue tones. Her living room walls were midnight blue, with accents of white trim and baseboards, and a big white rug on the wood floor. She had to vacuum this often because of Boris, who was a shedder, but she said it was worth it to have both carpet and dog. She had a lovely antique sideboard with all sorts of cubbyholes, and this had been refinished in a distressed pale blue crackle finish; it was a remarkable piece of furniture and gave distinction to her whole apartment. Above it hung a framed reproduction of Anquetin's *Avenue de Clichy*, a wonderful city scene that contrasted the cool blue of night with the warm yellow glow of shops on a boulevard.

Margie had fantastic taste in art, and in her bedroom, above the bed, hung another compelling reproduction, this one of Max Ernst's *Portrait of Dorothea*, a mysterious likeness of his wife, done all in shades of blue. The only furniture other than her bed (white coverlet, blue and green throw pillows) was a little wooden computer desk and a long, dark wood dresser with an attached mirror.

Perhaps my favorite room was her office, where she did all of her design work. There was a wide central window, in front of which she had placed her architect's table. Wooden umbrella urns sat on either side, and her rolled-up designs sat in these. A multicolored rag rug sat on the floor. Against the north wall sat a plump red easy chair, and beside that was a basket for Boris (he was in this, snoring away despite our presence in the room). On the opposite wall was an antique library card catalog, which she used for a variety of storage, from scarves to screwdrivers. Margie was remarkably organized.

Some framed pictures sat on top of the card catalog, including one of my brother, smiling widely, on what I had learned was their first date.

Margie came up behind me as I did my traditional tour of her apartment. "That's still my favorite picture of him," she said. She was happy and bright; she thrived in her own space, and she almost seemed extroverted on these pizza nights.

"He looks pretty good. He's not making one of his stupid faces."

"What stupid faces?" Domo called. He was setting the table while we waited for the pizza.

"The ones Mom has albums full of," I said. "The 'I'm uncomfortable in my own skin' photos."

"Oh, *those*," Domo said. Once again, my brother refused to be insulted.

"Now that I think of it, you really do owe Mom and Dad

a nice photo of yourself. Margie, you should make a copy of that one and share it."

"I will!" she said, pleased. "Your parents are great." She picked up a photo that sat slightly to the left of Domo's on her card catalog. "Did you see this one, Hana?"

It was a photo of Margie and me on one of our outings together. We had asked our waitress to take it when we went to a diner and ordered ice cream sundaes. (I had made Margie talk to the waitress.) We were both using the toothy smiles of people who didn't know each other that well but were making an effort. It was a cute picture, though. "Yeah—that was fun. And such good ice cream. We should go back."

"Okay," Margie said. "Now come out here and tell Domo and me what's been going on."

I followed her back to the dining room; the doorbell rang, and Domo jogged to answer it. He returned a minute later with hot pizza, which he set in the center of the table. "Yeah, I was working late yesterday, so I only talked with Mom today. She sounded kind of frazzled, so she told me to have you fill me in tonight. What gives?"

"Well—the most dramatic thing is, someone sent Grandma a package with a teapot in it, and a thank-you note, and a poisoned tea bag."

Domo's hand paused halfway to reaching for a slice of pizza. "What? You're saying someone tried to *poison* our *grandmother*?"

"Yes."

"Through the *mail*?"

Margie looked distressed. "Have they caught him, Hana?"

"No. But I'm sure they will. There must have been all sorts of clues on that box, or in it. Fingerprints and stuff. I'm sure they'll figure this out soon."

"So why is Mom all upset?"

I sighed. "There was a write-up about Ava's murder in the *Star.* It implied that we were somehow culpable, or at least careless. Like we should have been scanning the room for poisoners. Anyway, today's clients canceled. Mom is worried that more might follow suit."

"Oh, man. This is bad news," Domo said, his handsome face solemn. "But getting back to Grandma. Do they think this is the same person who killed Ava? If so, what's the connection? Some lady gets her tea poisoned, and then someone tries to poison Grandma's tea? Why Grandma, is what I'm saying. She's a little old lady."

"I don't know. I feel so bad for her; she has a cold, and then she got this package."

We all ate for a moment, thinking about these facts. "This pizza is good," I said.

"Montenegro's," Margie piped. She looked youthful this evening in blue jeans and a pink blouse. She had tied her hair into braids, which normally would have earned sarcasm from me, but of course on Margie it looked elegant.

"Domo," I asked, "did you ever think that Great-grandma Natalia had . . . abilities?"

Domo stared at me, brows raised. "What sort of abilities?"

"Like . . . psychic ones."

He chewed for a while, thinking. Margie got up and played with an iPad that sat on her pretty sideboard; soon we heard quiet music in the background. It sounded like a torch song. Domo said, "It's funny you should ask that. I do have one thing I've always remembered about Great-grandma. Way back from when I was a tiny kid."

"Yeah?"

"She had to walk me to school one day; Mom and Dad were busy doing I don't know what. This was like preschool or kindergarten. I was pretty small. Normally I liked school, but on this day it was going to rain, and I was afraid of thunderstorms. I was terrified of the idea of being at school during the storm, and I didn't want to go, but I was too scared to say anything to old Grandma."

"Poor little Domo," Margie said, her face softening with sympathy.

"So we were walking down Paris Street, just about two blocks from our house, and suddenly Natalia stopped walking. She was holding my hand, so I stopped walking, too." He looked surprised at the memory, or perhaps about how much of it was coming back to him. "She knelt down and looked into my face. She had that sweet old face; it was never mean. She said, 'You don't want to go.' I shook my head and started to cry a little. She said, 'We don't go then, Domonkos.'" He said it with Natalia's accent, long remembered by us both. "She said, 'We get breakfast. Now you help me up.'"

I laughed. "Poor Natalia and her creaky knees."

Domo nodded. "It was great, though, because I was helping her, and she was laughing, and then I was laughing. And she took me to a diner for pancakes. We actually had to walk home in the rain, but she told me some crazy story about fairies and raindrops, and I had a great time. I have no idea what she told Mom and Dad. Maybe she didn't. They never said anything to me."

Margie said, "That's sweet. But anyone could see if a child was nervous, right?"

Domo chewed on the inside of his cheek for a minute, thinking. "Yeah. But the way I remember it, she never looked at me. She was just walking along, and then she stopped short, like she had slammed into a wall. And *then* she looked at me, with this surprised expression."

This sounded entirely plausible to me.

My brother looked at me expectantly. "Why do you ask?"

I told him about the moment with the box—how I had suddenly realized it was bad, and that Grandma had, too, and we called the police.

"That's so interesting," Margie said. "Do you think it's some sort of gene that the women in your family have?"

"My mother doesn't buy into it. And she doesn't like Grandma to talk about it. But Dad said Mom has it, too."

Domo lifted his bottle of beer and took a sip. "This has been a very educational dinner."

I sighed. "Anyway, it's good to get away from it all. I just needed an evening out. I've been obsessing over this Ava thing, to the point that I was hanging out in the bathroom at the last event, trying to eavesdrop on ladies talking."

Domo laughed. "You're a dork."

"Really? Because one of the policemen told me I should be a cop."

They responded with blank expressions. "Because you hang out in bathrooms?" Domo asked.

"*No*, because I ask good questions." I stuck my tongue out at him.

"Did you ask those questions in the bathroom?"

"The bathroom didn't pay off that much. My good questions came later. All I learned in the bathroom was who was pregnant, who was cheating, who bought a new couch, and stuff like that. Although I did get a tiny conversation about Ava and the fact that she was musical. That she played the piano *for* a musical, in fact."

"Really?" Margie asked. "Like, in Chicago? That's pretty cool."

I shrugged. "It sounded like community theater. It had a weird name. They said it was a play about a woman and her dog. Freddie something. '*Freddie* and Something,' that's what the lady said."

Margie went to her sideboard and typed on the iPad. "There was a play called *Freddie and Felicia* at the Riverwood Grand Stage Theater. It closed last month."

"That's the theater right on the water—it's pretty nice. I took Marguerite there for our third date," Domo said, smiling at her.

"Does it say what the play was about?" I asked, picking at the crust on my plate.

Margie read from the computer: "'A sweet and funny drama about a woman, the dog she loves, and the people he brings into her life.'"

"Soon to be a major motion picture," Domo joked.

"It has a link here to the playbill," Margie said.

"Oh, click on that, Margie! Maybe it's got a biography of Ava."

Margie tapped some keys, and then came back. "It's printing," she said.

"The whole playbill? That's a waste of paper."

"No, just the page that had Ava Novák's name and photo."

Another moment, suddenly, of time slowing down; it allowed me to notice there was a small scratch on Domo's cheek, a smudge on the window behind him, a dead lightbulb in the chandelier above us. I turned to find Boris, lured finally by the smell of food, his face hairy and concerned as an old sea captain's, his gait sleepy as he came toward us. His nails sounded too loud on the wood floor.

"Hana? You okay?" Domo asked.

"Yeah. Fine." What was I supposed to tell him? I feel that something significant is about to happen? "Did it print out?"

Margie nodded and walked swiftly into the next room. She came back with two sheets of paper; on them were three biographies. My eyes moved to the picture of Ava. It was a professional photo; her blonde hair was swept up in an elegant twist, and she wore a gray off-the-shoulder dress. She looked beautiful, like an old Hollywood star. Underneath it was a caption and a brief biography.

Ava Novák, pianist and musical director.

Ava Novák was originally from a small town near Lake Balaton in Hungary. She loved music from the time she was a child, and would sing and dance with her family. She lived in Austria for many years before coming to America in 2015. She said, "Hungary remains in my blood, from its music to its food to its people. When I was a child, I loved playing with my sisters and my friends in our beautiful little town. I recall running through the blossoms that fell from the spring trees; my friend and I would make necklaces and hang them around the neck of my dear dog, Farkas. Even though I love the United States, I still smell the flowers and hear the music of Hungary in my dreams." Ava was trained in classical piano and sang with a traveling choir in her college years. She greatly enjoyed directing the cast in her first American musical.

I looked up at Domo and Margie, whose faces seemed to blur before me. "Why does this all sound familiar? Does this seem familiar to you?"

They shook their heads. "Have some more pizza, Han," Domo said.

"Lake Balaton," I murmured. "And Farkas. *Farkas*."

"What's FAR-kosh?" asked Margie, cutting into her pizza with a fork.

"It means 'wolf,'" I said. "Oh my God."

"Clue us in, for God's sake," said my brother, getting impatient.

"I have to call Erik," I said.

Now Domo was really interested. "Who's Erik?"

"He's the cop—the detective—investigating this. He and another guy, Benton."

"Wait—is that the Detective Wolf you told me about when I came by your place? And how do you happen to be calling him Erik? And know his number by heart, apparently?" he said as I pulled out my cell phone and pressed a number.

"Yes, Erik Wolf," I said.

"Everything is wolf," said Margie, furrowing her brows.

"I know his number because"—suddenly I got Wolf's voice mail— "Hi, Erik! It's Hana. Are you at work? If you're leaving soon, could you stop by an apartment on Heath Street? I'm visiting my brother and—it's important, and I want to explain—Erik, I think this might be big. Okay. Thanks." I left the address to Margie's apartment and then ended the call.

My two companions were both staring at me, waiting.

I sighed. "The fact is, we talked several times and it turned out there was this—attraction between us," I said.

"What?" yelled my brother.

"We—think there's something there. To explore when the case is over."

"Does Grandma know this? She'll go back to Hungary before she lets you bring a wolf into the family."

I nodded. "That's how she felt, at first. But then—Erik and I had a fight, and—"

Domo held up a hand. "You've known this guy for like twenty minutes, and you've already connected romantically and had a fight?"

"Yes. And Grandma gave Erik advice about how to win me back."

My brother looked at Margie, his mouth agape. "Was I unconscious for a long time, like Rip Van Winkle? Because it seems like I missed many months of events."

Margie looked at me, assessing. "I'm guessing he's dreamy," she said.

I shrugged. "He's not—unattractive."

She grinned. "You can tell me later, when Domo's not glaring at you."

I stared down at the playbill. "It's just that when the police took the statements of all these Hungarian women, they said things that seem to mesh with what Ava said here. This is the most information about Ava I've ever seen. Most people just said she was sad and she dated several men. This is more personal. It's crucial." My phone buzzed with a text. I looked down and saw it was from Wolf: I'll be there in an hour.

I took a sip of the wine Margie had poured me and said, "Do you have Diet Coke? Wolf likes that."

"Geez," Domo said. He frowned and shuffled toward the kitchen like an old man.

~

Wolf arrived on time. He still looked tired, and rather rumpled, but it was attractive on him, that work-worn look, and Margie was clearly impressed.

"Erik, this is my brother, Domo, and his girlfriend, Margie."

Erik shook their hands. "Domo—is that short for something?"

"Domonkos," he said. "The Hungarian version of Dominic."

"DOE-mun-kōsh," Wolf repeated. "Nice to meet you."

"Would you like some pizza? Or Diet Coke?" Margie asked politely.

He nodded. "I would love both, thanks."

I sat him down at the table and said, "Ava was the music director for a play called *Freddie and Felicia*."

"Yes—her husband told me about that. He said she was very talented."

"Did he show you the playbill?"

His brows shot up. "No. I take it you found something interesting?"

Margie set food and drink before him, he thanked her and took a bite of pizza. I took the printout and handed it to him. Then I watched him read; I could almost see the places where he paused, recognizing details.

"Farkas," he murmured.

"That's what Hana said!" Margie shouted.

Wolf was still reading. "And Lake Balaton."

Margie clapped.

I waited until he looked up at me. "Do you have your notebook? Or the statements?" I asked.

"Both." He took out his notebook; copies of the statements I had pored over were folded up inside. He began to flip through them. "It was one of the first three women, wasn't it?"

"Yes. It was either Kalas or Pinkoczi, I'm sure. She said something about Balaton right up front."

Wolf consulted his notebook, then looked uncertainly at Domo and Margie.

"Domo's Hungarian; he can offer insights," I said. "He's entirely trustworthy. And Margie is totally discreet. You need the Hungarian connection; we all have a certain—awareness."

He hesitated, but he seemed to realize that he was in Margie's domain, not vice versa. He returned to his task, found the page he wanted, and held up a finger. "Mrs. Pinkoczi. She said she grew up on Balaton, the Hungarian Sea. And then later—she said Ava reminded her of a dear friend. Mrs. Pinkoczi remembered playing with this friend and her dog, Farkas."

I nodded eagerly. "So now the question is: did Ava *remind* her of the friend, or *was* Ava that friend?"

Wolf pointed at the notebook. "When I asked her what we should know about Ava Novák, that was the last thing she said: 'You should know she was my friend.' Was she playing *games* with me?" He stared at the notes in disbelief.

"Or maybe she's divided. Right—like Jekyll and Hyde? Maybe she loved and hated Ava."

"Why would she hate her?" Domo asked.

"That's the million-dollar question," Wolf said. "Could this be about the husband? Armin? Lili is still married to him, yet Ava was dating him. Did she lie? Did she really hate Ava for dating him?" Wolf scratched his head and stared hard at his notes. "In any case, let's assume that Ava and Lili grew up together. They were good friends. They played with this dog. Ava had two little sisters; we can probably assume they played with them, too. Maybe they were tiny kids, or toddlers."

"And one of those sisters had a stone that she got as a gift, or found somewhere? She treasured it. But years later, before she died, she gave it to Ava and told her to live her life."

"A child died?" Margie asked, looking crestfallen.

"So what are we missing?" Wolf said. "What makes these two friends—with a friendship so strong, they both mention the childhood connection—Ava in the playbill, and Lili in her statement because she apparently cannot resist the veiled reference—have a falling-out so intense that one would kill the other?"

"Exactly," I said.

Domo took a swig of his beer and said, "Maybe they didn't. Maybe this Lili is not your perp."

Wolf shook his head. "She lied, though. She went to the trouble of saying she didn't know Ava, but that Ava *reminded* her of someone who most likely was Ava. That makes no sense, unless she had a reason to dissemble."

I sat back in my chair. "So as a policeman, what do you do now? Because if you confront Lili Pinkoczi and say *Aha! We know that Ava had a dog named Farkas, and you played with him,* she could always say that lots of people had dogs by that name."

"Is that true?" Wolf asked.

"Doubtful," Domo said. "You've met my grandma, right?"

"But is that fear of wolves a Hungarian thing? Or just your grandma's own superstition?" Wolf asked. I was amazed anew at the sharpness of his questions.

Domo and I shrugged. He said, "I don't know. My mom has never made a big deal of it. And I don't think Grandpa has."

Wolf smiled a little. "The truth is I don't know what comes next. Whatever I do, I might need you Keller women to sit in again. We don't have a Hungarian translator—I was told that Hungarian is considered a rare language in the Chicago area, and it's hard to find a native speaker on short notice. For obvious reasons I can't pull someone from one of these Hungarian parishes where everyone knows everyone else. So I will be calling you into service when I set up this next interview."

I drummed my fingers on the table. "If only you had

something else. Something that could be a one-two punch that you could use on her. That way, if she denies the dog connection, you could say, *Ah, but I also have this information!* and then she might cave in."

Margie looked sad. "You sound like you want her to be guilty. Some little old lady. Maybe it was someone else who did it. Someone who wasn't at your tea party."

Wolf looked at her. "Margie, is it?"

"Yes." She blushed a little.

"This woman, Ava"—he pointed at her picture on the printout—"was poisoned and murdered at the Magyar ladies' tea event. And the only suspects are little old ladies."

"That's just unbelievable," Margie said. "How could that even happen? It's not like you can buy poison at a store. Or even like you can get out poison and pour it in a cup with all those people around. So how would she have done it?"

We all sat pondering this. It was true: the room had been full of women, and yet no one had told Wolf that they saw someone carrying the beautiful butterfly cup to Ava's table, no one had seen a person go there at all. I thought of my lovely teacup, tarnished forever with a terrible act, still sitting sadly in a box in the corner of my room . . .

I sat up straight. "There was a box!" I said.

"What?" Wolf asked. His focus flicked to me.

"When we were cleaning up that day, I found an empty cardboard box on the floor. I figured someone had brought flowers or candy or something for a friend. For a moment I thought it was significant; it was like my brain did this close-up on the box—I don't know. But then I dismissed my instincts. It was a box and it was empty. I threw it away."

Wolf winced. "I don't think any of you women—Kellers or Horvaths—should dismiss your instincts. They've been valid so far. You don't still happen to have—?"

I glanced uncertainly at my brother and Margie, then at Wolf. "No. The garbage was taken away. I mean, I think your people searched through it, but they wouldn't have thought it was anything, either. But *now* I wonder if someone slipped the cup in there. Brought it somewhere to write in their ugly message, then came back in the room to pour in some of the tea—we had pots at several stations—and then to bring it near Ava. They could have waited until people were lining up for the tea leaves and then just casually passed by, slipping the cup out of the box and tossing the box away. Saying *I'm sorry for our fight, here's a peace offering. I'll be right back.* Setting it down in front of Ava, giving her a hug, moving away again. It could all have happened in seconds. And then she could just go somewhere, wait for her evil poison to take effect."

Wolf nodded. "It's an interesting theory. It certainly seems more likely than anything we've come up with so far."

Domo said, "But why did she do it? *How* could she do something like that, to a friend? How could any person just watch another person die?"

We stared at one another, unable to answer that essential question.

Later, I realized it was because we had innocent hearts, and my grandmother had always told me that the innocent heart cannot see the evil one, but that evil could see evil because "they live in the same darkness, and they learn to see in the dark."

Wolf left soon afterward, thanking Domo and Margie for the food and briefly squeezing my hand before he disappeared into the hall.

Margie was absolutely glowing; I should have realized she was a romantic by the zillions of anniversaries with Domo that she kept track of. "Oh, Hana, he is so *handsome*! He looks like a blend of Paul Walker and Chris Hemsworth."

Domo snorted. "He looks exhausted. They should give the guy some free days."

"They did," I said. "He spent them working."

Domo began clearing the table, looking troubled. "Should I go stay with Grandma tonight? Do I have to worry that some vengeful old lady is going to show up with a gun, or something?"

I shook my head. "She has Grandpa, and Wolf has a police car watching her house. And she—would sense if something is wrong, apparently."

My brother looked truly confused. "I just can't fathom what is going on here."

I was thinking about the words "vengeful old lady." I said, "What's odd to me is that someone killed Ava, who seems to have been a kind person, and a talented one. The killer called her a witch, a Vasorrú Bába. But this person, who watched Ava die, who sent poison to our grandma in the guise of a friendly thank-you gift, this person is still walking around, wearing a smile."

A sudden revelation lit up my mind. I sat up straight and stared at Domo. "Hana, stop being weird with your big eyes. You're freaking us out," my brother said, looking uncomfortable.

"Domo. She wrote 'Vasorrú Bába' in the cup. But what if she wasn't calling Ava that name? What if it was a *signature*!!? What if she was revealing *herself* as the evil witch with the iron nose?"

"So her goal would be to frighten Ava, rather than to

suggest she hated Ava for being a mean old witch?" Margie asked.

"Either way it's pretty horrible," Domo said.

I nodded my agreement. "But the second way is more terrifying. Because, after all, she had to know that people other than Ava would see that teacup. And she was okay with it. So what if she wanted to say to the world: *I'm a witch, and I walk among you, but you don't know who I am*?"

I told them of what Mark had seen: the woman outside the tea house, shrieking at the sky, her hair in disarray, her hands digging in the ground.

Domo stood up and gathered some dishes. "Okay, enough of this. If I want to be scared I'll watch a horror movie. Stop trying to make us lose sleep, Hana." He walked toward the sink, bearing his load of plates.

"I'm not! I'm just trying to think like this person, to figure her out . . ."

"Like a profiler," Margie said, trying to be helpful.

"Yeah. I guess so. I want to profile this woman, think like her, so I can figure out why she did it and then maybe determine who she is."

Domo came back and put his hands on my shoulders. "Isn't that Wolf's job?" he said.

"Yes, of course. But he needs our help, because—I don't know, because we understand the culture."

"What culture? Not all Hungarians are the same. No group has identical members."

"No. But we can help. I can help. And I'm going to." I took out my phone and texted Wolf my latest thoughts about the note in the teacup. Then I looked at my brother. "Now if you will kindly walk me to my car and check the backseat, I would appreciate it."

Domo smiled wryly. Minutes later, after I had thanked Margie and promised we would go out again soon, he did accompany me to my car; he looked in every seat and even underneath the vehicle; he shone his flashlight all around the parking lot, and he turned the ignition key for me in case our evil witch had decided to blow me up.

"Clearly your paranoia has affected us all," Domo said. But he hugged me and told me to go straight home and then to call once I was safely inside my apartment.

What we learned that night was the power of legend. None of us believed in witches, and yet the word "witch" still had a powerful effect. I contemplated this as I drove home, and I concluded that words themselves are loaded weapons. We used them to make others feel good or bad, and the lore of witches had lasted for centuries because the notion of voluntary evil was one that could creep into a person's mind, her cells, her blood. It could make her cast aside logic and believe what was foolish.

And when that hypothetical person was *me*, it made her run all the way to the entrance of her apartment house, half-fearful of the clutch of cold fingers on her shoulder, fumbling with her keys, and breathing a huge sigh of relief on the other side of the door.

Chapter 22

The Clue of the Wolf

We had a Girl Scouts tea scheduled for the afternoon, but I had planned a breakfast visit with my neighbor Paige Gonzalez and her daughter, my little friend Iris. Paige was five months pregnant and almost always hungry; once in a while I liked to cook for her and her daughter (and her husband, when he wasn't working), and I had made pancakes this morning. Naturally I had set out some of my Herend teacups and a large white teapot.

Paige poured some tea into her Queen Victoria blue Herend cup; with her blonde hair tucked neatly behind her ears, she looked like Alice at the table of the Queen of Hearts. "I know we can't talk in front of little ears, but that was a pretty weird thing about your tea house. I didn't even totally understand the text you sent me, and then I saw that article in the paper. I would have come up sooner but I had a job to finish for the company I'm working for part-time, and I've been working weird hours."

"No problem. There's not much to say yet, until the police figure things out."

Iris, who had been stowing away pancakes with the enthusiasm of a starved sailor, paused with her little fork over her next bite. "What is the police for?"

Paige waved away her concern, calm and mother-like. "Just something at Hana's job. She's not in trouble, the police just have to solve a mystery, like Nancy Drew or the Scooby-Doo gang or something."

Iris nodded. "I like mysteries," she said. She ate some more pancakes, offering me an openmouthed smile that revealed chewed-up food.

"Iris May, you stop that right now. Be polite," Paige warned. "Other people don't want to see your food."

Iris shut her mouth but continued to smile; she was always sort of giddy at our tea parties because she loved them so much.

"Do you know anything about the new baby?" I said. "The gender, I mean?"

Paige brightened. "Yes—we left it up to Iris whether she wanted to find out or wait until the baby was born. What did you say, Iris?"

Iris sat up straighter in her chair and pointed a tiny digit at me. "I said *yes*!" she said. "And my sister is a girl, and we will name her Daisy, because all our kids are going to have flower names."

I clapped. "Oh, that's great! Congratulations to you both. I can't wait to meet Daisy."

"Me, neither," Iris said to her plate as she poured more syrup on her food. Then she took a dainty sip of her tea. I had given her a lovely blue rose–covered teacup that I had purchased at a yard sale for one dollar. Iris didn't know the difference, and I didn't have to worry that she might accidentally break a Herend piece.

I pictured Iris with a little sister, bossing her around and loving her, and it brought Ava's little sisters to mind. On a whim, I said, "Can I ask you a question, Iris?"

"Sure!" Her bright eyes were back on mine.

"I was—um—reading this story in an old storybook. It was about three sisters. One of them was older, like a big girl, and then there were two little girls. They all loved each other very much, but one of the little girls had an illness. She had this precious stone, a beautiful red stone that she treasured as one of her favorite possessions. The little girl got very sick. And she knew her older sister wasn't happy at home, but stayed there for her. So she told her older sister to leave home, go far away, and have a happy life, and she gave her the precious stone to take with her."

Iris nodded wisely. "Did the little girl die?"

I darted a glance at Paige, who inclined her head, indicating that I could be truthful. "Well, she did, because this was a long time ago when there weren't a lot of doctors and cures for diseases."

"That's too bad," Iris said. She went back to eating.

"I only told you the story because I wanted to ask you, as a little girl yourself: why do you think she gave her sister the stone?"

Iris looked up at me with wide eyes, surprised at my apparent ignorance. "Because she loved her older sister. And she couldn't take the stone to heaven. So she put it with the sister who would go far away, so that her stone could go all over the world. The stone was like her heart, and then her heart could travel everywhere."

Paige and I exchanged a stunned glance. Iris had always

been verbally precocious and occasionally philosophical, but this was perhaps her most wonderful inspiration yet. "Do you know what, Iris? I think Daisy is such a lucky baby, to have you as her sister."

"I know," Iris said. "Can I have more butter?"

Wolf called me at noon as I was packing my things for the tea house. "I wanted you to know that I questioned Lili Pinkoczi today. She laughed about the Farkas dog connection, saying that many people in Hungary named their dogs Farkas, especially if they had a Mudi, a dog which looked rather like a wolf. She said it was coincidence, although she had known Ava when they were younger; they had both lived near Balaton, had gone to school together."

"But she never mentioned that in her testimony! No one mentioned it!"

"No one knew," Wolf said. "Mrs. Pinkoczi claims that she never really thought about the old days, and apparently Ava didn't, either, so it never came up."

I thought about this, clutching my apron in my hand. "I don't believe that," I said.

"I don't, either. But I have no grounds to arrest her; I'll keep on it. Thanks for your insights. I'll need anything you can come up with. I encouraged Benton to be with his son—the boy's feeling better, but they all had a scare with his unexpected illness, so they need some family time."

"Is there anyone else working with you?"

"Yes, when I need them. But you're the closest to this case, and your intuition has been on target so far. I have to go chase a lead, but keep sending me your texts, okay? They're helpful."

"Okay."

"Talk to you later," Wolf said, and he ended the call.

I stood still, holding the phone and my apron, smiling a little. This was the second time that Wolf had given me a compliment about my analytical skills. I found that I really wanted to help him get to the bottom of this; perhaps it was for Ava, or for him, or for me. I wanted answers, and I felt that if I dug deeply enough, I would find them.

The Girl Scout event was going well; the young faces were as bright as the teacups before them, and the girls giggled and whispered for half an hour before their troop leader started making a speech. Apparently some awards were going to be given. I scanned the room; we had hustled to keep the tea hot and the sandwiches plentiful; now I would see if François needed help.

On my way to the back room I fell into step with my mother, who seemed to have the same idea about our pastry chef. Her bright blue eyes above her embroidered apron made her look like one of Grandma's Hungarian dolls. "How are you today?" I asked her quietly.

"Fine. So far I haven't gotten any other cancellations, but I have fielded some calls from people who had questions. *How did it happen? How will you keep it from happening again?* As though psychopaths walk through our door on a regular basis." Her face was troubled; I put an arm around her shoulder.

"It will be over soon. The police are working really hard on it."

She gave me a sharp look. "And how would you know that?"

"Wolf called me today with some questions. And I saw him at Domo's last night."

Her gaze was almost as intense as Wolf's. "What was he doing at Domo's?"

I glanced at the crowded tables; no one was looking our way, but I was as paranoid as Domo had suggested. "Come in the back." I led her to the back room, where François was putting green "GS" lettering on white cakes.

"You're amazing, François," I said.

"*Oui*," he agreed with a little smile. Clearly his mood had improved since the police had stopped invading his territory.

"Do you need anything from us? Should we help with the frosting?" my mother asked. We had done this in the past, but only when François was extremely pressed for time.

"No, no. You can go back to your little chattering girls."

I laughed. "In one second. I just have to talk to Mom." We sat down at the table in the back of the room, the table at which Wolf had interrogated my grandmother and almost lost my affection forever.

"Tell me," said my mother.

I sighed and said, "I don't know where to start. You already know the police interrogated Grandma, and I got very mad at them for that."

"At *them*?" she asked, with a little smile.

"Then last night at Domo's I mentioned something I overheard in the bathroom, here at the hall." I told her what the ladies had said, and how Margie had found the playbill, and how significant it had seemed. How Ava had grown up near Balaton, where Mrs. Pinkoczi said she, too, had been born.

"Balaton!" François said, looking up from his work. His eyebrows were pulled together as he studied his thoughts. "They said this, the two that I overheard."

"What did they say?" my mother and I said in unison.

He touched his forehead, as if to prompt the memories. "I don't know. The angry one said it. Something about leaving Balaton."

I leaned forward. "Did you hear any names? Especially the name Ava or Lili?"

He shook his head. "I don't know. Maybe. This I don't recall."

"Thanks, François," I said. "If you think of anything else, let us know."

He nodded. "I will put on trays now; we can deliver in two minutes."

"Right." My mother turned back to me. "So you found the playbill. And how did the police get there?"

I shrugged. "I called Erik."

"And who is Erik?"

"Wolf. Detective Wolf."

"Is there something I should know?" she asked, curious but gentle. "Or maybe something I already do know?"

"I like him," I said. "I kissed him."

Her smile widened. "Oh, my little Hana. You are such a romantic."

"Margie's the romantic. I just—I like the way he looks at me."

I noticed then that François had paused in his task and was grinning at us. "*En sa beauté gît ma mort et ma vie*," he said.

"What does that mean?" I asked. "Something sarcastic?"

He shook his head. "I would not make fun of love. You know how beautiful is my love with Claire."

"So what does it mean?" my mother asked.

He set the last tray on the cart. "It is words of Maurice Scève," he said. "'In her beauty resides my death and my life.'"

My mother said, "Ah," and smiled at me. I'm sure my face was quite red as I wheeled my cart out of the room, escaping into the happy chaos of girls anticipating dessert.

Later, as the event wore to a close, I puzzled over several things that made me think Lili Pinkoczi was lying. First, it was too much of a coincidence that she and Ava had lived in the same town. Second, it was too much of a coincidence that they had both loved a dog named Farkas. Third, it was odd that in all the rambling testimony she had given to Wolf, she had never mentioned that she and Ava were both from the Balaton region, even though she mentioned right up front where she had been born. There was a clear pattern in her statement—she talked and talked but concealed things at the same time. That made me think she was clever, but the coincidences made me think she was hiding the truth.

Wolf already knew all this, so there was no point in telling him these conclusions, but I did take a moment, after bringing a cart of dishes to the back, to call Domo at work. He sounded slightly distracted. "Hey, Han. I'm about to go to a meeting—what's up?"

"Domo, have you ever heard of a Mudi? It's some kind of Hungarian dog that looks like a wolf?"

"Aw, yeah, those dogs are great!" he enthused in my ear. "The black ones are especially cool, I think. And they do look like wolves. Dad and I thought about getting Mom one, a few years ago, as a birthday present. You know how Mom loves animals, and we thought it would be cool, the whole Hungarian connection."

"So why didn't you?"

"Oh, because they're super rare and expensive. Dad

found out there are, like, only a thousand of them in the world."

My ears were ringing a little. I pushed the cart up to the sink and sat down in a chair. "So they wouldn't be in every household?"

"No way. They're great dogs, though. Supposed to be super loyal and great guard dogs, but not mean or anything."

"Thanks. That's good to know."

"Gotta go!" said Domo, and he hung up.

I pulled up Wolf's information and sent him a text: Mudi dogs are very rare. They would not be in every Hungarian household. Check for yourself. Also, François heard the women in the bathroom say something about leaving Balaton.

I went to the sink and began to carefully wash teacups—some of them were too delicate to be placed in a dishwasher, and those we cleaned by hand. Lili Pinkoczi, I thought as I rinsed a cup, might be a murderer. She had killed a woman who had once been her friend, a woman she had played with as a child, and she had planned this killing in advance in all aspects but one: she had not expected to see the butterfly cup, and when she did she could not resist it. She wrote a message on this cup with a wax pencil of some kind; she put in her dose of poison (where had she gotten it?), and she poured tea into the cup. And then she offered it to Ava Novák, probably while smiling at her. *Drink*, she had said.

I stared at the cup in my hand, horrified by the image I had just created for myself, but sure that I was right: Lili was guilty.

I simply had to find a way to prove it.

Chapter 23

Memories of Balaton

When the last Girl Scout had left, clutching one last cake in her hand (François's confections truly were that good), we locked up and started our cleanup job.

My mother had put on some music—Monti's *Czárdás* this time—and it inspired us, haunted us, invigorated us as we swept and polished. At six o'clock we were all at the door, bound for home. "What are you plans, Hana? Are you going out with your girlfriends?"

I hadn't actually seen my "girlfriends" from school in quite some time; I needed to remedy that, or Katie especially would be pounding on my door and accusing me of what she jokingly called "callous disregard." But not tonight; Katie and I had agreed that in a week or two we'd have more time to get together. I shook my head. "I want to dig a bit more. Maybe online, or maybe through making phone calls. It would probably be too obvious to talk to Lili's children, right?"

My mother shrugged. "Why not talk to her granddaughter? You're already friends. Maybe she can give you some insights. Although I wouldn't lead with the idea that you suspect her grandma of murder."

We had started walking to the parking lot, but I stopped and stared at her. "Why do you assume that I'm friends with her granddaughter? I don't know any Pinkoczis."

"No, I think her last name is Miller. Maria Miller. She's one of Lili's granddaughters."

I shook my head. "Nope. The only Maria I know is from the grocery—oh my gosh! She is Hungarian! But I had no idea. She's Lili's granddaughter?"

"Yes, I'm quite sure." She had been looking at her phone, but now she looked up at me. "Okay, I texted Dad to pick up Grandma and me. Are you okay on your own?"

"Of course. Take care of Grandma, and I'll see you soon."

My father pulled up in his Ford, and the two ladies climbed into the car. They sat and waited until they saw me buckle into mine. I made a show of locking my doors, and my father gave me a thumbs-up. We drove out together, turning onto Wild Heather Road, but we parted ways at the first stoplight, when I turned left onto Prentiss. I spied Fair Price Grocery a few minutes later, and on a whim I pulled into the parking lot.

I knew that the store closed at seven, so if I timed it right I could chat with Maria while she rang me up and then potentially walk out with her, giving me a chance to speak to her at more length. I waited for about fifteen minutes in my car, then went into the store and started collecting the ingredients for *palacsinta*, a Hungarian delicacy I wanted to make for Wolf. I already had what I needed to make the delicious, superthin pancakes, but I needed some strawberry *lekvar* to put between the layers and fresh berries and cream to serve on top; Fair Price now carried some Hungarian ingredients because the tea house was a regular customer.

Basket in hand, I took my leisurely time, keeping an eye on my watch, and at about five to seven I went to Maria's aisle. "Hey," I said. "Sorry to cut it so close. I realized I needed some staples." I started unpacking items onto her conveyor belt.

She tucked a strand of dark hair behind her ear. "Isn't that the worst? Sometimes I just can't be bothered to leave the house. I give you credit for your get-up-and-go."

I seized an opening. "That sounds like a grandparent expression."

She laughed as she ran the jam jar over her scanner. "It is. My grandpa uses it all the time." I thought back to the statements people made to Wolf. Maria might have been referring to Lili's estranged husband, Armin.

"I tell you," I said with a casual smile. "Don't these old Magyars drive you nuts sometimes?"

"Of course. When they're not being adorable," she said, running the jar of *lekvar* over her scanner. Then she looked up at me and laughed. "I'm kidding. They always drive me nuts."

I looked over at the door, where the manager was putting up the "Closed" sign. "Hey, are you off now? Do you have a minute to chat? I feel like I just need to vent to someone who understands."

Her eyes widened, and then she looked pleased. "Yeah, sure. That will be eighteen fifty-two," she said.

"That's the year I was born," I said automatically. Then I pointed at her. "And that's a joke I got from *my* grandfather."

"Hilarious. Here's your receipt. Just let me punch out,

and I'll meet you outside. There's that nice little bench on the sidewalk—do you want to sit there?"

"Yes, great." I went outside and strolled through the parking lot, up a grassy parkway, and to the sidewalk that looked onto the main thoroughfare of Prentiss Road. It was a pretty street; Riverwood was good about acknowledging the changing seasons, and the shops were already decorated with white and gold lights, and little pumpkins sat in store doorways and on windowsills here and there, while tubs of marigolds sat on the sidewalks every twenty feet or so.

The bench was one of several on the sidewalk, facing traffic and offering passersby a chance to admire the town while resting their feet. I sat down on the bench and took a deep breath. Moments later Maria was there, too, her dark hair splashed in dramatic contrast to her red Windbreaker. "Ugh. At last. Fair Price is a nice enough store, but, boy, am I getting sick of being a checkout girl," she said.

"What would you like to do?"

"Get my master's in math, maybe teach. I'm working on it. I've got applications out to a few schools."

"That's great," I said.

With a frank expression she studied my face. I could hear Domo's voice in my head, assuring me that Hungarians stared at people. They really did, I realized, looking at Maria. I suppose we were staring at each other. "So what do you need to vent about? Has your grandma been hitting the Pálinka too hard?" She laughed a little at her own joke.

"No, not lately."

Maria grinned.

"It's just—you probably know about this whole Ava Novák thing."

"Oh God, yes. Every Hungarian in town is talking about it, about her. You hear a lot in the checkout lane."

"I'll bet. It's just—hard to go to work, after something like that happens. Hard to imagine it really happened at our tea house."

"I get that. I'm sorry to hear it. My grandma loves your tea house. She goes there all the time, I think. My mom, too. I've never actually been inside, but it's so pretty from the outside. I actually think it's one of the most distinctive things about Riverwood."

She wasn't the type to flatter people; I couldn't help beaming. "Thank you very much! We try. And I guess we're adapting to clients' needs as we go along, you know." I realized that particular conversational strand was going nowhere. I tried another.

"And speaking of old Hungarian ladies, my grandma has been going on and on lately about her past in Hungary—in Békéscsaba, and then in Budapest. Maybe all this stuff has brought it back for her, but if I have to hear one more time how the baker in her town was driven out because he couldn't make a proper Dobos torte, I'm going to lose it." (This was unfair to my grandmother; she had told me this only once or twice.)

Maria nodded, chuckling. "Oh yes. The older my grandma gets, the more she returns to her childhood. Heaven forbid if anything bad happened in your childhood, Hana, because apparently you will never, ever forget it." She gazed out at the street, her eyes squinting in the sun as she contemplated a passing car.

My skin began to tingle. "What do you mean? Does she have bad memories?"

"Good and bad. She's always talking about her parents, of course, which makes sense because she was an only child. She was probably lonely. But she had three 'sisters,' as she calls them—her surrogate sisters—because she had some friend back then who was her bestie, and the friend had two little tiny sisters that Grandma loved like her own. I've been hearing about them since I was a tot. She called them The Bárány Sisters—the Lambs. Just affectionate, I guess. I don't know their real name. No one likes to encourage the stories—isn't that terrible?" She seemed to realize how it might sound to a stranger, and her face looked distressed.

"No, I get it. So did the Lamb Sisters come to America, too?"

"No, that's why she's always going on about them. They stayed in Hungary. But—this is the sad part. Grandma really loved them like her own sisters, almost like her daughters, in the case of the little ones. The oldest sister was her true friend, and Grandma doted on the young ones. She carried them all over the place on her shoulders, taught them words from her schoolbook, made special treats for them. She called them her baby dolls."

"That's sweet." I sat on my hands because they were trembling slightly.

"Yeah. I think she was a little jealous of her friend, though. Because it was her family, and my grandma wanted it to be her own family, her little sisters. You know? It makes me feel bad, that she could be that lonely. But I think she was just convinced they were hers. They were her blood." She thought about that for a while. I stopped sitting on my hands and folded them together in my lap, squeezing tightly. Maria sighed. "Anyway, she claims the oldest one changed, became selfish. The littlest one was sick with some disease. They all doted on her because Grandma said she was sweet and happy, even in her illness. The little girl had some special ruby or something that she got as a gift from the family doctor. Some healing stone that he said could help her. He probably just wanted to keep her positive, you know? He said it was because she was such a good patient. She loved it—took it everywhere, showed everyone."

"Wow, you really do know the story," I said.

She rolled her eyes. "You have no idea. Everyone in my family knows it by heart. So anyway, the best friend started to act weird, talking about how she wanted to leave their town. She had a chance to go to some wonderful university, I think. The parents were reluctant to let her go; they all assumed she would stay around for the sake of this baby sister. She still wanted to leave, though. This confused my grandma; to her their town was paradise. She said, 'You can't leave, your sister needs you.' They were both, like, eighteen at this point."

"So she stayed, right?"

Maria's dark eyes studied me for a moment. "No. The morning after they had that conversation, the older sister was gone. And then to make things worse, the little girl lost her stone. It was like the two things just took the life right out of the little sick one, Grandma said."

My lips felt slightly numb. "That's sad," I said.

"Yeah. My grandma was so mad at the older sister for leaving, because a couple weeks later the little girl died. Grandma was there, with the family, holding the baby's hand. That's what she called her, the baby, even though she had to be eight or nine. I guess that's the part she can't forget. Who really could though, right? The death of a child. Especially a child that you loved. You don't get over that. Hey—I thought it was pretty nice out here, but you look like you're getting cold."

"You know what? I am a little. I wonder if I caught whatever my grandma had."

"Time to have some of her chicken soup," Maria joked, standing up. "Well, I don't know that I let you vent. I think I did most of the venting."

"It was great. We'll do it again sometime," I said. "Thanks, Maria!"

"Sure thing. See you in the checkout line," she said. She turned and walked down Prentiss Road; apparently she lived close enough that she didn't need to drive.

I waited until she was about a block away; then I ran to my car, tossed in my bag, and dove into my seat. I locked my doors and took out my phone. I pressed my contacts, where Wolf now resided.

"Detective Wolf," he said.

"Are you still at the office?"

"Hana? Yes, I'm working late."

"Arrest Mrs. Pinkoczi."

"What? Why?"

"I just spoke with her granddaughter. We're sort of friends, but I didn't know until today that she was related to Lili. She told me a story her grandmother always tells." I relayed it all to him: the Lamb Sisters, Lili's love for them, the little girl's "ruby," and Lili's discussion with Ava the day before she left.

"Think of what she said in the bathroom," I said. "When François heard them. She said 'all these years I thought it was lost.' She meant the stone, and then she must have seen Ava with the stone. Maybe right before this tea event. That's the only thing that makes sense, right? Because that would be the thing that would make her murderous, when for four years she wasn't. It must have brought back a flood of emotion. It must have felt—like time reversed itself."

"That's it," he said. "We got her. She didn't even bother to be discreet!"

"Yes. I mean no. Can you get her tonight? What if she talks to her granddaughter? What if she tries to run away?"

"We'll keep an eye on her. And I'll have her in first thing tomorrow for questioning. I'll want as many of your tea house ladies as I can get. Definitely your grandma—she's the most fluent, right? In case Mrs. P. slips into Hungarian."

"I can't believe this. Lili Pinkoczi."

"I can," he said in a somber tone. "I was just following up on another lead when you called. We have the puzzle pieces now, Hana. We have them all. We just need Lili to put them in order."

With a sudden burst of insight, I yelled into his ear, "Oh my gosh! Remember what Mark said the witch called out in the darkness? 'Fear, murder, fear, murder.' What if it was 'Vera, Magda, Vera, Magda'?"

Wolf said, "You're brilliant. I have to go."

He hung up, and I double-checked the locks on my car.

When I got home I felt restless. I cleaned my kitchen and scoured my sink. I fed the cats and brushed them. I tried to watch television, but found I couldn't concentrate. Had Maria said anything to her grandmother? Had she noticed that I became upset after she told me the story of the Lamb Sisters?

I brought some cleaning materials into my room and began to polish the shelves and the china on them. When I finished, and everything gleamed in the light, I moved across to my bed and gave a special cleaning to Fairy, gently polishing her green-blue surface and admiring the bold lift of her chin. The cats padded around on my quilt, watching me with what seemed to be concern. Could they sense my agitation?

I sighed and left the room, tucking my cleaning things back in the utility closet. I went to the kitchen and made myself some non-caffeinated tea. I drank it and looked out the window at the darkness—not rainy tonight, but windy and cool. The tree outside my window seemed to nod and bow, its motions gentle and protective.

"Okay, I think I've calmed down now," I told the cats, who sat together on the kitchen mat. "And I'm probably ready to sleep."

Five minutes later I was in bed, with the cats tucked in beside me. I said a brief prayer and dozed off into troubled dreams.

I woke at two a.m., sitting up in bed as though pulled by a string. Something was wrong and I knew it, just as I knew to walk into the hall, then into my living room, and to peer out the picture window that looked down on the parking lot and the field beyond.

There, near the one streetlight, I saw her: her white face tilted upward, her silver hair disheveled, her eyes black in their sockets. She was searching, searching . . . and then she seemed to see me. My muscles clenched in a paroxysm of fear. "Vasorrú Bába," I whispered. The creature in the parking lot began to move, crookedly, toward the front door.

I dove for my phone. With a trembling hand I pressed the button labeled with Wolf's name.

It rang one, two, three, four times before his voice, tired and confused, said, "Hana?"

"Erik, she's here."

"What?" He was awake now.

"She's here, a woman, she looks like a witch, like the bad fairies. She's moving toward my front door."

"I'll send a car. Hang up, I'll call you back."

I ended the call and peered out the window. I couldn't see her anymore; this was far more terrifying than seeing her had been. I forced my hand to the window latch, made myself crank open the window. I heard the sound almost immediately: a soft keening, eerie and high-pitched. At first it sounded like singing, like a woman singing a melancholy song in my parking lot at two in the morning. But then I made out the Hungarian words: "*Hana engedj be!*" "Hana, let me in."

I dropped the phone, then picked it up again with sweat-slippery hands. It rang in my palm.

I touched it with a trembling finger. "Erik?"

"Hana. A car will be there in one minute. I'll be there in six. Are you okay?"

"She's calling me. She's calling to me in Hungarian. She's telling me to let her in."

"Do *not* let her in, Hana! Wait there for the police."

"No danger of that," I said, my voice shaking. "This is weird, Erik. It's scary."

"Do you recognize her? Is it Lili?"

"I can't see her anymore. I'm afraid she got in. I'm afraid she's coming to my door." The cats ran past me, their tails high and puffed with fear, their eyes glowing gold in the dark. "Even the cats are scared."

"Just hang on, babe. I'll be there soon. I just ran a red light and that will save me time."

"Don't get pulled over."

The lot was illuminated now by red and blue lights: the best sight I had ever seen. "They're here. The police are here."

"Stay where you are. They know what to do."

"I'll stay right here. But what if she's inside? What if she's in my hallway? At this point I feel like she can move through walls, sidle through cracks, slither under doors . . ."

"Hana. Take a deep breath. Do it."

I took a deep breath, then several more. "Okay."

"You can't let panic win. Your door is locked. She won't get in. She's an old woman."

"It just feels—this whole thing has felt so—strange. Not human."

"She's human. Tell me what you see outside your window."

I peered out again. One officer stood next to the car, talking into a radio. Then, a moment later, another officer appeared, guiding the silver-haired demon toward the car. The witch-woman was silent now, and still. This, too, made me nervous; what was she planning? Wolf's car tore into the parking lot then and squealed to a stop. In my ear, he said, "I'm here. I'll call you back." He got out and spoke to the officers, then bent to talk into the face of the woman. She said nothing, but peered up at him in apparent surprise.

They persuaded her into the back of the police car, and the car drove away.

Wolf looked up at me and waved, then moved forward to ring my doorbell.

Chapter 24

Jekyll and Hyde

We were there at nine o'clock, all three of us Hungarian women, behind the one-way glass, with a view of the interrogation room where Wolf intended to speak with Lili Pinkoczi. We talked together in hushed tones, horrified yet invigorated by the intensity of it all. Not one of us had ever been inside the Riverwood Police station, and yet here we were, helping the detectives, providing crucial detail and the ability to translate.

Wolf peeked in our door. "Can I get you anything? Coffee? Tea?"

We all declined. We were far too keyed up to consume anything. Lili Pinkoczi didn't know what she was about to face. She had told the officers the previous evening that she must have been sleepwalking, that she had no memory of driving to my apartment house, and that in fact she had a history of walking in her sleep. Wolf didn't believe her, nor did I, but she had fallen back into the guise of a sweet old woman, and now she claimed she was confused and frightened by her own somnambulation. I felt briefly bad for Lili, walking into an ambush, but I thought of Ava, and my pity melted away. How cruel, how horrible, Lili had been.

She was ushered into the room by Wolf himself a few minutes later. She had been escorted home the night before but told that she would be picked up in the morning to answer questions for Detective Wolf. Despite what must have been a night of minimal sleep, she looked presentable and well rested; her hair was back in a neat bun at the nape of her neck. He offered her coffee, which she declined. She seemed as unperturbed as she had at her first interview, despite the events of the early hours. "My daughter has made some lovely *töltött káposzta*, Detective. Stuffed cabbage. Very good. I could bring for the officers here."

"Mrs. Pinkoczi, I need to ask you some questions. Detective Benton will once again be taking notes." Sure enough, Benton, carrying his trusty computer, walked into the room. He looked much better—his face was less pale, and he looked more plump. My grandmother nodded her approval.

"Fine," Lili said. She folded her hands on the table and looked at Wolf. "But I need to be done in one hour. I have to meet with Armin," she said, her expression prim and contained. I noted that the gray hair she had pulled back was actually quite long. If it fell out of the bun and floated in waves around her face, it could potentially look witchlike to a frightened boy like Mark, or to a frightened Hana, looking down from her window.

"Before we begin, I must tell you the following," Wolf said. "You have the right to remain silent. Anything you say can be used against you in a court of law. You have the right to consult with a lawyer and have that lawyer present during the interrogation. If you cannot afford a lawyer, one will be appointed to represent you. Do you understand these rights, Mrs. Pinkoczi?"

She shrugged. "Yah, just like the cop shows. I don't need a lawyer." She flashed a smile at Benton as though the two of them were in on some private joke. "I tell you, I was sleepwalking last night. Sleep-driving, I guess!" She smiled again. "I did not know that Hana lived at this place. I think I just probably pull over in that big parking lot."

"Hana informs me that you called her name. That you called to her to let you in."

She shook her head, as if amazed by life's surprises. "Is that so? I wonder what dream I could have been having. I will have to apologize to Hana, in case I scared."

Wolf cleared his throat. "Very well. Mrs. Pinkoczi, tell me about your relationship with Ava."

She sighed. "I tell you. She was my friend. A nice lady. A fun companion for Armin for a while."

"Tell me about your relationship with Ava in your childhood. At Balaton," Wolf said.

She squinted at him. "I don't know her much then. Yes, to see around town, but not so much as good friends."

I exchanged a glance with my mother and grandmother. Lili's lies were going to trap her.

"And yet, we have testimony that indicates otherwise," Wolf said. "Suggesting you two were actually the best of friends, for many years."

"Testimony from who? Ava?" She snorted at him, trying to make a joke.

Wolf took a paper from his file and slid it toward her. "Yes, from Ava, to start. Read this, please." I realized it must be Ava's quote from the playbill.

Mrs. Pinkoczi leaned over the paper and read it, her lips

moving slightly. "So? We are back to this dog? I told you. Everyone had a dog named Farkas. A common name, for Mudi."

"But a Mudi is not a common dog. Very rare, in fact. Ava had one, though. We had confirmation from her sister Vera."

Lili's head came up sharply. "Vera? When did you talk to her?"

"She's in the United States, actually. She's staying at the home of Joe Novák."

Again, we three women behind the glass exchanged a shocked glance.

Lili Pinkoczi showed her first signs of distress. "Vera Fodor. I have not seen her in many, many . . ." She stopped, realizing her mistake.

Wolf's voice was quiet, but firm. "Tell me about the Bárány Sisters, Mrs. Pinkoczi."

"What?"

Wolf remained silent as Lili sat thinking in her chair. Her eyes darted around the room; clearly her thoughts were colliding in a chaotic way. "What—who said this to you?"

"I understand that you called the Fodor girls this, because they were your dear friends, your sweet lambs. Especially the little girls, who were almost like daughters to you."

Lili's eyes were angry. "You can't just take stories and say they are true. This—you don't got evidence."

"I understand that you loved Magda most of all. What illness did she have, Lili? Was it a lung ailment?"

Lili shook her head. "Don't speak of her," she said.

"Did you love her? She must have been just a child when she died. Was she seven? Eight years old?"

Lili pounded a small fist on the table. "Stop. I will not speak of Magda."

"Why not, Mrs. Pinkoczi? Is Magda the reason you hated Ava so much?"

"Stop. I want my husband here. I want Armin Pinkoczi."

"Why? Did Armin know how you felt about Magda? She must have loved you, right? Did she see you as an alternate mother? I heard the stories, about how you put her on your shoulders and walked all over. How she was so happy and kind, even in her illness. How much you loved seeing her little face, hearing her voice each day . . ."

She pounded her fist on the table again, but this time her eyes were full of tears. "You will not. You will *not*. You will not speak of my child."

Wolf looked surprised. "Your child?"

"Yes, like my own child. My sweet baby. An angel. A lamb. All she wanted was our affection, Ava's and mine. But she was my special girl. Her parents were busy, busy providing, and I was the one who gave her attention and love. That's all she asked. And she had one precious thing, this small red stone. One thing that made her happy. The people said it might even heal her. Make her better. It seemed to be doing so."

"That's just a legend, Lili. She was going to die anyway."

She shook her head, dashing away tears with fisted hands. "She was getting better. Her color was good. She laughed, happy like a bird, each day. Very happy, barely coughing at all. Even though—" Suddenly her eyes looked black in her face.

"Even though?" Wolf prodded.

"One night her beloved sister disappeared into the darkness. Without thinking how this might affect the health of the poor child! My poor little baby, my sweet Magdalena, my child . . . she had lost her health stone as well, that's what we thought." She rocked in her chair; she could no longer contain her crying, and she sobbed with the rush of memories.

Wolf and Benton waited, saying nothing, still as statues in their chairs. Lili found a tissue in her purse and wiped at her eyes. "She died soon after. Without the stone, without her sister's love, she get sicker. Sick and sad, poor child. Her mama and daddy can do nothing for her. It was Ava she loved. I tried to be everything for her, be her sister for her, but I could not save her."

"Do you feel guilty about Magda's death?" Wolf asked.

She shrugged. "It is hard, to watch a child die. I willed it to be otherwise. But two losses, at once. It was hard to fight against them."

Wolf looked blank. "She had a terminal disease."

She shook her head. "You weren't there. She was fine; Ava left, and she declined. Later, much later, I found out the stone is not lost. Ava had taken it. Taken it! The *cruelty*! Like murder."

Her eyes glittered now with some unrecognizable emotion, and I saw why she had frightened Mark so much in the darkness, why she had frightened me.

"We've been told a different version of events, Mrs. Pinkoczi. That Ava's little sister knew Ava had always wanted to leave, to travel. That Ava sat at her bedside, and Magda said that her greatest wish was to know that Ava was out in the world, and she wanted her to take the stone with her. This was her last request, and Ava granted it."

Lili shook her head, her face bitter. "A lie. She left the baby, she left us all. She left me."

Benton cleared his throat. "I wonder," he said. "When she came to America—didn't she explain it all to you? Didn't she clear things up four years ago, when you two became friends again?"

Lili held up a hand. "We were friends again. I said it was a long time ago. I could not understand why she left, but I forgive her."

The room grew quiet again. Wolf said, "And in four years, you never tried to harm her."

She shrugged. "Like I said, I forgive her. We were friends, united again."

"Mrs. Pinkoczi, did you kill Ava Novák?"

She looked at her hands. "No."

"Did you find a butterfly cup that reminded you of an old Hungarian fable?"

Her eyes flew up, surprised, and briefly met Wolf's gaze. Then she looked down again.

"Did you write 'Vasorrú Bába' on the inside of the cup?"

We three ladies all looked at one another in surprise; Wolf's pronunciation had been excellent.

"And did you put several drops of cyanide poison in that cup and fill it with tea? Did you go to Ava Novák at her table in the tea house and apologize for the fight you had with her in the ladies' room?"

Now Lili's face showed some fear. "No. None of that."

"Did you apologize and ask her to accept your gift of tea?"

"No, *Jaj Istenem*, no."

Wolf went back to his file. "Mrs. Pinkoczi, you told us last week that your son worked in a research lab. Do you recall telling us that?"

"No."

Wolf took another piece of paper out of his file folder, but he kept the sheet in front of him. "I wonder—what made you choose the day of the tea party? There were more private ways to poison Ava, more private places. What set you off, Mrs. Pinkoczi? Because this was a crime of rage, of fury. You wrote the signature of a witch inside the cup—or were you calling Ava a witch? Either way, there was anger there. Enough anger that you came to the party prepared with a small syringe of cyanide."

Her face changed then, but she said nothing. She stared at the paper in front of Wolf, her eyes wide.

"But I'm wondering," Wolf said. "What happened the day before? What set it off, this rage that had been lying dormant in you? What could poor Ava have possibly done?"

Lili swallowed, then bit her lip. Then she smiled, rather bitterly. "You are a smart detective. You have evidence on that paper, ya? Not just stories, I see. So I tell you. We were at the church hall for a chicken dinner. An end-of-summer parish dinner. And Ava talk to one of the old priests about the old days, and Balaton. I was close by, listening. She talked of the girls, her sisters, how she loved them. I start to feel angry, resentful. She could not claim to love them, after leaving them alone. But I could have gotten over this. We were friends, it was in the past. And then she took out the stone. She had it right there, with her, her bloodstone with the blood of baby Magda on it, took it out and showed it to that priest at the table. The *witch*, I thought. The terrible old murdering witch."

Her face was wild now; her eyes didn't seem to be focusing on anything or anyone. "I went home soon after. I made some *gulyás* and brought it to my son Michael's house. Driving there, all I could see was Magda's face, little Magda. It all came back, flowing back, the pain of losing her, her little hand in mine when I said good-bye—"

She swallowed back a sob and forced a grisly smile. "He invited me in. He loves my cooking, he and his wife. I said

I had to use the bathroom; I know where his sample bag is, which he has to take to the medical facilities. I knew what I wanted."

The room was quiet except for the sound of Benton typing.

Wolf said, "And the next day, you took that cyanide and you put it into the teacup of Ava Fodor Novák."

Lili clutched the edge of the table as though she intended to break it in half. "She had the stone again! On her purse, like a murderer holding the head of her victim for all to see." Her face was twisted with fury. "I watched her, when she sipped it. I was back at the tea-leaf table, pretending to wait for my reading. My eyes were on her, just on her. I wanted her to read it, understand, look up at me. Show that she was sorry, or frightened, or sad. But she never saw it. She sipped, once, twice, three times. She make this face"—Lili acted as though she were in pain; she clutched her stomach—"and then she run toward the bathroom. That's it. So quick. She never come back. I went to the table and took the red stone."

The room we were in suddenly felt too bright. I covered my eyes, taking deep, calming breaths. My grandmother cleared her throat a few times; I could tell she was fighting back tears.

My mother sat like something carved from wood.

Wolf hadn't moved. Now he said, quietly, "You lost the stone, though. You dropped it in the grass, am I right?"

Her face creased with distress. "That is where it was? In the grass? I got home and realized I had lost it—after all this time, and I still didn't have Magda's stone. I wanted to make a shrine to her, my lost child. I went to search, used a light on my phone to search in the darkness, but I never find."

Wolf sat quietly while Benton made more notes. Then he said, "I wonder—how did you get the butterfly teacup from the display table to Ava Novák?"

She slumped in her chair. "The officers get corsages. I used my box. A cardboard box. I act like I was throwing it away."

Wolf was quiet for a moment, looking at his notes. Then he said, "Why did you try to poison Juliana Horvath? I am confident that the fingerprint we found on the teapot will be yours—won't it, Mrs. Pinkoczi?"

I took my hands from my eyes and looked at my mother and grandmother; their faces were shocked, but curious. I looked back to Mrs. Pinkoczi, who was still stunned by the rapid deterioration of her defenses. "I—the ladies say she knows things. I was . . . afraid. I don't got nothing against Juli. I was just afraid."

Wolf's voice changed slightly. "Ava Novák was your best friend. She was like your sister. Have you felt any regret, Mrs. Pinkoczi, about what you did to her?"

I leaned toward the glass to study Lili's face, and there I saw, displayed in a way that I would never forget, the duality of human nature. I saw her love for Ava, never extinguished, visible as a kind of longing in her eyes. At the same time I saw hatred, the sharp, barbed protection over a grief so raw that it had not ebbed in more than fifty years. Lili said, "Yes, she was my friend. But *she* chose evil, not me. She was the witch, not me. She was the one who killed, not me—killed with her thoughtlessness and cruelty."

Wolf set his pen down and said, "No, *you* killed, Mrs. Pinkoczi. Magda died of tuberculosis. The stone would not have saved her; it made her happy to know that her beautiful Ava was taking her stone, her legacy, and traveling with it to other places in the world. It made her feel that she would live forever. You understand? Little Magda wanted to live through Ava, and Ava gave her that."

Lili's face went slack. "No," she said.

"We were told as much by her husband. Not a day went by, he said, that she didn't think of her sisters and pray for them. She kept in touch with Vera, but hadn't seen her in decades."

"No, it—Ava would have told me. She only said she left because it was too painful, seeing her sister. So selfish."

Wolf consulted his notes. "Ava's husband told us that you told her not to speak of the past. Perhaps she didn't go into detail because she felt it would upset you. Do you really think, Mrs. Pinkoczi, that your childhood friend wanted to kill her own sister, or hurt her in any way? Do you really think she would steal a talisman from that child's hand? Is it more likely that she would have done what she did out of love? Isn't that the Ava you knew?"

Mrs. Pinkoczi seemed to shrink before our eyes. Her skin, white as paper, looked unhealthy against the dark material of her suit. "She was good once," she said. "I loved her."

Wolf stood up. "Lili Pinkoczi, I am arresting you for the murder of Ava Fodor Novák . . ."

Lili didn't respond. Since Wolf's final speech she had become like a dead woman herself—expressionless, lifeless, and still.

Chapter 25

A Thing of Beauty

I knew Wolf would be busy for several days, so I stayed away from him, sending only the occasional text message of encouragement. I'm proud of you, I said. But also sad, about everything.

The papers had the story the next day, and our tea house was in the news once again, but only as a backdrop to the surprising story of murder in Riverwood—murder committed by an old woman who had never recovered from a tragic loss.

"Her husband is with her," my grandmother said at our family Sunday lunch. We sat around her extra-long wooden dining table in her house, which smelled of paprika and onions. "I heard from Mrs. Guliban. Armin is being good, visiting her every day, acting like the husband he should be. She said she had boyfriends, but she lied."

I sighed, leaning back in my chair. "All she had to do was talk to Ava. Just talk to her and work it out. It doesn't take a therapist to have a conversation."

My father looked thoughtful as he forked into a pile of *haluska* on his plate. "Can you imagine how many murders could have been prevented in just that way?"

This made us all sad again. My grandmother had been humming some Hungarian song under her breath, and I didn't dare inquire what it was about. I had asked my mother once why my grandmother seemed to sing only melancholy Hungarian songs. She had smiled grimly. "Because they're *all* sad, Hana. Even the happy ones are unhappy underneath. You just have to listen to the lyrics."

My grandmother, in a different conversation, had assured me that the Hungarians were "a sad people with a sad history." And that, she told me, was my legacy.

Now, at my grandma's crowded table, my father smiled at me. His contribution to my DNA was standard American stock, with roots in Germany. Perhaps I would be spared the life of sadness after all. I returned his smile, and he said, "You never did come over Friday to tell me about your boyfriend. I'll have some more goulash, Juli," he said, holding up his plate as my grandmother whisked past with a pot full of food.

Grandma served him, but all eyes at the table were on me. They meant well, my family, and they were all present: Grandma and Grandpa, Mom and Dad, Domo and Margie. I sighed. "He's not my boyfriend."

I was confronted by a wall of disbelief.

"He could *become* my boyfriend, though. We'll see. He's very busy, as you know. He just arrested someone for murder. As Mom and Grandma witnessed, he is very good at his job, and very detail oriented."

Domo finished crunching on a bite of *uborkasalata* and said, "What I saw was what a good cop *you* are, Hana. Maybe you should quit the tea house and become an investigator."

Margie nodded eagerly. "Hana knew all these things about the case, and she found important details that she shared with the police."

My mother raised her glass. "They couldn't have done it without you, sweetheart. Without all of us, really—we Hungarian tea house ladies who became translators for the police."

"I wouldn't be surprised if we got more business because of all this media attention the murder has gotten," I said.

My mother nodded. "We will. I've already gotten three calls since the article came out. I assume there will be more. Someone said that the article referred to us as a place that served European high tea, and they thought it sounded 'classy.' I guess press is press." My father leaned over and kissed her cheek for no particular reason; her skin grew rosy and she smiled at him.

The doorbell rang, and my grandfather rose to answer, winking at me before he left the room. He returned in the company of two people I had never seen—a gray-haired man with a kindly face and a younger woman, pretty and European-looking. "Everyone," he said. "I think you might know Joe Novák? And this is his sister-in-law, Vera, who is visiting from Hungary."

We stood up, acknowledging them both, and Grandma invited them to find a seat around her table. She could not have been happier to have a chance to feed this many people. "How are you both holding up?" my mother asked, her voice sympathetic.

Joe smiled, but his eyes were mournful. "Day to day. Day to day. Ava was a good wife, a good person. We were happy. She was hoping to see Vera this year, but she—well. It never happened. Vera came earlier than planned, to meet me and to attend the funeral." He looked at my grandfather, shrugged, and said, "*A szerencsetlenseg lóháton jön, gyalog megy el.*" My mother later translated this for me: "Misfortune arrives on horseback and goes away on foot."

Vera Fodor put a soothing hand on Joe's arm. "Poor Ava," she said. "She hated to leave us, back when we were children. She loved us so much. But I know she is in heaven now, with Magda and her mama and daddy."

I met Vera's eyes. "What will you do now?"

She took a plate that my grandmother handed her, filled with a sample of every food my grandmother had made in the last several days. Joe had received a similar plate. "I don't know. I have some time for a visit. Joe says he would like me to stay—his only relative. He wants to show me this place where Ava lived."

"Don't judge America by the actions of one angry woman," Domo said. "We are welcoming here."

Vera nodded. "In any case, that woman was Hungarian. So do not judge us, either." She sighed, holding a fork but not using it yet. "I loved her, that Lili Pinkoczi. I can't believe she came to this. I can't believe she killed my sister. She once loved Ava, more than anything."

My grandmother appeared behind Vera to offer her some Pálinka. Apparently Grandma believed it even had the power to cure broken hearts. Both Joe and Vera drank some of the strong fruit brandy, though, and they managed to laugh later on at one of Domo's silly stories and to smile when my grandfather spoke about the church fall fest.

When they left together an hour later, they had been comforted with generous helpings of my grandmother's delicious food, healing doses of Pálinka, and many assurances that they were always welcome beneath my grandparents' roof. I watched them from the window as they walked to the car. Joe took her hand as she navigated a large puddle (it had rained in the night), and after she stepped over it, they kept their hands joined. It looked natural, sweet, and I wondered if in fact Vera would become the next Mrs. Novák, regardless of how many pots of *paprikás* the Hungarian widows were currently making for the newly widowed Joe.

When I got home I greeted the cats and went into my room. The bag sat where I had left it, against the wall and half-concealed by my big bookshelf. I went to it now and took out the carefully wrapped parcel. First I retrieved the saucer, with its blue butterfly and carefully detailed green leaves, its hand-etched gold border, its tiny chip beneath the rim that had made it affordable to me. I set it down on the carpet and unpacked the cup. As Wolf had promised, it was clean and perfect, bearing no trace of the words that had been scrawled inside it, or (I assumed) of the deadly substance it had once contained. The cup was still lovely, with its huge orange flower painted on its front and the sapphire-blue butterfly that composed its handle. "A thing of beauty is a joy for ever," Keats once wrote, and I found that I did still take pleasure in looking at the beautiful cup, its artistry and its inspiration.

I would never drink out of it. I stood up, holding the cup and saucer, and set them on the topmost tier of my bookshelf. The teacup was a piece of history; thinking of it that way would allow me to view it with more objectivity. Its beauty would never fade—it was permanently a work of art, a thing of beauty, a benefit to the world, just as Ava Novák had been: a talented musician, a good and kind woman, a devoted wife, a loving sister.

Chapter 26

A Buried Grief

That evening I stopped at the Fair Price to buy a few things and to face Maria. I didn't know what I would say to her, so I was half-relieved when I saw she was not working one of the registers. I started back toward the exit, but spied Maria leaving the back room. She saw me, too, and I couldn't escape then without actually running away. She moved closer, smiling with half her mouth. "Do you have a minute to talk?" she asked.

I nodded, and without speaking we both understood that we would return to the bench. Today Prentiss Road was rather gloomy; it was one of those September twilights that contained no vestige of sun; it had been cloudy all day. She sat on the chair. "Normally I wouldn't be here, but I had to pick up my paycheck. I took some days off to be with the family. People are pretty upset about Grandma."

"I'm sorry," I said.

She studied me with her frank stare. "I figure you told the police what I told you."

There was no point in denying it. Now that I contemplated it, I realized I had nothing to apologize for. I nodded. "I did. Because even as you told me, I realized that your grandma was the one who poisoned Ava Novák. But I'm sorry for your family. I know it's hard, for Lili and all of you."

She nodded. Her eyes filled with tears. "I can't believe she did it. It's—so cruel. And she's my gentle little grandma."

I turned toward her on the bench. "People bury their pain. For years. And then it can come out—as fear, or anger, or hatred. She probably barely knew what she was doing."

Maria wiped her eyes and gave me a wry smile. "No, she knew. She admitted it to my dad. She's sorry, though. She's sorry now, when it's too late and a woman is dead and a husband has lost his wife."

"It's a terrible situation."

"I called her, after I talked to you. I asked her, what was the name of those Lamb Sisters? She said why did I want to know?" Maria sent me a guilty glance. "I said I had been chatting with you, and it came up. I heard what she did later, coming to your house. I don't—I can't explain it. That's not her, at all."

"Just desperation. It would drive any of us outside of ourselves."

She raked a hand through her dark hair. "I know this is selfish, but I keep thinking—what will people think of our family? How will this affect *us*?"

"I doubt that it will affect you, outside of your grandma's

situation. Few people will know, and those who know won't care."

Her eyes were bitter. "Really, Hana? What about you? Would you really want to hang out with someone related to the notorious Mrs. Pinkoczi?"

"I'm doing it right now. I came here looking for you."

She seemed to appreciate this. She let out a shuddering sigh. "I'm so mad at her, Hana. But then I think—what if I hadn't been so impatient when she told me her stories? What if I had asked more questions, encouraged her to talk it out? I think my whole family feels that way. Like we bear the burden of guilt for not preventing this."

I shook my head. "I think the guilt lies with one person. And she'll have to find ways to earn your forgiveness, and maybe one day to forgive herself."

She shook her head. "And my uncle—God—I hope he doesn't get in trouble. He's always been very responsible. He never would have imagined his own mother was rifling through his bag. He has samples of all kinds of toxic things in there—it's been a family joke for a long time, his weird job."

I sighed. "I saw Joe Novák today. He said this Hungarian saying—misfortune comes on horseback and leaves on foot."

"I get it," she said. "I totally get it."

I drove back to my apartment in the last of the light and found Detective Wolf's car in one of the visitor spots. He was leaning on his back hatch, his blond head bent over his phone, his thumbs moving.

I parked and climbed out of my car, then walked toward him. He put his phone away and glanced at me with cool green eyes. "You haven't been answering my texts." I couldn't tell in the dimness if he were angry with me, or concerned, or some other inscrutable Wolf-like emotion.

"I'm sorry. My phone was off. I was with Maria—Lili's granddaughter. She needed to talk."

He nodded.

"How long have you been waiting here?"

"About twenty minutes."

"Come inside. We can have some dinner." I took his hand and started leading him toward the door.

"I was hoping to get an invitation. That's why I'm hanging around in your parking lot; I must have looked like a vagrant. I got some stern glances from a tiny little girl who seems to be the sheriff of your building."

"That's Iris. She is kind of the sheriff, but also a princess and a mermaid and other things," I said as we climbed the stairs. Outside my door, we could hear Antony and Cleopatra clamoring. "Oh, those insatiable cats. I'm going to let you feed them while I run to the washroom. Their food is next to the fridge."

We went into my apartment; I turned on the coziest lights and jogged to the bathroom, where I combed my hair, washed my face, and walked through one spritz of Éclat d'Arpège. Then I went back into the kitchen, where Wolf was smiling down at the cats while they stood crunching food at their bowls, occasionally turning their heads to observe each other. "They're great," he said.

I pointed at the cabinets above the sink. "You can find dishes in there. I'm going to heat up some chicken soup, and I've got some nice crusty bread."

"Sounds delicious." Wolf did some investigating and located some white and blue bowls, which he set out on the table.

At the stove I poured the last of my soup into a pot and set it on simmer. I pulled the bread from my pantry and began to slice it on a wooden board. Wolf came up behind me and touched my shoulders. "Need any help?"

I turned around. "No."

It was strange, having Wolf in my space without the case to talk about. I wracked my brain for a topic of conversation. I didn't know who was worse at casual romantic patter, Wolf or me.

"What in the world are we going to do with ourselves?" I said, only half joking.

"We'll find all sorts of things. We just need practice," he said. He lowered his head and pressed his lips to mine. "I like those little noises you make when I kiss you," he said against my mouth.

"What noises?"

He smiled. "Just—little happy noises."

I touched some stubble on his jaw. "Can I ask you a question—about the whole Ava thing?"

He scowled slightly. "I thought this was our time."

"It is. But I was thinking back to that first day and the way you walked around the room and took things in and talked to people. Then the next day you had an order of names for the interviews. And the ones you put first were Kalas, Pinkoczi, and Guliban. I just wondered—why were they first?"

He raised his eyebrows. "Well—because they were my prime suspects."

"How did you know? That first day, and already by the time of the interviews, you put Mrs. Pinkoczi second."

Wolf shrugged. "I based it on who knew Ava best, who had the most access to her, who people said were her best friends or her strongest connections. I had a whole list of things I looked for, and those three came out on top."

"Well, you're brilliant. I was so impressed with your work, from beginning to end."

Wolf's smile was almost boyish. "Thank you," he said. "I was very impressed with yours, too. I couldn't have done this without you. But now it's over, Hana."

"Yes." It was strange to me that this fact didn't fill me with euphoria. I had hated not being able to see Wolf, to invite him over if I wanted to do so. Now I could, anytime, but I found myself dwelling on those invigorating moments when we had found out something important, or when Wolf congratulated me via text.

He read my mind. "You've got the bug, haven't you? Solving puzzles exhilarates you."

I shrugged. "That's not the only thing. But yeah, sort of. Hey—what did you find out about Steve Sarka? I mean, why did no one mention him as someone Lili dated?"

He let out a short laugh. "It turns out none of the women considered Steve Sarka a serious contender. He has a reputation as one who flies away. That's how Mrs. Kalas put it when I asked. So no one thought to mention him."

"Huh. And the sisters? Guliban and Cseh? Did we find out why they don't sit together?"

He nodded. "Mrs. Guliban says her 'little sister' has her own group of friends, but that they get along fine. Who knows if there's more to that story, but I've looked under enough rocks for the time being."

I rested my hands on his shoulders. "It was interesting, though. So—compelling."

"I'm telling you—become a cop. You'd be great." His hand sifted through my hair, and he bent to breathe its scent.

"I think I'll just date a cop, for starters. If that's okay."

"That is okay, Hana. More than okay. It's the best news I've ever gotten."

"Now you won't have to try to woo anyone else," I joked, thinking of our labored courtship.

This surprised him. "Why would I want to woo anyone else?"

For some reason I recalled my grandmother leaning forward to talk to Wolf, in the back room of the tea house, when he had confronted her about her letter to Ava. "Erik? What did my grandma say to you, that time when she was whispering to you in the tea house? Right before Benton walked up. She was talking for a long time, and you were listening."

He smiled and tucked my hair behind my ears. "She said that she knew the moment she saw her husband that he was the one for her. She said they were at a grape festival in Hungary, and she saw him standing with a group of young people, but only he had light around him, a gold light. I still remember her words because I was miserable and I knew you were glaring at the back of my head, but I still thought what she said was poetic. She said, 'This gold light made him look like a king, or a man who had emerged from the sunrise.' She said she couldn't wait to take his hand in hers."

My eyes watered slightly. "I've always loved that story. I never heard that particular version of it, though. I always used to think she was just being metaphorical. But she really saw it—that gold light. She really . . . sees things."

"She certainly saw how I felt about you. And I was trying to hide it."

A burst of warmth went through me, but a concern bubbled to the surface. "Erik, there is something that—we might have to deal with. Maybe you won't want to date me when you know."

"What?" His eyes were wide.

"I—the night that Lili came to my house, I knew. I woke up and I knew. That she was there, and where she was. I saw it all inside my head."

He nodded, thinking about this. "We already thought there might be something, after your grandma got that package. You said that you *both* knew it was bad."

"Yes. I guess I was thinking—hoping even—that I was just sort of absorbing her instincts. But there have been other things. On the day of the poisoning, my body didn't want to go into the tea house. My legs just stopped walking. And my grandma knew; she understood. And when I picked up the cardboard box that Lili used to transport the teacup, I knew that was important, too. And I knew that the playbill was going to be important before I read it. When I start to dig, there's a lot of evidence. But I—don't know how I feel about it. I don't really want to have whatever weird inherited ability I have."

"It probably won't manifest that much, now that the danger is over. Just little bursts of insight, like your grandma and your mom have. That's not so bad, right?"

I thought of my grandmother's instant love for my grandfather, captured so beautifully in the story she had told Wolf. I thought of the "golden light." "No—there are some nice parts. I just wouldn't want you to find it off-putting."

His hands slid up and down my arms, enjoying the softness of my sweater. "Nothing about you is off-putting. I can barely stay away from you."

I smiled and turned to stir the soup. He peered into the pot and said, "Hey, I learned to say something in Hungarian."

I looked up, expectant, and he said, "*Az ételed finom.*"

A laugh bubbled out of me because, even with my limited knowledge of Hungarian, I knew what that meant: "Your food is delicious."

Chapter 27

Omens of the Future

On the first day of October we sat in my mother's big kitchen, just as we had done on the day that poor Ava died. We weren't polishing teacups this time, but drinking tea together and celebrating the anniversary of the opening of Maggie's Tea House. "Thirty years," my mother said. "It's hard to believe."

'It's been a success," her mother said. "From the very start. You are smart, Magdalena. Always a smart girl. The college was a good investment."

I nodded. My mother had majored in business, and she ran the tea house with a shrewdness that had served our family well.

Domo wandered in, eating one of François's petit fours. "God, these are good. Can I bring some home to Margie?" he asked. "Poor girl is slaving away on her drawings."

My grandmother pointed to a tray on the table. "We have *kiflis*, too. Four flavors."

"I'll get around to everything," Domo assured her. "I'm just pacing myself."

As Grandma studied him, her face took on a pleased expression, as though she'd just had an idea. "You can take home," she said, "if you let me read the leaves. All of you."

My mother and I groaned, but Domo came forward eagerly. "Sure," he said. "I hear you have quite the gift, Grandma. Not a fake one, but something real. Right?" he asked, looking into her hazel eyes.

She shrugged. "We shall see."

We got new cups of boiling water and scattered in our loose leaves. We drank the tea and then turned over our cups so that Grandma could study the leaves for each of us. Domo went first. Grandma righted the cup and stared at the tea left inside, her eyes narrowed. Domo started to look nervous. "Don't tell me anything bad, now. I don't want to know if someone's going to poison *me*."

My grandmother swatted his words away and continued to stare into the lovely green cup. Then she pointed. "See this? You have a man, yes? See his figure? And he has a staff. This is a shepherd, but good. And no Vadleány to lure him into danger. He points his staff at the future. You are moving on."

"Okay," Domo said. "To what?"

She smiled into the cup. "New job," she said. "And marriage."

Domo made a huffing sound. "You're just making that up," he said.

She shook her head. "Look at the leaves, you don't believe me. Next."

My mother handed over her cup, smirking slightly. My grandmother stared into the cup, first with a tense expression, then a more relaxed one. "Devotion," she said. "The joined hands."

I realized she was no longer using any sort of standard tea-leaf symbolism. She was following her own instincts with vague touchpoints from Hungarian mythology. Frankly I found it more interesting and a bit frightening.

My mother said, "So I am devoted?"

"Yes. To everyone. But especially your man. The other hand is him, devoted to you."

"That's sweet, Grandma," I said.

My mother nodded her agreement. "Yes. A very nice reading, Mama. I'll tell Jack when he gets home from school."

I handed my grandmother my cup, emptied of all but the dark leaves. She peered inside, and her brows furrowed. "Dark woods," she said. "Unknown. But see here—you have a guide. Maybe the good shepherd, maybe something else. But here? The heart. The connection is the heart."

"Okay. So I won't have to face the dark woods alone, because I have a guide who is connected to my heart," I said.

Domo sat down and took a *kifli*. "That sounds exactly right. That's been Hana's life for the last few weeks, right?"

I sighed. "I don't know what to think of my fortune. It's pretty vague."

"It's good fortune," my grandmother said, daintily stirring tea in her pink and gold cup. "Much better than mine." She stared down at her tea, and I realized that her lower lip was protruding slightly. My seventy-eight-year-old grandmother was pouting.

I laughed. "Look at Grandma! What could your fortune have possibly been that would put that expression on your face?" I reached out to pat her hand.

She sighed. "An omen of the wolf." She gave me a significant, baleful glance. "Means I am getting a wolf in the family."

Domo handed her a little chocolate cake, and she bit into it with a resigned expression.

Author's Note

My grandparents (on my father's side) were both born in what was, at the turn of the century, still Hungary—my grandmother in Doroslovo, which is now officially in Serbia, and my grandfather in Bodva Vendégi, now called Hostovice, on the border of the Bodva river, now in Slovakia. After they emigrated from their homeland, my grandparents eventually met each other in a citizenship class that was offered in a Chicago church basement. When they married, they settled in Burnside, an area of Chicago with an interesting history: Before the Civil War, it was nothing but undeveloped swampland. Later, after industry reshaped Chicago, it was bounded by three railroads: the Illinois Central, the Rock Island, and the New York Central. Not surprisingly, immigrants lived in Burnside, because many of them, including my grandfather, worked for the railroads.

In 1960, Burnside was made up of 99 percent European immigrants; twenty years later they had all but disappeared. It wasn't that Hungarians made a mass migration out of Burnside; it was more that many of the original immigrants died, and their children, who had no remembered ties to the area, moved away. Those children, like my father, had grown up speaking Hungarian at home and English at school, and they had adapted to American life. Hungarian Burnside became a thing of the past.

Our Lady of Hungary, at 93rd and Kimbark, was a place in which Hungarians came together—not just to worship, but to connect with people who spoke their language. My father attended the parish school as a child. When he started first grade he could speak only Hungarian, but this was also true of many of his classmates. The church was the hub of Hungarian immigrant society in Chicago at that time. When we were children, we played ball in the parking lot of the rectory of this now-defunct parish, and my grandparents' old house was right across from the church on a street called Avalon.

This novel is set in the present, about fifty years after the setting I have described, but in creating Riverwood I have borrowed many cultural details from my memories of Burnside; this might make parts of the story seem anachronistic, but at the same time I think any Hungarian readers will find some authenticity in the story of the Horvath family.

From Hana's Recipe Box

Note: All *measurements below would be shrugged off by my grandmother Juliana Horvath, who cooked by instinct, not by amounts. Therefore, you can take some liberties with the quantities listed.*

Chicken Paprikás
(Csirkepaprikás)

Makes 4–6 servings

1 chopped onion
1 tablespoon shortening or butter
1 tablespoon paprika
¼ teaspoon black pepper
2 tablespoons salt
4–5 pound chicken, disjointed
1½ cups water
½ pint sour cream

Sauté the onion in either shortening or butter. Add paprika, pepper, and salt and stir well; lay chicken pieces in pot and simmer for about 10 minutes. Add water to the mixture, cover, and simmer until chicken is tender. Remove chicken (place temporarily on plate or platter) and add sour cream to the spices and drippings; mix well. Add dumplings (recipe below) and place chicken on top of dumplings. Heat and serve. If more gravy is required, add ½ pint sweet cream to the sour cream mixture.

DUMPLINGS

(Nokedli)

Officially, nokedli *are meant to be passed through a noodle grater so that they come out long and thin, similar to German spaetzle. However, when you're in a hurry and making several dishes at once (a recurring dilemma for my grandmother), you can do it her way and use a teaspoon. I am including the spoon-flicking method here, but it requires practice and a deft hand.*

Makes 4 servings

3 cups flour
1 tablespoon salt
½ teaspoon paprika
3 eggs, beaten
½ cup to 1 cup water

Boil water in a large pot. In a large bowl, whisk together flour, salt, and paprika. With a wooden spoon, stir in eggs and enough water (½ to 1 cup) to make a wet, lumpy dough. Let dough rest while waiting for water to boil.

When you have a rolling boil, lift your dough above the boiling water and, using the tip of a standard coffee spoon or teaspoon from your silverware drawer, flick round bits of dough into the boiling water. The dough will sink, so after you have flicked in several dumplings, use your wooden spoon to make sure the dumplings are not sticking to the bottom of the pot. They will almost immediately rise to the surface and float. Once you have several floating dumplings, remove your *nokedli* with a slotted spoon and put into a bowl, first making sure to coat the bowl in butter or oil to keep the *nokedli* from sticking.

Repeat this process until you have used all your dough and you have a full bowl of dumplings.

Serve with Chicken Paprikás and gravy.

STUFFED CABBAGE

(Töltött Káposzta)

Makes 6–8 servings

1 large head of cabbage
1 large white onion
3 tablespoons shortening
¾ pound ground pork
¾ pound ground beef
2 tablespoons salt
2 tablespoons paprika
½ teaspoon black pepper
1½ cups rice, uncooked
1 small can sauerkraut
Large can tomato juice
½ pint sour cream

Bring a pot of water to a boil. Core cabbage and add to water, separating leaves gradually with a fork.

In a separate pan, sauté onions and shortening. Add meat, seasonings, and rice. Mix well.

On a plate, place a tablespoon of meat and rice mixture on each cabbage leaf, tucking edges tightly. Place cabbage rolls in a pot and cover ⅔ full with water. Put sauerkraut and tomato juice on top.

Cover and cook slowly for 1½ hours or until rice is tender.

Pour sour cream on top and cook for 5 more minutes.

DESSERT CRESCENTS

(Kiflis or Kiflik)

Makes 3–4 dozen crescents

6 cups flour (unsifted)
3 teaspoons baking powder
½ teaspoon baking soda
¾ cup sugar
1 pound butter
5 egg yolks
½ pint sour cream
1 teaspoon vanilla extract
Filling of choice (see below)

In a large bowl (my grandmother recommends glass, for some reason), mix together the dry ingredients. Cut in the butter, then add the remaining ingredients. Mix well, using your hands if necessary. Divide the dough into 2 portions, then refrigerate for 1 hour. Flour a board and roll out each dough portion. Cut the dough into squares approximately 3 inches wide (your total yield will depend on how large you make them), and spoon the filling onto the center of each square. Roll straight and put on a greased cookie sheet.

Filling options: raspberry, strawberry, or apricot *lekvar*; or almond paste, nut blend, and sweet cheese.

Optional: After rolling *kiflis*, brush top with milk and dip into a mixture of ground nuts and sugar.

Bake at 350 degrees for 15 minutes or until light brown. Cool and sprinkle with confectioners' sugar. Serve with coffee or tea.